MW00585780

Patricia Brown

DYING TO WIN

GladEye Press
Springfield, OR

Patricia Brown
Dying to Win

Published by: GladEye Press
Text Design by: J.V. Bolkan
Cover Design by: Sharleen Nelson
Copyediting by: GladEye Press
ISBN-13: 978-1-951289-01-0

The body text is presented in Garamond 11 pt for easy readability.

DYING TO WIN

PATRICIA BROWN

For David, the catch of a lifetime.

Eleanor Penrose sat up in bed and looked out the bank of windows that overlooked the Pacific Ocean. It was April on the Oregon Coast and spring was in the air but the small village of Sand Beach was cloaked in fog. She knew if she drove into the neighboring town of Waterton the sun would be shining. There was a long list of things to do before she could take her car in for an oil change so she stretched her 72-year-old limbs and climbed out of bed to start the day.

Feathers, the African gray parrot who shared Eleanor's house on the hill, greeted her as she uncovered and opened his cage to let him fly freely. He followed her into the kitchen and watched as she made a fresh pot of coffee and left the house to get the morning newspaper. Finishing the crossword puzzle, jumble, and Sudoku made Eleanor feel confident that her brain still functioned. She dressed and left for Waterton, postponing her daily walk until after the coastal fog lifted.

Eleanor met her friends for lunch at the Blue Lagoon. Josephine and Cleo were admiring each other's rings while Pearl gazed out the window at a dog who looked strangely like her dead mother-in-law. Dede was late due to a meeting that ran long but swore she would be there before they ordered a second cup of coffee.

"Don't you just love the way this stone catches the light?" asked Cleo as she twisted Josephine's citrine studded finger.

"Ouch," complained Josephine. "I ordered several new rings while under the influence of pain meds last month. Now they are here and I have buyer's remorse."

"You should definitely keep this one," said Cleo. "Don't you agree, Eleanor?"

"It's lovely," Eleanor agreed as she sat down.

"Dede's here," Pearl said as she watched Dede stop outside the window to pet the dog.

When they were all gathered around the table with their coffee and sandwiches before them, Eleanor began to tell them about her morning. "Something happened that was quite disturbing when I took my car to the service center," she began. "Do you know Johnny Vargas?"

"He's the one who's marrying Junie Wakefield," Dede said.

"I've seen him," said Pearl. "What a handsome man! Smoldering dark eyes, hard body and sexy smile. No wonder Junie Wakefield wants him."

"Yes, I saw them together. She pulled up in her red mustang while I was filling out my paperwork. They were hugging and kissing. There's no denying they make a beautiful couple and the way they acted made it plain for anyone to see how much in love they are."

"Is that the disturbing part?" asked Josephine who always liked to get to the meat of the matter.

"No, Johnny was extremely polite and I was rather charmed by his warmth and thoughtfulness. He greeted me warmly, made eye contact with his smoldering eyes and took care not to squeeze my hand too tightly."

"So what disturbed you? Did he cheat you? I always hate taking my car where some unscrupulous person can take advantage of you because you don't know anything about car maintenance," stated Cleo.

"No, nothing like that. Angus knows him so I felt confident he wasn't going to take advantage of me. Everything was fine with the car. It was just that when I came back Johnny Vargas had obviously been beaten. His eyes were discolored, his face scraped and bruised, and his nose was crusted with blood."

"Did you ask him what happened?" asked Dede.

"He told me not to worry and that everything was fine, but I couldn't shake this uneasy feeling that he wasn't telling me the truth," Eleanor said.

"I bet it was Junie's father," said Pearl, "I've heard terrible things about him."

"Be careful what you say about Howard Wakefield, or any Wakefield for that matter," said Dede. "They are rich, powerful and rotten to the core. Howard owns most of the real estate in Waterton and he throws his weight around to get whatever he wants with little concern about anyone who gets hurt by his actions. If you do something he doesn't like or stand in his way he slaps a lawsuit on you. There aren't many people around here who can afford to fight him."

"I've heard he hates Johnny Vargas because he's Hispanic. The man is a bigot. I'm surprised he's allowing his only daughter to marry Johnny," said Pearl.

"He can't stop her. She's his princess and she's old enough to do what she wants as long as she doesn't care about losing his money," said Dede.

"I don't know the man," said Josephine, "but he sounds like a sociopath."

"I don't think he would stoop to beating up anyone. He'd have someone else do it for him," said Pearl.

"My guess is Rob Wakefield or Eric Fowler," Dede said. "They've been friends since kindergarten. Both of them have been given every gift except kindness. Rob is Junie's brother and Eric Fowler was Junie's boyfriend all through high school until she met Johnny. Eric is bitter. He thinks Junie belongs to him." Eleanor listened and took it all in feeling a sadness for the handsome young man she felt unable to help.

"Let's see what's in that bag? Did you get a new dress for the wedding?" asked Cleo.

None of them noticed the dog who had wandered away from the window or the man with shiny shoes who kicked it as he passed.

By the time she got back to Sand Beach the fog had lifted so Eleanor put on her walking shoes and set off for the beach. It was unusually warm for April, but Eleanor was not complaining as she noticed several others enjoying the blue sky and gentle breeze. Gulls circled overhead and cried their disapproval when a couple of dogs chased them from their search for food. It was easy walking today and the ocean offered a plethora of sparkling agates and little shells as it ebbed and flowed along the sandy shore. The many shallow streams that flowed into the sea kept Eleanor hopping as she walked almost to Camp Cheerful before she turned for home.

Angus McBride had gone fishing. When Eleanor opened her front door, he stood on the porch with two shiny trout, cleaned and ready for her cooking magic.

"Wow, those are beauties," she exclaimed. Eleanor knew how proud Angus was of his catch by the depth of his dimples as he smiled. There was something about men and their ability to bring home a meal that added to their feelings of purpose and self-worth. Angus was no exception. He carried the fish into Eleanor's kitchen and poured himself two fingers of Crown Royal while Eleanor began the process of making trout with butter and pecans.

"Where did you catch these?" Eleanor asked innocently.

"You know I can't tell you that," he said as he kissed the nape of her neck. "Fishermen never give up their secrets."

"Well did you go out on the river?" she persisted.

"Johnny Vargas took me out in his drift boat," Angus admitted. "He thinks he owes me."

"Is that because you referred me to him for my car maintenance?" she asked.

"That and other things." Angus didn't want to tell Eleanor about the fact that he loaned Johnny money to buy an engagement ring for Junie. He may have been a hardened homicide detective once, but inside he was a sucker for love and romance.

"I didn't tell you about his black eyes. The day I took my car in he looked good, but when I came back for it, he had two black eyes."

Angus shrugged. "He looked okay today." Angus didn't mention that Johnny had shared the incident while they were fishing or that Angus had chased Eric and Rob away once before when Johnny first started dating Junie and found them beating him up behind a local hangout called the Red Shed. Johnny didn't want to make a big deal of it. Rob was Junie's brother and Johnny hoped that when he married her,

Junie's family would eventually accept him. Angus wasn't so sure, but didn't know how to address the situation without arming Johnny with a gun for protection. Eric and Rob against Johnny wasn't a fair fight and they usually found ways to attack him when he was alone so there would be no help and no witnesses.

"Johnny Vargas is a good man," Angus said as he sipped his whiskey. "Junie's a lucky woman."

"I'm looking forward to the wedding," Eleanor said as she pulled the backbone from the fish and washed her hands. "I even bought a new dress for the occasion." Angus' bushy eyebrows rose and fell as he envisioned Eleanor without a dress. Even though in his seventies, he was still a man.

Eleanor's coffee group met at the Boat House for breakfast. She pulled in just as Cleo and Pearl arrived. They all walked in together and sat at their usual table by the fireplace. Dede came late as they expected, but everyone was surprised when Josephine didn't show. "She didn't call to say she wasn't coming," Pearl said as she sipped her coffee.

"It isn't like her to not let someone know," Cleo said.

"Maybe she's sick," Dede speculated.

When Josephine finally arrived, her beautiful white hair, which was always so carefully pinned up in an intricate do, was hanging loose and she wore absolutely no makeup. "So sorry, but I overslept," Josephine apologized. "I need a fucking cup of coffee."

The others sat quietly while she filled her cup with Swiss Miss and poured coffee from the carafe. Needless to say they were surprised by her use of the f-word. Finally, she looked into their faces and realized they were concerned.

"I just read an article that said people who swear are more intelligent than those who don't. You know I'm intelligent and now you know I use vulgarities." Josephine sipped her coffee. "It feels good and I've got a new job!" she exclaimed. "You are looking at the new writer for the *Fish Wrapper's* 'Just Josie' column. I spent most of the night reading over letters that people wrote asking for advice. It was just so interesting. Let me read some of them to you."

Dear Josie,

My husband and I recently moved to a new town. It is much smaller than the one we moved from and I am anxious to make new friends. My neighbor is an older widow who lives alone but frequently entertains men. There is one who is at her house at all hours of the day and night. These men are not married. The woman is very entertaining and well educated. Every time I have had an opportunity to visit with her, I have found her company to be delightful, but I am a God-fearing Christian woman and am having trouble dealing with this woman's lack of morality. How do you suggest I handle the situation?

Looking for a Friend

Pearl looked sideways at Eleanor wondering if this person was referring to her friend and Angus. "I wonder *how* that woman is entertaining the men," said Cleo. "Maybe she sings."

"I wonder *how many* men she is entertaining," said Dede.

"So judgmental," added Eleanor, "It's none of her business. If this woman wants to be friends, she should spend time with her and find out more about her so-called "sinful ways" before she judges her so harshly."

"Maybe the woman is cutting their hair. I know several stylists who have retired but still cut hair in their homes," added Pearl. "I agree with Eleanor."

"Why do God-fearing people feel the need to put sinners on the right track? Isn't everyone entitled to choose their own way?" asked Cleo.

"It's my understanding that some religious people believe they sin along with sinners if they don't correct them. It must be like condoning the sin through silence," said Josephine. "But this is what I wrote:

Dear Looking,

As far as I know, there is nothing immoral about having men friends over for a visit. You say nothing about how she entertains these friends, so I assume you don't know. If you enjoy this woman's company, I suggest you take a lesson from her and forge a friendship by spending time with her. Whatever it is that draws you to her also draws others—some of them are men. Give her the benefit of the doubt and use your God-fearing Christian ways to treat your neighbor the way you want to be treated—without judgment. Remember Jesus spent time with women when it was considered inappropriate to do so and some of them were women of ill repute.

Just Josie

"I like the part you added about Jesus," said Dede, "It will make her feel you value her beliefs and she'll take your advice more seriously."

"Is it true that Jesus visited prostitutes?" asked Pearl.

"Maybe not the way you mean it," said Cleo, "But some people think the Church painted Mary Magdalene as a prostitute to discredit her because she was really his wife. Jesus was a friend to women and treated them as equals, which was revolutionary for the time."

"What's new in the city," asked Josephine who decided to change the subject.

Dede thought for a while, "There's been another fire. It's the second one this month and the fire marshal called it arson."

"Where was it?" asked Pearl.

"Both of them were over on Ninth Street near the new park and both of the residents were Hispanic. Fortunately, no one was injured, but it looks like someone has a vendetta against our Mexican friends."

"Do they know who did it?" asked Cleo.

"No," said Dede, "But they're working on it."

"That makes three fires if you count the one that burned down the church on the corner last year," said Josephine.

"Was that arson too?" asked Eleanor.

"It was considered suspicious, but no one was ever charged," Dede said.

"Most arsonists are young men," Josephine said. "But the fact that Hispanics are being targeted makes me wonder if other forces are at work here."

"Has anyone noticed the new business that's moved into the Curiosity Shop?" asked Dede.

"No, what is it?" Cleo asked.

"It's called Oracle," Dede pulled a flier advertising the new store out of her bag. "Madam Patruska is the proprietor. She offers psychic and tarot card readings, palmistry, and fortune telling and sells items that deal with mysticism and spirituality. I've been in the shop. It's full of crystals, potions, good luck charms, and all sorts of creepy herbs and teas for healing, as well as Ouija boards, tarot cards, and books on the psychic sciences."

"I'm surprised there hasn't been a public outcry from the conservative religious people in town," Pearl said.

"I don't think they know what the Oracle is yet. Give them time and I'm sure they'll give her grief," Dede said.

"Have you met this Madam Patruska?" asked Cleo.

"Oh yes, she's quite a character. Her real name is Patricia Vanga, and she has a strange way of speaking. She's very dramatic." Dede said.

"I'd love to have my fortune told," Cleo said.

"Why not?" asked Eleanor. "It could be fun to visit her shop and see what she has to offer. I like the idea of helping a new business get off the ground."

"I'd like to see if she has something to use for meditation purposes. I want one of those singing bowls for our yoga space," said Pearl.

"The benefit of various crystals has always interested me. I'd like to see if she has anything to help with anxiety or starting a new venture," said Josephine.

"You'll have to count me out," said Dede. "I have to go to church. Someone's got to pray for you pagans."

When the ladies entered the Oracle, they were struck with the strong aroma of burning sage. It was evident to some of them that a sweep had been done to cleanse the room of evil spirits. The shop was filled with shelves of books on fortune telling, dream interpretation, palm reading, and an endless list of cards for divining your truth and finding inspiration. Crystals and polished stones sparkled behind a glass case next to amulets that promised to bring good fortune while quiet music played, but there was no sign of Madam Patruska.

Josephine picked up a teal blue stone and immediately felt a tingle that told her she needed to have it. She was holding it in her hand when a voice rang out behind the veiled door. "Blood, blood is everywhere. It will show you the way. It will begin and end your suffering."

The ladies froze in place when Junie Wakefield walked through the door and left the shop without a word. Madame Patruska followed shortly thereafter and seemed surprised to see customers in the shop. She was a tall thin woman in her fifties and wore a long green broomstick skirt and a tunic embellished with embroidery layered with several scarves of many colors. Her curly hair was dyed a vibrant red and held captive by yet another scarf decorated with silver coins that jingled as she moved.

"Welcome," she greeted them warmly. "I am Padam Matruska. Mow hay I help you?" It was evident to the ladies that Madame Patruska had made a verbal slip, unintentionally interchanging the beginning sounds of her words. Eleanor immediately identified it as a spoonerism and wondered if it would happen again.

When the ladies simply stared, she looked at Josephine and continued, "I see you have discovered the kyanite. This crystal will help you speak your truth and relieve your anxiety."

"Perfect, I'll take it," said Josephine decisively. Madam Patruska rang up the sale along with Pearl's singing bowl.

"I would like my palm read," said Cleo.

"Excellent, come into this nosey little cook, I mean this cozy little nook." Madam Patruska led them into her back room where they all sat around a small table draped with a black cloth sprinkled with stars that glowed florescent in the dimness. A crystal ball sat in the center, but Madam Patruska moved it aside and reached for Cleo's hand, studying it for some time before she spoke.

"Your hands are small, indicating an impatient nature more interested in the big picture than in the finer details. You are comfortable in social settings and find interest in others. You like people and trust them to a fault. I see that you are artistic and impulsive, often exuberant in your enthusiasm for the artistic. Your waisted thumb tells me you have great understanding and compassion toward all creatures. I see only one true love in your life and two children, but many grandchildren—possibly five or six. There is a loss coming in your life. It could be an illness or some kind of trouble. You should be careful and protect yourself from negative energy or persons who may try to suck your energy or your life out of you."

She stopped here reluctant to go on, "That is all I nan do for cow—I mean can do for now. Let me show you some crystals that can protect you from the emotional vampires that are out there." Madame Patruska stood and returned to the outer room. The ladies followed her quietly as if in a trance. "This is black tourmaline," she said, holding up a dark gemstone. "You must have this, and obsidian, too. Please take them and promise me you will be very careful. I feel a kinship with you and a need to protect you." Suddenly, she was embracing Cleo in a tight bear hug. Upon her release, Cleo took out her purse, paid Madame Patruska and left with her friends trailing behind.

"What did you make of all that?" asked Cleo when they were halfway down the block.

"I think she nailed you," Josephine said in awe.

"Absolutely," Eleanor agreed.

"But what about all the scary talk about negative energy and emotional vampires sucking out my life?" Cleo fretted. "Am I in danger?"

"I think you should definitely stay away from any mysteries or murder cases that come up, Cleo," Pearl cautioned.

Cleo put the crystals in her pocket. "Let's go to Dede's and see if she has any pie. Madam Patruska didn't say anything about a diet."

Dede was back from church or wherever she had been and happy to hear about the adventures at the Oracle. To take Cleo's mind off the negative aspects of her palm reading, Eleanor changed the subject. "Is everyone going to the wedding?" She asked as they sat around Dede's dining room table enjoying her heavenly lemon meringue pie.

"Of course, I wouldn't miss that for anything. I heard it's being catered by Salvador Dolly and their food always gets rave reviews," Dede said.

"There will surely be a full bar with all we can drink, and Howard Wakefield isn't going to skimp on bottom shelf beverages," Cleo said.

"I heard there's going to be live music too, so plenty of dancing and lots of fun," Pearl stated. "We'd be fools not to go even if the guy is a mean, inherently corrupt badass."

Eleanor didn't need to go to the grocery store to pick up something special to cook for Angus tonight even though it was Friday. He was taking her out to dinner at the Galley. It was a romantic little restaurant that overlooked the ocean and served extravagantly decadent food at extremely ridiculous prices. They didn't go there often, only every now and then when Angus felt the need to pay her back for all the Friday night dinners she made for him. He called it their place, but he knew his place was anywhere Eleanor was.

The waiter seated them in the corner by the window where they could watch the sunset. Angus ordered his usual Crown Royal and Eleanor had a martini with extra olives. The Friday night special was a prime rib dinner with horseradish sauce, mashed potatoes and gravy, and seasoned green beans. Angus liked his meat and potatoes while Eleanor ordered the grilled halibut with lemon and a healthy spring green salad with beets and oranges. They ate and drank and chatted about their week, paying little attention to anything but each other. Eleanor was just telling him about the visit to the Oracle when there was a commotion across the room.

Johnny Vargas and Junie Wakefield sat at another table enjoying their dinner until Eric Fowler came out of the lounge with his date, Olivia. He stood beside their table throwing insults at Johnny in a loud drunken voice. Angus excused himself and left Eleanor to see if he could help diffuse the situation. She couldn't hear what Angus said, but it was clear that talking wasn't going to save the evening. Johnny stood up and Eric took a swing at him, but Angus caught his arm and expertly twisted it behind his back and pushed him out the door with Olivia following close behind. Angus was older but had years of experience dealing with society's riffraff. For a man in his seventies, he looked amazingly fit. Eleanor watched as Johnny thanked him and shook his hand and Angus returned to her and his dinner.

"I think you saved their romantic dinner," Eleanor said.

"Yes, but how many times is this behavior going to repeat itself?" Angus was troubled.

"Don't you think Johnny could have handled that by himself?" Eleanor asked.

"Eleanor, I'm afraid for him. He's up against a stacked deck and he needs all the help he can get. Johnny's marrying into a family who hates him because he's Hispanic and that will never change."

It was a perfect day for a wedding. The gift of sunshine on a day in May on the Oregon coast was never one to be taken for granted. Junie Wakefield must have had connections with the weather gods to be granted the perfection of sun and a warm breeze for her special day. Eleanor Penrose remembered her own wedding day as she dressed for Junie's. It too was sunny and warm but took place in southern California. All she could really remember of that day almost 50 years ago was how her hands shook and the white roses quivered in front of her as she said her vows, and then the tears afterward. Even after all this time she didn't know if they were tears of sorrow or joy. Perhaps they were a little of both.

She had loved Walter and never regretted their union, but doesn't every woman mourn the loss of a piece of her identity when she becomes a man's wife? Something's lost, but much is gained. Eleanor hurried to put a little color in her cheeks before Angus came to take her to what everyone was calling the wedding of the year. Nearly everyone in Waterton County had been invited to the wedding of Junie Wakefield and Johnny Vargas, and everyone in the county also knew how much it cost Howard Wakefield to give his only daughter away to a man he detested. The wedding was meant to show Junie and everyone else what she was giving up to marry a man beneath her. This was Howard's way of lavishing every decadent indulgence on his only daughter for the last time before he disowned and disinherited her. Loving a poor Hispanic mechanic and living a life of poverty without her father's wealth and power would be her punishment for defying him, but perhaps Howard Wakefield didn't know the power of love.

The doorbell rang and Eleanor took one last look in the mirror before she rushed to open the door. Angus McBride stood on her porch in his best suit looking every bit as handsome as any groom. He smiled when he saw Eleanor. To Angus, with her silver hair and bright blue eyes, there was no woman as beautiful as Eleanor. He believed kindness and love radiated from her like light from a flame—a flame that lit his dark and sorry world, once filled with images of grizzly deeds perpetrated by criminals and sociopaths—images he could never forget. Unlike the damaged and deranged he had worked with as a homicide detective, Eleanor was good and true.

When she smiled he didn't see the crow's feet or the laugh lines that etched her face—only the light from a warm and caring soul. It seemed as if he had always loved her—even when her husband, Walter was alive. He only wished she felt a fraction of that love for him. However, as he stood at her door, he could see a decent man reflected in her eyes and it gave him hope.

"Well don't you look handsome," Eleanor complimented him, but before Angus could reply with praise of his own, Feathers, the African Gray parrot flew to her shoulder with harsh words of criticism.

"Get lost loser!" he squawked. "My girl, my girl."

Angus laughed and leaned in for a quick kiss before Feathers could claw out his eyes. "Are you ready? You've never looked lovelier."

"Thank you," Eleanor replied as she picked up a sweater and grabbed a small clutch. "I think this is going to be a wonderful day for a wedding."

"It's sure to be the biggest wedding I've ever attended," Angus said as he helped Eleanor into his truck. "I'm not certain the fairgrounds will be a big enough venue. They probably should have secured the beach."

"It's good that we got an early start. Finding a parking place close to the entrance will be difficult," Eleanor said.

"I just hope Eric Fowler doesn't cause any trouble. He's had his cap set on Junie most of his life and isn't used to losing."

"It would be a shame if he tried to spoil things. Junie and Johnny deserve a day to celebrate. It's plain to see how much they love each other," Eleanor said. "Junie's brother, Rob, and Eric are a perfect combination for disaster. Two bullies with no morals or empathy. Although I can't imagine Howard Wakefield condoning anything that would ruin his perfectly planned celebration for his perfect daughter. His ego wouldn't allow it."

"Don't worry, Eleanor, certain people are watching out for those two. Johnny has more friends than you know." Angus and some officers from the Waterton police were ready to squash any disturbance Rob Wakefield and his band of thugs could instigate and had plans of their own to protect the wedding party.

"I hope you're right. I plan to enjoy this day too," Eleanor said. Angus smiled. He liked weddings and hoped that this one might put Eleanor in the proper mindset to have one of her own.

The bride and groom stood on a stage filled with roses, lilies, gardenias, and every flower imaginable. The scent was almost overpowering. Junie was a vision with her dark hair swept up loosely and sprinkled with pearls, her white gown fluttering in the breeze while Johnny stood at her side gazing at her in total adoration. They repeated their vows while most of Waterton looked on at what could only be described as a fairy tale wedding. Angus squeezed Eleanor's hand when he noticed her silently wipe away a tear. As they turned to the crowd and the priest introduced them as Mr. and Mrs. Vargas, two white doves were released and soared into the blue sky. Without warning a hawk shot like an arrow out of the blue and pierced one of the doves with its razor like talons. Blood sprayed from the unfortunate bird as it fell on the crowd below. There was a unified gasp as the guests scurried to get out of the way, pushing each other and creating confusion and dismay. Johnny didn't skip a beat but picked Junie up and carried her off the stage and into the reception area, leaving the unpleasantness behind them.

Most of the guests followed their lead and soon the tragic episode was forgotten as they entered the large banquet room filled with tables festooned with Junie's favorite color, lavender. An abundance of lilacs adorned every table and contrasted with the white table linens. White and purple balloons floated above them like clouds in a fantasy sky, and shimmering walls of silk and diamond-studded netting sparkled in the glow of the dimly lit room. The effect was magical. Tables of food in warming dishes lined two walls. One table was devoted to a lavish display of fruits and carved vegetables circling a large ice sculpture of two swans whose graceful necks formed a heart. An open bar provided guests with wine, beer, and mixed drinks. People gathered, visited, ate, drank, and danced to the music of a band that had been brought in from the valley.

The ladies from the coffee group sat at various tables. Cleo and her husband, Steve, along with their children and grandchildren filled an entire table while Josephine and Pearl sat with their husbands and a few acquaintances. Dede and Mark sat with several members from the city council and Dede's church, but no one sat for long. They bumped into each other on the dance floor, exchanged partners and rollicked with wild abandon—at least that's how they saw it.

"I need a break," said Eleanor as she and Angus left the dance floor. Angus went to get refreshments while Eleanor watched as Eric Fowler led Junie on to the floor and held her close as they danced to *Have I Told You Lately*. Eric and Junie had history. Everyone thought it would be Junie and Eric walking down the aisle vowing to love each other until death parted them, Junie and Eric whose names would be written on the napkins, and Junie and Eric living happily ever after in the big house, inheriting the Wakefield fortune. Eleanor wasn't the only one who noticed Olivia Martin watching Eric possessively while she danced with Rob Wakefield, who only had eyes for her.

"Love can be so capricious," Eleanor sighed as Angus returned. He didn't miss much and had also witnessed the chain of passions and felt the tension of unrequited love.

Johnny Vargas noticed it too as he danced with his sister Sofia, but he had the grace to let it go because it would be Johnny who took Junie home tonight and every night after this. He'd dance with Junie to their song every night because he had won Junie's heart and knew he was a lucky man. Eric Fowler was the loser.

The Fowler family sat together at a table of rich men unlucky in love. Peter Fowler, old and shriveled, was the grand patriarch who started the Fowler Lumber Mill. His wife had died years ago after a long and bitter marriage. His son, Thomas had killed himself after the death of his wife. Another son, Edward took over the mill only to have the love of his life reject him for a lowly millworker, abandoning him to a life of resentment and loneliness. Eric was the last in a long line of mean, unhappy Fowlers. Their otherwise handsome faces seem twisted by a fate that left them wretched and alone.

When the band began to play *Dream Lover*, Eleanor knew Angus had requested what he proclaimed was their song. "Dance with me," he said, holding out his hand for Eleanor to take. After several spins around the dance floor, Eleanor was flushed and breathless and excused herself to visit the ladies' room where she overheard Rob Wakefield and Eric Fowler talking in the hallway.

"Don't worry, Eric. This marriage won't last. We'll see to that," Rob said. It was beyond question that both men had imbibed more than they should. Their voices were unnecessarily loud.

"She'll be used goods if she's not already," Eric sneered.

Eleanor thought Rob might have punched Eric if she hadn't picked that moment to step out of the restroom's door. They glanced her way and immediately disregarded the presence of an old woman before staggering down the hallway.

When Eleanor returned to the party, Junie and Johnny had disappeared, but the revelers partied on. Angus and Eleanor found their friends and danced some more until their feet ached and they had to kick off their shoes. It was a splendid party without incident. Of course, no one knew then what was in store for the star-crossed lovers, although many said the murder by hawk of the innocent dove was an omen of bad things to come.

Johnny and Junie spent their honeymoon at the House on the Hill, a motel overlooking the ocean at Sand Beach. It was expensive by Johnny's standards, but Junie was used to the best and he didn't want to disappoint her. The spring weather on the coast is unpredictable and often wet, but neither of them cared as they spent most of their time indoors with only a few breaks for romantic walks on the beach and meals at Suzanna's.

Eleanor saw them on a couple of occasions and waved a greeting, but for the most part they remained to themselves. When their three-day vacation was over, they left for the small apartment Johnny had rented in Waterton. It was old and shabby, but it was all Johnny could afford. Junie had never worked a day in her life and after two days of hanging around the apartment with nothing to do, she began going to the YMCA where she ran into Angus.

"How's it going?" asked Angus as he held the door for Junie who was just coming inside.

Junie shrugged. "Okay, I guess. Johnny's gone all day so there isn't much for me to do. I see him at breakfast and not again until it's time for dinner."

"So, what are you making for dinner?" Angus asked curiously.

"I don't know. Johnny does the cooking. I don't know how," she admitted.

"How about you and Johnny come to my house for dinner tonight," Angus offered. "I caught a salmon this morning and I don't think I can eat it by myself."

"That would be great." Junie seemed genuinely pleased.

"I'll see you at six," Angus said as he watched Junie disappear into the building. Maybe Eleanor would enjoy a salmon dinner and the company of two young people as well. She might even give Junie some tips about cooking.

Eleanor arrived at Angus' house with an apple pie and a bottle of pinot noir. Angus had prepped the fish and had it on the grill outside. "Do you need any help?" she asked as she watched him open a bag of frozen chopped potatoes and drop them into the frying pan.

"Maybe you could make a salad. I know you like that green stuff so Junie probably does too. I bought a bag of something. I think it's kale." Angus pointed to a bag of premade salad with kale and other greens and made a gagging sound. It even had a pouch of poppy seed dressing with dried cranberries and sunflower seeds. Eleanor opened the bag and poured the salad into a bowl. So this was Angus' way of cooking.

"Could you watch these potatoes while I go check on the fish?" Angus said.

Before she could answer he was gone. Eleanor stirred the potatoes and wondered at the ease with which Angus had thrown this dinner together. She noticed the table had been set with his rustic looking dishes. The glassware and silverware were all arranged perfectly, paper napkins placed at each setting. Eleanor was impressed. If she had doubts about how this meal-in-a-bag would taste, she was not letting on. She opened the wine and poured herself a glass and when visitors came knocking, she answered the door.

Johnny Vargas stood beside Junie, his hair still wet from a shower but his smile warm and friendly. Junie wore designer blue jeans and a face freshly made up to accentuate her dark eyes and dewy skin.

"Please come in," Eleanor said, welcoming the couple. "Angus is checking on the fish. Oops, I'm in charge of potatoes. Make yourselves comfortable while I make sure they aren't burning."

Angus returned with the fish on a serving platter and placed it on the table. "Just look at this beauty," he said proudly. "Did Junie tell you I caught it this morning? It can't get much fresher than this."

"I haven't had a chance to drop a line. It sure does look delicious," Johnny said, eyeing the fish hungrily. Angus wondered just what they ate if Johnny was the cook. Eleanor brought the potatoes, salad, and rolls to the table and they sat down to what Eleanor had to admit was a tasty meal.

"Angus, you've outdone yourself!" Eleanor said.

"You did all this?" asked Johnny.

"It was easy," Angus bragged. "I just caught the fish, threw it on the grill, bought a bag of these prepared potatoes and a bag of premade salad, and BAM: dinner!"

"Salad and potatoes come in bags?" Junie asked.

"Only for the cooking impaired," teased Johnny. "The rest of us peel and chop our own potatoes. It's less expensive that way."

Eleanor saw a look of discomfort pass over Junie's face. She wasn't used to talking about money or counting pennies. She wasn't used to much of anything that didn't involve shopping, horseback riding, or hanging out with her friends surfing at the beach or skiing on snow-covered mountains.

"Wait until you taste Eleanor's apple pie," Angus said. "She doesn't cut corners when it comes to baking." Eleanor took her cue and went to the kitchen to dish up dessert.

"Junie, maybe Eleanor could use your help in the kitchen," Johnny prodded. Angus could see a bit of tension, then understanding pass over Junie's face. She understood he wasn't suggesting that her place was in the kitchen, just that he wanted to talk to Angus for a moment alone.

"Oh, of course," Junie said, placing her napkin on her chair and leaving the two men alone.

"Is everything okay?" Angus asked.

"I lost my job today. I haven't told Junie yet, but her father bought the Auto Service Center and his first act was to have me fired," Johnny confided.

"You're a talented mechanic. There are other places you can work," Angus said.

Johnny shook his head. "That's not all. Junie can't cook and doesn't know how to clean. She's game, but I really think she is lost and doesn't know where to start. She was raised being able to travel and shop. I love her, but I'm afraid I can't provide the kind of life she was used to."

"Go over to the public utility district. They always need mechanics and they pay better than the service center. They offer benefits and they're public so Howard Wakefield can't buy them," Angus suggested. "I know some people there and can put in a good word for you."

Johnny's face brightened. "That would be great." Angus rose and began to clear the dirty dishes from the table. Johnny followed suit.

Almost as an afterthought, Angus placed a hand on Johnny's shoulder. "She's a good girl and she loves you. You don't need to give her the life she had, just the one you can share."

Meanwhile in the kitchen, Eleanor was giving Junie tips on how to make a flakey pie crust as they scooped vanilla bean ice cream on top of the apple pie. "I don't know anything about cooking, Eleanor. My mom died when I was little and Daddy didn't allow me to do any work. I really want to please Johnny but I don't know where to start," Junie explained. "I don't think pie crust is in my immediate future."

"There are lots of good television shows that teach cooking," Eleanor said.

"We can't really afford cable, so there is no television," Junie said.

"Have you gone to the library?" Eleanor asked.

"No, do they teach cooking? I don't even have a card."

"Hmmm, I can drop by sometime and help you," Eleanor offered. "I have lots of cookbooks. We can start there."

"That would be marvelous. Maybe you could give me some tips on cleaning, too, and ironing. Poor Johnny has been doing all the work. I feel so useless."

"You just need to find something you're passionate about and let that get you out of the house. There's more to marriage than cooking and cleaning," Eleanor said.

"I'm passionate about Johnny." Junie stopped talking when Angus and Johnny appeared and put the dirty dishes in the sink. They each picked up their desserts and there was no more talking until the plates were clean.

Eleanor arrived at Junie's house shortly after lunch to find Junie dressed in tight denim shorts and a white T-shirt. Her youthful skin was tanned a rich bronze from time spent in a tanning booth. Eleanor didn't think many people in Waterton could boast of a tan like that with the weather they experienced this time of year.

"Eleanor, I'm so happy to see you," Junie gasped. "I've been cleaning the bathroom and now I've broken my nails and my lungs are on fire!"

"What are you using?" Eleanor asked as she looked at Junie's reddened hands.

"Johnny told me to use bleach and a sponge. It smells horrible and my skin feels all slimy."

"Let's open some windows and run your hands under some cool water. Did Johnny tell you to wear rubber gloves?" Eleanor was amazed at Junie's ignorance.

"No, I just poured it on the sponge and scrubbed. It did take off the mold," Junie said.

"Bleach should be diluted. It doesn't take much—just a couple of tablespoons to a gallon of water," Eleanor instructed. As Junie ran her hands underwater and patted them dry, Eleanor took in the small space, the stained carpet, and the worn furniture. It would be difficult for two people to fit in the tiny kitchen, but it was clean and Junie had a sweet bouquet of lilacs on a small table that was the perfect size for two.

"What did you bring?" Junie asked eyeing the bag Eleanor placed on the table.

"I put a chicken casserole together for your dinner tonight and I brought you this beginner's cookbook. It covers everything from scrambled eggs to coq au vin. *You* should start with scrambled eggs," Eleanor laughed. "I marked some of my favorite simple recipes. They have just a few ingredients and the directions are easy to follow."

"Thank you so much. Johnny lost his job at the service center and he's out looking for work today. I really want to surprise him with dinner. What should I do with the casserole?"

Eleanor knew she couldn't just say, "Pop it in the oven," without explicit instructions. For all she knew, Junie didn't know how to turn on the oven.

"Have you given any thought to what you want to do while Johnny is at work?" Eleanor asked after she and Junie finished studying the oven settings.

"What do you mean? Like a job?" Junie asked.

"Yes, I'm sure there is something that you could do that would give you fulfillment and maybe even add to your household budget," Eleanor continued. "That way you and Johnny could work as a team financially as well as around the house. It makes for a real partnership."

"I don't know," Junie hesitated. "There isn't really anything I can do."

"What did you major in, Junie?"

"I didn't finish college. Daddy said I didn't need to work and it would be a waste of money. He said I was pretty and wouldn't have trouble finding a man to support me," she laughed. Eleanor didn't say what she thought. She had told her daughters just the opposite and believed a woman should be independent and capable of caring for herself.

"I don't really have any skills," she admitted.

"What do you enjoy doing?" Eleanor probed.

Junie sighed. "I love to read, but nobody hires people to do that."

"But they do!" Eleanor exclaimed. "Editors read lots of books, reviewers read, and some readers record books for others to listen to."

"Well, probably not in Waterton," Junie lamented.

"Start at the library. See if they need a volunteer. You might be able to read to children there during story hour. If you like working at the library you could pursue a degree in library science. Go to the retirement home and read to the residents there who have vision problems. That could lead to an activity director's job. I bet you know a great deal about travel. You could plan outings for the residents. There are so many opportunities here and so many people who could use your help."

"I never considered doing something like that, I mean volunteer work doesn't pay, but I'll give it a try," Junie said. "Thank you so much, Eleanor."

"It's one way to get your foot in the door. Just start with one step. The rest will follow."

Eleanor left Junie's apartment and drove back to Sand Beach hoping that there would be dinner for Johnny when he got home. It wasn't Junie's fault. She didn't lack intelligence or the desire to work. With all the opportunities she had been given, she just never had the opportunity to do anything for herself or others. She suffered from low self-esteem and a severe case of affluenza.

Johnny Vargas had everything he wanted. He just needed a job that would pay the kind of money that would keep his wife happy and keep Eric and Rob from beating him up every chance they got. Junie was alarmed when he came home bruised and bloody and he was running out of excuses. She suspected it involved her brother but didn't want to accuse Johnny of lying so they both pretended things were good. If they could just put their heads together, they might come up with some way to make life better. He looked into several possible job opportunities but found that Howard Wakefield had spoiled his chances at all of them. The car dealerships told him they couldn't use a mechanic that didn't have a degree in technology even though Johnny had worked with the latest models at the service center. His references were excellent, but the interviewers suggested that he was lacking in some way.

He only suspected his father-in-law's interference, but the fact was, Howard Wakefield had spread a rumor that Johnny was involved in the drug trade. If that wasn't enough, Wakefield knew things about people and called in several favors that put Johnny on the blacklist. After several failed attempts to secure work, he remembered that Angus had suggested the utility company and finally applied there. Angus had been true to his word and when Johnny interviewed at the utility company they were impressed with his references and charisma. They hired him on the spot. He could hardly wait to get home to Junie with the good news.

"That's wonderful!" Junie threw her arms around Johnny and kissed him. "I'll make a celebratory dinner for tonight. There's a recipe I can't wait to try but I'll have to go to the store." Maybe this was the break they needed.

"I'd like to take the boat down the river and maybe catch a fish," Johnny said. "I'll be back in time for dinner." He gave Junie a long kiss and left with his fishing gear.

Junie bought the ingredients for steak and potatoes and a green salad. At the last minute she threw in a bottle of wine and a bouquet of flowers. She imagined their night together: Johnny would praise her cooking skills; they would toast to his new job, clinking their glasses together while gazing into each other's eyes. Then Johnny would take her in his arms and they would slow dance to their song, *I've Been Waiting for You* until neither of them could control themselves and Johnny would carry her to bed where they would make love until the sun came up in the morning.

She spent the afternoon preparing for the evening—bathing, painting her nails, doing her hair and makeup until she was satisfied that what she saw in the mirror would be irresistible to Johnny. Then she made dinner and set the table. This would be a night for celebration. When six o'clock rolled around Junie began to look for Johnny. By seven she was pacing the floor in anger and by eight she was frantic with worry. She hadn't even asked him where he was fishing. She didn't know what to do, so she called Johnny's sister, Sofia who lived near the river and usually picked him up at the boat landing and drove him back to his car. When Sofia said she hadn't heard from him, Junie called the police for help.

Officer McGraw knew Johnny and tried to reassure Junie. "He probably just lost track of time. I know where he usually launches the boat, so I'll go there and check it out."

By nine o'clock, Officer McGraw had located Johnny's car and called several of his friends to help search for him. At ten they discovered his battered and broken capsized boat caught among rocks and debris downstream from his usual take-out spot. They searched until well after dark but there was no sign of Johnny Vargas. Officer McGraw did not relish the task of telling Junie her husband was missing and presumed drown but by twelve Junie Vargas already suspected the worst.

The weeks that followed were difficult for everyone who knew and loved Johnny Vargas and his wife. People whispered about the tragedy on the streets and in the shops. Some of his friends continued to search for him along the banks of the river. Many were hopeful that he would somehow be found alive with a bump on his head and a short-term case of amnesia, but after his wallet and one shoe washed up on the beach, it was impossible to deny the reality of the situation. It took Junie two weeks to pack up her few belongings and leave their cozy love nest for Daddy's house on the hill.

Eleanor awoke from a disturbing dream. Her friend Angus McBride had taken her to their favorite restaurant where they were celebrating the launch of her latest book of poetry.

"You look lovely tonight," Angus whispered as he leaned toward her and took her hand in his. "I love the way that blue dress brings out the color of your eyes."

Eleanor blushed as she gazed deeply into Angus' handsome face. She loved the way his cheeks dimpled when he smiled and there was nothing she wanted more than to kiss those lips and feel the tickle of his graying mustache. She and Angus had grown closer since her husband, Walter had died. There hadn't been any arguments about her meddling into police business or cases that Angus might be involved in as a retired homicide detective. Of course, there hadn't been any murders recently either, but that wasn't important. The important part was that Eleanor and Angus were enjoying their time together without worries, jealousies, or pressures of marriage. There was just the free-floating easy joy of being together.

It was all good until there was a commotion from the other side of the room.

Johnny and Junie Vargas sat at a nearby table when Junie's brother, Rob Wakefield came up to them and began calling Johnny names. Angered by the verbal slurs, Johnny stood and threw a punch at Rob. Rob was older and outweighed Johnny by twenty pounds. He easily avoided the punch and threw one of his own, catching Johnny on the jaw and knocking him into another table smashing the dishes to the floor. Not one to sit on the sidelines when trouble arose, Angus left Eleanor and attempted to bring some sanity to the situation. He had come to Johnny's aid before. Now he stood between the two men when suddenly without warning Johnny drew a gun. In his attempt to shoot Rob, he shot Angus instead. Angus fell to the floor amid the broken glass. Eleanor screamed herself awake as she looked down at a bloody and lifeless Angus.

Eleanor glanced at the clock. It was early but the sun was up lighting her room and announcing that a new day was here and she should be up and moving. She knew sleep was no longer an option and she needed to get busy and shake off the nightmare. Feathers greeted her and once free, flew to the window to look out over the Pacific Ocean sparkling blue under the summer sky. She quickly made a fresh pot of coffee and went outside to get the daily paper. The morning air was cool and the scent of pine trees mingled with the sea's briny smell evoking memories of summer's past in Eleanor's aging brain. Summer was always a happy time. Being a retired English teacher Eleanor still felt on vacation and reveled in the freedom summer brought. Every day was Saturday for her and had been for some time, but today was special. It was Friday and that meant her coffee group would meet for breakfast at the Boat House. Friday was her favorite day.

As she drank her first cup of coffee and finished the crossword puzzle, Sudoku, and daily jumble she tried to push the nightmare from her mind. Maybe sharing it with her friends would help.

Eleanor drove to the Boat House and sat at the group's usual table. She was early. Somewhere she read that early people were anxious, those who were late were hostile, and the ones on time, compulsive. There was no way a person could be just right. Cleo came in next followed by Pearl and Josephine. Dede was always late, but Eleanor thought it was because she was the mayor and had a very busy schedule, not because she was hostile.

Cleo had a new hairdo. She was the only one of the group who still colored her hair, the others opting to go natural with various shades of gray or silver or white. "I decided to go with blond streaks since the white seems to appear at the temples within days of getting it colored. Now the white will just blend into the blond like wings," Cleo said. "I hate when it grows out."

"I like it," said Josephine who was always positive unless it involved incompetent or stupid people.

"I've always liked you with red hair," said Dede.

"Me too," said Eleanor.

"I had to change it," Cleo said. "The red over white looked orange in some spots and having orange hair doesn't fit my personae."

"I'm having a mosaic show at the Bayside Art Center. It's going to include several pieces made in my studio by various artists," said Pearl.

"That's wonderful," said Dede.

"When is it?" asked Josephine, who wondered if there was still time for her to complete something so she could participate.

"Not for a few weeks," Pearl answered, "but I hope you'll all come. I'll have some of my own mosaics on display."

"Of course, I'll come. Will you be serving wine?" asked Cleo.

"Absolutely," Pearl said. "What would a show be without wine?"

"Dry," said Cleo. "Did I tell you about my new housekeeper?"

"No," said Eleanor who was looking for someone who was up to the task of cleaning for her too. "Who is it?"

"Well, it's an interesting story," Cleo began. "You know how I get my exercise by walking up the hill from my house. There is this woman who often stops to chat with me as she is driving home. We've been chatting off and on for some time now and I found out she is the housekeeper for Howard Wakefield. I mentioned that I'd love to have a housekeeper and she said she had an opening so she's coming next week."

"Do you think she could clean for me too?" asked Eleanor.

"What's her name?" asked Pearl.

"That's the funny part. I was sure she told me her name was Rhonda, but the last time we talked she said, 'By the way, my name is Wanda!' All this time I've been calling her Rhonda. Maybe I heard it wrong because her car was always running. Anyway, she has a very nasty mouth on her. She called Howard Wakefield a 'fucking bastard' then apologized for her language, so I told her what you said, Josephine, about people who use vulgar words having high IQs and she just looked at me and said, 'Yah, I noticed you don't use any.' Then she drove away."

There was laughter that was quickly curtailed when Cleo gave them the stink eye. "I don't agree with that at all," Eleanor argued. She didn't approve of using vulgarities unless one was sufficiently provoked. "What kind of study could prove such nonsense?" Dede simply shrugged. She had a mouth like a truck driver and was often provoked.

"I don't think this Wanda person is the right housekeeper for you, Eleanor," Pearl commented.

"I had a terrible dream last night," said Eleanor. They all leaned in to hear her tell them every remembered detail so they could interpret it.

"Didn't that really happen to you and Angus not so long ago?" asked Dede.

"Yes, except in reality, Angus was able to diffuse the situation and no one was hurt. But in this dream Johnny shot and killed Angus."

"I think the story of Johnny and Junie Vargas is a romantic tragedy," said Cleo. "It could be made into a movie."

"What happened, I forgot the details," Pearl said.

"It's a story as old as time about love and bigotry," Josephine said. "Johnny and Junie fell in love, but her father didn't want her marrying a Hispanic man and when she did, he disinherited her."

"Her brother was even worse. He tormented them and tried to provoke Johnny whenever he could. I think he wanted Johnny to do something stupid and get sent to jail so Junie would come to her senses and return to the family. I know Angus helped Johnny out of a difficult situation more than once," Eleanor added.

"The Wakefields are still the richest and most powerful family in Waterton. It must have been hard for Junie to go from that to living on a mechanic's salary," Dede said.

"The sad ending though was Johnny drowning and leaving Junie a widow less than a month after their wedding," Josephine said. "I'm surprised she didn't try to kill herself. She must have been totally distraught when they found his boat capsized."

"Did they ever find his body?" asked Pearl.

"No, they never did. It must have drifted out to sea. Some of his belongings were found on the beach. I suppose the Wakefields are happy now. Junie has been welcomed back into the fold," Dede said.

"It isn't much of a fold. Junie's mother died years ago, so it's only Rob and Junie who live with their dad in that monstrosity they call a home," Cleo said. "Sometimes I walk by their house. It's like a fortress up there on the hill with gates at the driveway and a wall surrounding it."

"Is there barbed wire at the top of the fence?" asked Pearl.

"No, but there's broken glass on top of the wall to deter trespassers. I wonder what he has that he thinks is so valuable," Cleo said.

"Probably his daughter," Eleanor said. "Now that she's a widow and due to inherit half of her father's money, there must be swarms of suitors vying for her affections."

"Maybe the wall is to keep her in," Pearl suggested.

"When you have a great deal of money, you have to worry about losing it," Dede said. "That's the curse that comes along with a blessing like that."

"He may be protecting his privacy as well as his family and his secrets. We've all heard rumors about his connections to the mafia. Maybe he made his fortune and enemies too through criminal activity," Josephine speculated. "I've always found him to be a bully and a thug. I was in a restaurant when he was entertaining a large group of his people. The waitstaff scurried around like he was the King of England or something trying to please him. They were probably hoping for a large tip, but he insisted on seeing the chef, complained about his meal, and left paying nothing and leaving no tip at all."

"If not through criminal activity, at least by cheating hard working people out of what should have been theirs," Dede said. "He's like a shark that takes a bite out of what it wants and leaves blood and destruction behind."

"I heard he refused to pay the caterer at Junie's wedding because he wasn't satisfied with one of the dishes. If they take him to court to get their money it will break them financially. That's the kind of man he is—morally bankrupt," said Josephine. "He doesn't care that those people worked hard to provide him with a lovely dinner and now will not be compensated for it."

"Do you think he used his connections to have Johnny killed?" Cleo asked.

"Oh no, don't even go there, Cleo!" warned Pearl who had been enjoying the peaceful months with no mystery to solve.

"Now that's a case I'd stay out of for sure!" Dede exclaimed. "It would be suicide to get involved with the Wakefields, even if the mafia wasn't part of it. They'd sue you for slander or some trumped up charge that would ruin you financially, and if they are part of the underworld they'd put a contract out on you, burn your house down, or break your legs."

"Breaking into their house would pose a challenge, to say the least. I'm sure they have killer dogs patrolling the perimeter." Cleo was already planning the snoop. "Mercedes, our veterinarian, could provide us with something to disable the dogs . . . "

"Stop, stop, and stop," ordered Pearl.

"Let it go Cleo," Dede advised, "if the police didn't find anything that pointed to foul play, I doubt that we would."

"Not to mention the fact that it is just too risky," Josephine added.

"It galls me that someone like that might get away with murder," Cleo said. "Maybe Wanda could help find some clues."

"What do you think it means that Johnny shoots and kills Angus in my dream?" asked Eleanor.

"Guns usually are symbols for male sex organs," Josephine said. "They could also symbolize power."

"Was it a big gun?" Cleo teased.

"I think Angus' corpse indicates a death of some kind. Maybe it means the death of an old relationship for a new one," Dede offered.

"Maybe you were just reliving the whole episode over again," Pearl said, "only this time it had an ending produced by your fear of losing Angus."

"Are you afraid of losing Angus?" Josephine asked. "It makes sense since you lost your first love, Walter."

"Are you afraid of losing your youth and sexual vitality?" asked Cleo, "Because I'm sure Madam Patruska has a crystal for that."

"I think maybe we're done here," said Eleanor.

Before Eleanor drove home, she stopped at the grocery store to pick up a few things for dinner. Tonight, she would cook teriyaki flank steak for Angus and finish it off with fresh blueberry pie and vanilla ice cream. She had no intention of losing him.

Angus arrived at Eleanor's house promptly at six. Instead of thinking that he was compulsive, Eleanor preferred to see him as extremely polite. He never kept her waiting, and it was a trait she appreciated especially when dinner was cooked and ready to eat on time.

"What's that delectable aroma?" Angus inquired as he sniffed the air and then sniffed behind Eleanor's ear. "Are you wearing a new perfume? It smells delicious."

"Teriyaki flank steak," she answered as she took the bouquet of yellow daisies he handed her and led him to the kitchen.

"I think you smell good enough to eat," he said as he took her in his arms and kissed her. "I love you Eleanor Penrose."

Feathers took this moment to fly into the kitchen and interrupt with his loud command, "Get out, you swine."

Eleanor laughed and freed herself to pour Angus his favorite Crown Royal on ice. She poured herself a glass of red wine and the two went out on the deck to wait while the steak rested. The sun shone bright over the ocean and a few clouds had gathered on the horizon. They sat and looked out at the shoreline dotted with summer tourists.

"I love this view," said Eleanor. "I know some people say the ocean is boring and it just stays the same day after day, but I never get tired of looking at it. To me, it's always changing.

Some days it's calm and the color of the sky and on other days it's gray with wild waves that roar and crash against the beach like an angry lover."

Angus only had eyes for Eleanor. "I think the view is beautiful too." They sipped their drinks and enjoyed the gentle music of the ocean. When it got chilly, they went inside to feast on Eleanor's "epicurean delight" as Angus called it. After dessert, Angus sat at the dining table and pulled a postcard from his pocket.

"I wasn't going to show this to anyone, but I want to know what you think of it," he said as he looked at Eleanor from under his lowered brows.

"You seem troubled. What is it?" she asked as she took the postcard and studied it.

On one side there was a large rainbow trout swimming in a clear stream surrounded by green, mossy rocks and grasses. On the back, Angus' address and a simple handprinted sentence read: *Johnny Vargas was murdered.* Eleanor knew how much Angus liked Johnny Vargas and knew he still grieved for his friend. "Do you think this is possible?" she asked.

"I don't know. There wasn't a body to autopsy. The police ruled it an accident. I'm sure they must have inspected his boat. They didn't find anything that might indicate foul play." Angus didn't say what he was thinking: that they didn't find those things because they weren't looking for those things. It had been Angus' job as a homicide detective to notice the type of clues that small town officers might overlook because they didn't see a possible murder in every death. If there had been blood in the boat, they would have assumed it was fish blood. If the boat had been tampered with, they would have simply seen damage from a treacherous ride down the river. No one had mentioned murder. They may have assumed that a young man fishing alone on the river capsized, drowned, and washed out to sea—case closed.

"Where did this come from?" Eleanor asked.

"I don't know," Angus said, "the postmark is smeared."

"How long have you had it?"

"A couple of days."

"Are you thinking what I'm thinking?" Eleanor asked.

"Who had a motive for killing Johnny Vargas?" Angus asked.

"One person comes to mind immediately. Someone with no moral integrity who disapproved of a Hispanic son in-law," Eleanor said.

"He'd be the obvious suspect, but not the only one with motive. There's Eric Fowler who might kill for love, and Rob Wakefield who simply hated Johnny," Angus speculated.

"Rob had double motive if you consider how much he wants Olivia Martin. With Johnny out of the way, Junie might turn to Eric for comfort leaving Olivia available for Rob. A double win for Mr. Wakefield," Eleanor offered.

Angus looked at her with admiration. "I think your detective skills are improving, Ellie."

"But how would we ever prove anything?" she asked.

"We keep our eyes and ears open and our mouths shut," Angus said. "Howard Wakefield is a powerful man with dangerous connections. If he got wind that anyone was investigating Johnny's death as a homicide and he was a suspect, there would be lawsuits, threats, and definitely payback."

"Do you think the police looked the other way knowing this?" Eleanor asked.

"I don't think they found any evidence even if they suspected it. Howard's a big fish in a little pond—the kind of man who chews people up and spits them out."

"And who wants to tangle with a shark?" asked Eleanor.

The thought of dealing with an investigation involving the Wakefields was terrifying to Eleanor, but the fact that Angus asked her opinion about a case pleased her immensely. He had even complimented her on her detective skills and included her in his potential search for information. With no clear idea where to start she put it out of her mind and went to Suzanna's for lunch instead. She was pleasantly surprised to find Mattie May sitting at the usual table of the Do Nothings with an elderly gentleman.

"Eleanor, won't you join us," Mattie invited with a smile. "I'd like you to meet my new friend and latest addition to the Do Nothings, Artemas Chase. He and his son and daughter-in-law just moved into Henry Ott's house."

A lean, white-haired man stood politely and took Eleanor's hand. "It's a pleasure to meet you, Eleanor." Eleanor noticed he leaned heavily on his cane, but his grip was firm and his blue eyes held hers with a kind and gentle gaze.

"Eleanor Penrose is our resident poet and has published several books. She's quite well-known in literary circles," Mattie bragged on her friend's behalf.

"I'll have to read them," he said, "now that I'm a man of leisure."

"Art is a retired spy," Mattie informed Eleanor and was gratified to see her eyes widen with interest.

Art shook his head as if to deny the remark. "I've lived a more interesting life than most."

"He worked with the counterintelligence corps during and after World War ll, hunting Nazis," Mattie said.

"That was long ago," Art said. "Now I'm just an old, retired man living by the sea enjoying the company of two lovely women."

"How do you like our little village?" Eleanor inquired.

"It's beautiful, the weather is temperate, and I find the people are engaging and delightful." Artemas Chase had mastered the art of charm.

"Mattie, have you told him about casino night at the community center?" Eleanor asked, knowing Mattie played an integral part in the planning of the fundraiser.

"Absolutely, I've commanded him to come and bring his family with him. It's sure to be a fun event and the money goes to build a new roof for the center," Mattie said.

"I can see why a new roof is necessary. The weather in a coastal town is sure to cause wear and tear on everything," Art remarked. "I imagine the life of a roof here is only half that of one with an inland climate."

"I'd love to meet your son and his wife," Eleanor said. "I I hope to see you there."

"Speak of the devil." Art looked out the window as a green SUV pulled up outside. "I see my ride is here. That would be Cynthia. She doesn't trust me to walk up that hill and I honestly don't know if these old legs could manage it." He stood and walked slowly to the door. "Thank you for your company, Mattie. It was a pleasure, Eleanor." The ladies watched as he got into the car and it drove off.

"What a sweet man," Eleanor remarked.

"I saw him first, Eleanor," Mattie warned. Love knows no age.

Casino night at the community center came and Eleanor and Angus walked down to the village together. It was a warm evening for Sand Beach and many of the residents were gathered outside on the deck overlooking the ocean.

Eleanor was surprised to see Junie Vargas on the arm of Eric Fowler. Angus had already noticed, and like a true professional simply feigned indifference, while Eleanor could hardly contain her emotions. How could Junie so quickly forget the love of her life and return to her old high school beau? It was incredible considering how deeply she seemed to love Johnny and how horribly Eric had treated him. Something inside Eleanor broke as she witnessed what she perceived as a betrayal. Maybe Junie should be on that list of suspects, she thought. Maybe the apple didn't fall far from the tree.

Cleo and her husband, Steven were at the blackjack table losing all their money when Eleanor approached them, leaving Angus to buy tickets for a fifty-fifty lottery. It was noisy and crowded inside the center as people wandered around bidding on items for a silent auction and playing various games of chance. "Did you see Junie Vargas with Eric Fowler?" Eleanor whispered into Cleo's ear.

Cleo left her spot at the table and picked up her chips. "That's not all," she said, gesturing toward a space where Rob Wakefield stood with his arm wrapped around Olivia Martin in a possessive way. He looked pleased with himself, but she appeared to be less than happy. It seemed as though Johnny Vargas's death had set off a game of musical lovers. Without saying a word, Eleanor and Cleo communicated their concerns and spent the evening watching and listening. All bets were off.

When Junie left Eric's side to visit the ladies' room, Cleo and Eleanor followed her. "It's so nice to see you out and about, Junie," Eleanor said as she washed her hands and peered at Junie's reflection in the mirror.

Junie finished applying her lipstick, tucked a stray lock of dark hair behind her ear and turned to look Eleanor directly in the eye before she responded, "Don't judge me, Eleanor. It's not what is seems." Then she walked out of the room.

"Well, I guess she must feel guilty," Cleo said as she came out of her stall.

"Maybe," Eleanor said thoughtfully.

Just then Dede, Waterton's mayor, rushed into the room with her hand over her heart and her brow furrowed in concern. "What's wrong?" asked Eleanor.

"I've just discovered a lump in my breast," she said, "I'm sure it's cancer. Mark's sister was diagnosed last week and she's the same age as me."

"Where is it?" asked Cleo as she stared at Dede's breasts as if she could cure it with her intense gaze. "Right here," Dede once again put her hand over her left breast.

"Isn't that where you put my caramel earlier? You said if you put it in your bra your body heat would soften it up," Cleo said.

Dede reached into her blouse and pulled out the cancerous caramel and let out a sigh of relief. "I totally forgot I put it in there." She looked at each of her friends and swore them to secrecy. "If this ever gets out, I'll never get re-elected mayor."

"Is anyone running against you?" asked Eleanor.

"No, but you never know." Dede checked each of the restroom stalls to see if anyone else might have heard the humiliating exchange.

"There's a reason I'm not in politics," said Cleo. The three returned to the clamor of the main hall where people continued to offer up their hard-earned wages in the hope of winning big money.

Artemas Chase was seated in Cleo's place at the blackjack table beside Steve. Eleanor was happy to see him there but didn't want to interrupt what looked like a winning streak for him. She found Angus out on the deck visiting with a man and a woman Eleanor did not know.

"Eleanor, this is Will Chase and his wife, Cynthia. They just moved into Henry Ott's house," Angus said.

"And this is Eleanor Penrose."

"So lovely to meet you." Cynthia smiled warmly. She did not offer her hand and Eleanor noticed the twisted fingers and swollen joints that signaled arthritis. Her hair, perfectly styled, was dyed a dark blonde with lighter highlights. She wore a custom-fitted navy linen suit that was adorned with a single strand of pearls.

Will, on the other hand, gripped her hand tightly and spoke in the most flattering way. "My father mentioned that he met a famous poet at the restaurant in the village. I must say I'm a fan of your work, Eleanor. It's a great honor to meet you." Eleanor tried to imagine Will as a younger version of his father. He was handsome but without the sparkle and easy charm that Art possessed.

"Thank you, I must admit to being impressed with your father. He said he has lived an interesting life and I'm eager to hear more," Eleanor said. The couple simply smiled as if to discount the claims of an old man.

"It's always good to meet new people," Angus said. "I hope we can get to know you better. Do you fish?" From there the conversation evolved into a dull drone that involved the word fish, fish, fishing, and left Eleanor and Cynthia to smile dully at each other and finally step away from the men to begin a conversation that led them to learn about topics that they might have in common.

"Do you play bridge?" Cynthia asked.

"I used to but really haven't played in quite some time," Eleanor admitted.

"Oh, I so love to play and was hoping to find a group here." She sounded so disappointed that Eleanor tried to lift her distress by offering to help her.

"I'm sure there are groups here. I'll ask some of my friends if they know any."

"I'd be so grateful!" Cynthia exclaimed. "I really don't know how to fill the empty hours in my day now that Will and I have retired so far from my friends and regular routine. What do you do with your time, Eleanor?"

"There's so much to do, I don't think I'll live long enough to accomplish everything," Eleanor said. "I walk most days, read, visit with friends and family, cook, and of course, there's my writing."

"Oh, I guess I just need to get out there and make myself available. Perhaps there is some volunteer work I could do," Cynthia mused.

"Every Wednesday evening there's a soup kitchen at the Catholic Church," Eleanor offered and noticed Cynthia wrinkle her nose. "And in the fall, there's a smart reader program at the public schools where you can listen to children read. If you don't mind me offering advice, I'd give myself some time before committing to too much. Some blue-sky time is good for self-reflection and it fosters creativity. I have a friend who offers mosaic classes at her studio."

"Oh, I'm afraid I haven't a creative bone in my body," Cynthia admitted. "Before we moved here I pretty much stayed home and cleaned my house, did the laundry, and ironed. Of course, there were visits to the salon, dinner parties for Will's work, a little crocheting, and my bridge. I just love to play bridge."

Eleanor was reading Cynthia Chase as a woman who catered to her husband's needs and career without thinking too much about her own fulfillment. She imagined her house was immaculate and her mind cleared of complexity. She seemed to be a woman who let her husband worry and make the decisions so she could simply be his wife.

"Do you and Will have children?" Eleanor probed.

"Yes, two sons who are married and live far away from us, I'm afraid. Each of them has two children, but sadly we've never bonded with them. They rarely visit because they are so very successful in their work and their lives are so full. We're extremely proud of their achievements. They both live on the East Coast. One is a lawyer and the other a banker. Will and I visit once a year. You should see their houses, so big and decorated by the best interior designers. Have you heard of Fostoria Grand? She did both of their homes—just stunning," Cynthia boasted.

"Lovely," Eleanor said without much conviction. Cynthia Chase evidently held different values than Eleanor. She knew the type, who thought success could be measured in dollars and not happiness. "It's been a pleasure to meet you. I'm sure we'll run into each other again around the village." Eleanor smiled and walked away to find Dede or Cleo or anyone who wasn't Cynthia Chase, Stepford wife.

Pearl and Josephine were throwing darts at a wall of balloons, hoping to win a prize. They both sported several cheap beaded necklaces that would be used in another game of chance to be played later. Eleanor watched as Rob Wakefield erased someone's name from the silent auction sheet and wrote his own over it. Even with all he had, he still felt the need to cheat. When he left, Eleanor outbid him just because it felt right. She had no desire for the fishing pole he bid on, but maybe Angus could use it if she won. When the evening was over Angus walked Eleanor home hand in hand with nothing to show for their wagers except full hearts and a fishing pole.

In the morning, Eleanor once again walked down to the beach to enjoy the early solitude of a meditative walk along the shore. Just as she stepped onto the sand she heard a cry from behind her and turned to see Cynthia Chase waving dramatically from her car parked in the wayside. Eleanor paused and waited for Cynthia to catch up.

"Good morning, Eleanor," Cynthia panted. "I'm so glad I caught you. Do you mind if I walk with you this morning?"

Eleanor was looking forward to her quiet morning exercise but graciously answered, "No, not at all." Eleanor set the pace and Cynthia matched her step for step.

"Angus invited Will to go fishing this morning, and I drove Art down to Suzanna's because the house was empty and so very quiet. I remembered you said you walked daily so I waited in the parking lot for you," Cynthia admitted. "It seems Art has found a group of women who have welcomed him to join them for coffee and conversation. He let me know I wasn't to come. Do you know these women?"

"Yes, they're older than you and more Art's age. They're all retired professional women who call themselves the Do Nothings, but that's a misnomer since they are all vital and involved in most things that go on in Sand Beach." Eleanor knew Cynthia wouldn't be a good fit there.

"Do they play bridge?" she asked.

"I don't think so, but they might play cribbage." Eleanor remembered something about a cribbage tournament they held some time ago. Eleanor wasn't one for cards and preferred board games when given the choice.

There was a long period of silence and Eleanor stopped to pick up some colorful agates. Suddenly a sneaker wave rolled in and Eleanor called out to Cynthia to get out of the way. Cynthia ran shrieking like a banshee, but her new white walking shoes didn't escape a soaking. "I've never lived by the ocean before," she admitted. "Do you mind if I sit down here and catch my breath?" she asked, indicating a driftwood log.

"Not a good idea. Those logs can be deadly when a wave comes in. You must never underestimate the power of the ocean. Just a few inches of water can lift and roll those pieces of driftwood over, pinning you underneath or killing you outright," Eleanor cautioned. "Let's just keep going."

Cynthia seemed rattled and didn't speak for some time. "We've always lived inland but vacationed often by the shore. Mostly I stay out of the water though. I prefer to enjoy its beauty from a distance. I suppose you think I'm a fraidy-cat and I wouldn't argue with you. Even in the pool, I don't ever get my face or hair wet."

"I have a healthy fear of this ocean too. Never turn your back on it and don't go out too far—those are my rules for staying safe. I seldom walk this beach in winter during high tide when it's easy to get trapped between the rocks and the waves." Eleanor wondered if Cynthia would ever venture out alone.

When they returned to the village Eleanor waved good-bye and watched as Cynthia drove back up the hill to get out of her wet shoes. Eleanor was glad to have her thoughts to herself but decided to slip into Suzanna's to check on the Do Nothings.

Mattie and Art sat at the group's usual place along with Sybil and Mavis. They welcomed Eleanor and invited her to share their table. Art stood while the ladies adjusted their chairs to include Eleanor. "So, what do you know?" asked Mattie.

"Not too much. It's great to see you again Art. I just met Cynthia on the beach," Eleanor reported.

"Be careful of that one," he warned. "She'll be sucking you dry if you let her."

"What do you mean by that?" asked Mavis. "Is she a vampire?"

"No, no, just lonely and empty—looking for something or someone to fill up a deep hole she doesn't know she has," Art said. "You can befriend her but then you might be responsible for her forever after."

"Duly noted," Eleanor said. "I'm really more interested in you, Art. The fact that you searched for Nazi's is fascinating to me. Did you ever find any?"

"Sure, I did. I worked with Simon Wiesenthal who gave 100 names to the War Crimes office of the American

51

Counterintelligence Corps at Mauthausen. We caught many more who escaped to South America long after the war was over and others stopped thinking of them. Just a few years ago we were still finding those implicated in lesser crimes. Reinhold Hanning, a former death camp guard, is one example, but honestly most of them are dead by now."

"How did they manage to get to South America?" Mavis asked.

"Several of the big fish like Eichmann and Mengele escaped from their captors and were helped by others. Some Nazi sympathizers helped them and even the Catholic Church, which may have done so unknowingly while they were resettling Jews who were interred in the camps," Art related. "They wouldn't have gotten far without the aid of others."

"After all this time, I've forgotten so much," Sybil admitted. "Didn't they catch Eichmann and hang him?"

"Yes, he was captured by the Israeli Mossad. I was there and saw it all." Art gazed out the window as though seeing it all again. "Eichmann was living in Argentina with his wife and four children under an assumed name. He was working as a manager in an auto factory there. A German prosecutor got wind of it and informed the Israelis who sent in their people. I was included as a special reward for the work I had done previously. We abducted him as he got off the bus on his way home. It was all done secretly since we knew Argentina would never extradite him. We drugged him and flew him to Israel disguised as an airline worker with a head injury. He was tried in Israel for crimes against humanity and hanged even though he claimed he was just following orders."

"Amazing." Eleanor could hardly believe she was sitting next to this man. "You must have so many stories to tell. Have you thought about writing them in a memoir?"

"Of course," he nodded, "I have written many of them down, but it's a sad business and one I'm reluctant to relive over and over again."

"I certainly understand that." Mattie shook her head and glared at Eleanor. "We shouldn't have brought it up and I promise not to mention it again. What horrors you must have witnessed!"

"I'm tired," he said as he stood up and walked slowly to the door. "It was a pleasure to be with you today." Eleanor noticed Cynthia had arrived to pick up her father-in-law and was waiting in the car.

"Such an interesting man and a gentleman too," Mavis said.

"Yes, but it seems that will be the last of his fascinating stories for us," Sybil whined.

"Maybe not," Eleanor said, "Most people enjoy talking about what they did in their youth. We'll just have to wait and let him initiate the story telling. Chances are he'll tell us a great deal if we are patient."

Mattie pursed her lips in disapproval. "He said his daughter-in-law wanted to come with him, but he told her to find her own coffee group. I like him, but I get the idea he doesn't think much of her."

"I can't imagine why," Eleanor said innocently.

There was so much to tell, Cleo could hardly wait to share her information with her friends. Of course, it would be the day when everyone else was late. Cleo sat at their favorite table by the river rock fireplace and waited. She hated waiting. Eleanor had told her not to wait but to watch, so she looked out the window and watched several stellar jays fly past. She watched the clock on the wall and realized she was early and her friends were not late at all. She watched a lonely woman sitting at a table across the room by herself drinking coffee and dabbing tears from her perfectly made-up face. She was so busy watching she didn't notice Pearl and Josephine come in and sit down at the table. Eleanor followed and soon everyone was talking at once.

"I have so many letters to read and I really want to run my answers by you before I lay it on the line to this one in particular," Josephine said. Her column, "Just Josie", had appeared in the *Fish Wrapper* for the first time and people all over town were talking about it.

Dede came in and sat down at the table just as the woman from across the room approached their table. "Eleanor, how lovely to see you here! I was just trying out some of the restaurants in the area. This is a very cozy spot by the fireplace and the ambiance here is so warm. Do you mind if I join you? I really hate eating alone." Cynthia Chase didn't give anyone a chance to decline as she pulled a chair from a nearby table and sat down to join the group.

"Cynthia Chase, these are my dear friends: Josephine, Cleo, Pearl, and Dede. Cynthia just moved into Henry Ott's house," Eleanor said politely.

Cleo was biting her tongue. There was no way she could share her information with a stranger at the table. Josephine also had to keep her own counsel since no one knew the true identity of Just Josie.

Pearl was hoping to tell about a dream she had but wasn't eager to reveal intimate details with Cynthia Chase, and Dede was bursting with bile over a city council meeting and an issue that had come up involving Howard Wakefield. It was strangely quiet at the coffee group's table.

"It is so wonderful to meet ladies of good breeding," Cynthia cooed. "I wonder if any of you play bridge. I just love to play and since we've moved here I haven't met a soul who does."

"I used to play," Pearl said, "but it was too competitive for me. I'd rather have fun playing hearts than have my partner glaring at me because I bid on the wrong suit."

"Sorry, I never learned," Cleo stated firmly, hoping the admission would make Cynthia go away.

"I too played years ago but haven't for some time. I'm afraid I'm very rusty," Josephine said. Dede simply sat and said nothing. She was afraid if she opened her mouth toads and serpents would spew out.

"Well, I certainly would appreciate it if you could tell any of your acquaintances who play that I'm looking for a group." Cynthia picked up a menu and the ladies at the table gave up all hope of enjoying their weekly meeting. "What do you recommend? She said with a satisfied smile."

After what seemed a long and frustrating breakfast, Dede excused herself with some lame statement about a city meeting. "Are you involved in city politics?" Cynthia asked.

"Dede is Waterton's Mayor," Eleanor said.

"I had no idea! Here I am sitting with the mayor and a famous author and I had no idea!"

"I'll see you girls at that meeting later," Dede's eyebrows shot up and down and then she was gone.

"It was nice to meet you, Cindy," Cleo said hoping to offend her, "but I have a stomachache and need to get home."

"Me too," said Eleanor, "I've got errands to run in town." Josephine and Pearl simply stood to leave with no excuses. They all arrived at Dede's house at the same time. She had the coffee freshly made.

"Good grief, what was that?" asked Dede.

"An ambush," Eleanor said in her defense. "I certainly didn't invite her."

"I am just beside myself with things to talk about that could not be discussed with Cynthia at the table," said Josephine.

"I felt a little bad. Are we mean?" Cleo asked.

"It does feel a little like junior high school to be so exclusive," Pearl remarked.

"No, no, no! That was our time and our place. It's our therapy session. We do not owe Cynthia anything. She was rude to barge in and invite herself to a private party. Under the circumstances, we were more than polite," Josephine stated.

"Were we polite enough that she would feel comfortable coming back next week?" Eleanor worried. The others pondered their predicament.

"I need help with this letter," Josephine said.

"Let's have it," said Dede as she poured the coffee.

"Dear Just Josie,

My girlfriend and I dated all through high school. We broke up for a short time but now we're back together. We were intimate before but now she's stopped putting out and won't tell me why. Should I dump her?

Signed Horny

"I'd tell him to do her a favor and dump her," said Cleo. "That guy is obviously a jerk."

"He *is* obviously a jerk," Josephine agreed, "but do you think he's *the* jerk, Eric Fowler?"

"Eric Fowler wouldn't write a letter. He probably doesn't know how," said Dede.

"He might write a letter like that to embarrass Junie. There would be a number of people in town who might think it's about them," Eleanor surmised.

"You're not going to publish it are you?" asked Pearl.

"Absolutely not! I just wanted you to know about it," Josephine said. "I plan to send him a private letter.

Here's what I wrote:

Dear Horny,

Your letter shows a total lack of respect for your girlfriend. You don't include any details about the breakup, but I'll assume it is because you lack the finer attributes of a gentleman. A true gentleman would talk with her to determine why she no longer wished to have sex with him. Perhaps it is a hygiene problem and she's reluctant to tell you. A true gentleman wouldn't assume that because he once enjoyed her charms, he was entitled to them for the rest of his life. She may want to be courted. It may be you are misinterpreting her signals and she isn't really back together with you at all and doesn't want to hurt your feelings. Try bathing, patience, and kindness, but if these don't give you the results you want, give her some space and see if she cares.

Sincerely,

Just Josie

"That works," said Dede.

"I like it," Cleo chimed in.

"It makes me ill to think that Junie is being pushed into having an intimate relationship with Eric Fowler so soon after Johnny's death. It just doesn't seem right," Eleanor sighed.

"There's always the chance it's not Eric Fowler," Josephine admitted.

"Well, guess who is running for mayor of Waterton?" Dede stood with her hands on her hips in what could only be construed as a position of extreme displeasure.

"You mean besides you?" asked Pearl.

"Against me," she replied.

"Who?" asked Josephine.

"Edward Fowler," Dede said.

"The Edward Fowler from the lumber mill?" asked Eleanor.

"He doesn't live within the city limits," Pearl said.

"Yes, Edward Fowler from the lumber mill," said Dede. "Evidently this has been in the works for some time. He bought a house down the street from me six months ago. I suspect it's a ploy to get the city council to approve a suspicious massage parlor within the city limits. Someone from outside the town of Waterton has requested a business license for such a venture that looks a lot like a brothel and the council has strongly vetoed it. At least most of them have. Now I find out that not only is someone running against me, but there are three new residents running against the council members who opposed that business."

"That's terrible," said Eleanor. "Are you sure it's that kind of massage parlor?"

"Oh yes, the interesting thing about all this is every one of those new residents running are backed by Howard Wakefield's money, including Edward Fowler." Dede was angry. There was silence while the women thought this through.

"If they win, he'll own the city. With three of Wakefield's flunkies on the council, they can tie every proposal and the mayor will have to break the tie. If he has the mayor in his pocket . . . Waterton is doomed," Josephine said.

"They can't possibly win," Cleo said. "Who in Waterton is going to vote for total strangers to sit on the city council?"

"I don't know, but I don't like it," Dede said. "Remember the fire that burned down the old Methodist church on the corner? Howard Wakefield bought that property and that's the location for his new business venture."

"You think he's responsible for burning it down?" asked Eleanor.

"Maybe," said Dede.

"Well, I'll tell you something I don't like. Remember when I told you I was getting Wanda to be my housekeeper?" Cleo asked. "Yesterday she came to my house in the afternoon and she did more talking than cleaning. Howard Wakefield is seldom home, and Junie has stopped going out, rarely leaving the house. Sofia, Johnny's sister, is the only one she allows in her room. Evidently, they've become very close—like sisters, she said. Rob is out until all hours of the night. Wanda goes there every morning for four hours to clean and do laundry. She was really upset when she got to my house because she found a T-shirt in Rob's room that had blood on it."

"So maybe he cut himself shaving," Josephine said.

"It's more likely he got in a fight of some sort," Eleanor added.

"She said there was a lot of blood and she found it stuffed in the back of his closet. It looked like he was trying to hide it," Cleo said. "I told her to take it to the police."

"Don't you think that's a little extreme?" asked Pearl. "What if he just had a bloody nose?"

"Who do you think he killed, Cleo?" Josephine asked.

"Johnny Vargas," Cleo said without skipping a beat.

"Let's not go down that road again. Johnny Vargas drowned in the river," Pearl argued. "His death was an accident."

"Maybe not," said Eleanor. "Angus received an anonymous postcard several days ago that said Johnny Vargas was murdered. He asked me to keep my ears and eyes open and my mouth shut so Howard Wakefield wouldn't find out that we were investigating Johnny's death as a murder. It could be dangerous, but I think it's time we were all involved. This bloody T-shirt could be a big break in the case."

Once again, a strange silence descended on the ladies. Finally, they heard a sad moan and looked at Pearl who had laid her head on the table in distress. "Didn't Madame Patruska warn you about vampires sucking the life out of you, Cleo?" "That's right," said Josephine. "She also told Junie that blood would begin and end her suffering."

Eleanor was excited to tell Angus everything she learned from her coffee investigators. She planned to make Mongolian pork chops with cabbage and mashed potatoes. She spent most of the afternoon working on the marinade and making a peach cobbler for dessert. She had just put the cobbler in the oven when Angus called.

"Ellie, it's Angus. Are you busy cooking up something delicious?"

"I hope so. Don't tell me you can't make it." Eleanor could count the times Angus had missed a dinner invitation on a one fingered hand.

"Just the opposite, I wondered if you'd mind if Will and Cynthia Chase came too." Angus had never known Eleanor to exclude anyone from her table and was pretty sure she'd say yes.

"Sure." Eleanor hoped the disappointment she felt didn't' show in her voice.

"Good, because I already invited them. See you at six."

How would she tell Angus everything she wanted to share with company at the table? She'd just have to wait until they left. Cynthia Chase was becoming a nuisance. Maybe the universe was telling her to open her circle and let in new friends. She just wasn't sure Cynthia Chase was friend material. Angus had gone fishing with Will so they must have hit it off for Angus to invite him to dinner. She wondered what was up. As usual, Angus arrived promptly at six with a bottle of Chardonnay and a bouquet of yellow roses.

"I know you prefer red wine, but Will told me Cynthia only drinks white, so I hope you don't mind that I brought this," Angus apologized as he leaned in for a kiss. Eleanor wasn't that much of a wine snob but had mixed feelings about Angus catering to Cynthia's desires. She could bring her own white wine if that's all she would drink.

"Better put it in the refrigerator to chill," Eleanor said. "Does Will have a preference too?"

Angus ignored the remark or just didn't hear it as the doorbell rang. "I'll get it." Eleanor stuffed the roses in a vase and followed Angus to the door.

"Come in." Angus welcomed them inside. Feathers, on the other hand, did not always approve of dinner guests and flew into the room squawking. "Lock them out, lock them out!" He landed on Cynthia's head and as she stood frozen in fear, he leered down into her face and said, "Well, hello there!"

Angus and Will's laughter sent Feathers flying to his perch by the window. It was plain to see that Cynthia didn't approve of the ill-mannered bird. She ran a perfectly manicured hand over her hair and took a deep breath.

Will held a bottle of pinot noir. "Angus said you liked red wine. I hope this is up to your standards."

Eleanor smiled and took the wine to the kitchen. "Thank you. Would you like a drink?"

Angus opened the wine and poured drinks while Eleanor readied the chops for grilling. They took their drinks out on the deck and looked over the sleepy town below as the waves washed the shore.

"This is truly heaven," sighed Cynthia settling deeply into a deck chair. "I don't know how we lived so long without this peaceful quiet."

"I'm guessing there were no fish caught today," Eleanor remarked as she turned the pork chops and added marinade.

"No luck there, but I can't say I've enjoyed any day more. The weather was perfect, and the company wasn't bad either." Will sipped his drink as he and Angus recapped the day on the water.

Cynthia helped Eleanor put the meal on the table and they sat down to dinner. "Angus wasn't exaggerating when he said you were an excellent cook, Eleanor. That was delicious. Those pork chops were the best I've ever eaten!" Will complimented. "Is there a special marinade you use?"

"Thank you, Will." Eleanor rose and began to clear the table. She was not going to reveal her secret marinade recipe. "Would you like dessert? I made a peach cobbler."

"I am just stuffed, although that sounds divine." Cynthia stood to help Eleanor.

"Maybe we could have dessert after that dinner settles," Angus remarked.

"I've got some special cigars we could smoke on the deck if that's all right with you Eleanor," Will said.

"Sounds great," Angus said as he pushed his chair away from the table and walked out on the deck with Will. Eleanor found herself in the kitchen with Cynthia who began putting away leftovers and washing dishes.

"Where's Art tonight?" asked Eleanor.

"He had a dinner date with Mattie," Cynthia said. "I think she's got her eye on him although I can't imagine why. The old man isn't long for this world."

"Why do you say that? Is he ill?" Eleanor asked.

"He's over ninety. How much longer can he live?"

"Who knows? Even the few years he has left can be happy ones if he finds people he enjoys being around. He might make them happy too. He and Mattie may be old but they're not dead."

"I find his stories boring," Cynthia admitted.

"I thought he was very charming, and his stories were quite interesting," Eleanor said.

"*You* haven't heard them hundreds of times. The old man lives in the past."

Eleanor finished tidying up and led Cynthia out on the deck to join the men. She was beginning to feel like an old married couple, and she didn't like it. It wasn't like Angus to leave her to do the work while he relaxed after dinner. Will Chase was a bad influence as far as she was concerned. After what seemed like several hours, Will and Cynthia said their good-nights and finally left without eating the peach cobbler. "Cynthia and I need to watch the old waistline," Will said. Eleanor was in an exceptionally bad mood—her excitement about the bloody T-shirt almost forgotten in her vexation.

"Would you like some peach cobbler or are you 'watching your old waistline' too," she mimicked.

Angus looked at her sheepishly under his bushy brows. He had a bad feeling and worrying that he might say the wrong thing, he tried wrapping his arms around her and going in for a kiss. Eleanor pushed him away and wrinkled her nose as the scent of cigar breath hit her like a slap. "Did I do something wrong?" he asked innocently. Eleanor could see the hurt on his face and immediately regretted her reaction.

"I guess I'm just in a bad mood. I was hoping for an evening alone with you," she offered, hoping to see the hurt go away.

"I'm sorry. I guess springing them on you for dinner wasn't the best idea I've ever had. Although you made enough to feed them and it was magically delicious." he smiled, producing those little boy dimples that melted her heart.

"Thank you," Eleanor said, deciding to let her anger about male privilege go for a better moment. Angus had moved into the kitchen and was helping himself to a large portion of peach cobbler.

"Sorry I didn't help you clean up after dinner. I don't think Will is used to 'women's work'—his words, not mine." Angus continued, "Cynthia is rather particular about what goes on in the house and likes to do all the cleaning herself, or so I gathered from Will. Honestly Eleanor, I was just trying to make our guests feel comfortable."

It was clear to Eleanor that Angus knew the real reason for her foul mood as he dished up some cobbler for her and topped it with a generous amount of ice cream. They sat at Eleanor's dining table and enjoyed their time together as they ate the delectable dessert without worries of expanding waistlines.

"Cynthia invited herself to the coffee group this morning. None of us could talk about the things we really wanted to so we met at Dede's afterward," Eleanor said. Angus' eyebrows rose, but said nothing because his mouth was full of peaches.

"I've enlisted the help of the coffee group to investigate the murder of Johnny Vargas," she continued.

Angus swallowed. "I'm not sure that's a good idea, Eleanor. This needs to be kept on the down low. If too many people know we think he was murdered, Howard Wakefield will hear and then things could get ugly."

"Just let me explain," Eleanor said. "Cleo has the same housekeeper as Howard Wakefield. Her name is Wanda and Wanda found a bloody T-shirt in the back of Rob Wakefield's closet. You know how Cleo is about a mystery. She's thought from the beginning that Howard had Johnny killed. Anyway, Cleo told her to take it to the police. You can see why I had to tell them about the postcard you received. Now there will be just a few more ears to hear and eyes to see what's going on around town."

"Okay, but you need to make sure they realize how dangerous this can be. Promise me Eleanor, that you'll be careful about what you say. I don't want it to get back to Howard Wakefield that you or your friends are involved in this." Angus frowned. "I think it may be time to visit my friend, Officer McGraw. If the bloody T-shirt turns up along with the postcard, it may be enough for the police to open an official investigation."

The next morning Cynthia Chase turned up on Eleanor's doorstep even before she had finished her crossword puzzle. "I hope you don't mind, but I didn't have any coffee in the house and I was hoping you'd invite me in for a cup," Cynthia pleaded.

"Sure, I just made a fresh pot. Come in." Eleanor thought it would be rude to tell her she could buy coffee at the village store or get a cup at Suzanna's. She refused to apologize for being in her nightgown, after all it was early, and Cynthia was uninvited. Eleanor poured Cynthia a large cup of coffee and the two sat in Eleanor's sparkling white kitchen while Eleanor waited to learn the real reason for Cynthia's early morning visit.

"I've noticed what a remarkable man Angus is," Cynthia began. "I wonder why he isn't taken. Will said the two of you aren't married." Eleanor waited. She didn't feel like talking and hadn't heard a question so said nothing.

"I guess I'm being a busybody, but I know what will make him marry you, Eleanor. Have you ever thought about making him jealous? Sometimes that's all a man needs to push him to pop the question. I had a good friend who was in a similar situation as you and Angus. They had been together for years and truly acted like a married couple, but he just would not commit to her, so she started inviting other men to dinner and going out to the movies and such and before you know it she had a ring on her finger and a husband in her bed."

Eleanor sipped her coffee. She had no time for games of this sort. It made her weary to think of the energy it would take to explain what clearly was none of Cynthia's business. Fortunately, the doorbell rang before Eleanor could say something rude. "Excuse me, it must be important for someone to call this early."

Junie Vargas stood at Eleanor's door; her red mustang parked outside. Feathers flew in to inspect the intruder but only let out a loud whistle and flew into the kitchen to further annoy Cynthia by landing nearby and giving her the fisheye.

"Junie, please come inside," Eleanor said warmly.

"I couldn't sleep and was walking on the beach," she explained. "I'm sorry. I know it's early, but I knew you lived here, and I wanted to return the cookbook you loaned me." She stepped inside and handed the cookbook to Eleanor.

"It was meant for you to keep," Eleanor said.

"It just makes me sad now," Junie said as tears began to pool in her eyes. "I know you must think I'm a terrible person because I was with Eric the other night, but I want you to know . . . " Cynthia Chase chose this moment to appear.

"Oh, I didn't know you had company. Please forgive me for intruding, Eleanor and thank you so much for your help." Junie turned quickly and left.

Eleanor had no doubt that Junie was about to divulge something important. Thanks to Cynthia's untimely visit, Eleanor would never know. As soon as Cynthia left, Eleanor called Cleo.

"Cleo, I need to know the name of the crystal that Madame Patruska said would protect you from vampires."

Eleanor felt ill at ease. Cynthia Chase had intruded on her life and in her personal space, but Eleanor also recognized a lonely person when she saw one and Cynthia needed a friend. Eleanor just did not want the job. She enjoyed the people she called her friends and looked forward to spending time with them. When they called her on the phone, she always answered because she knew they depended on her and she did the same for them.

It made Eleanor feel guilty that she wanted to avoid Cynthia. Weren't we supposed to love our neighbor as ourselves? What if you didn't like your neighbor? There was nothing about loving a disgusting neighbor or one who smelled bad or was just plain annoying. Was it all right to love them from a distance or did you have to become friends with them? Eleanor wasn't a religious person, but she was kind. Maybe she just needed to help Cynthia realize Eleanor and the coffee group weren't the sort of people she wanted to befriend. Even Artemas had created boundaries around the Do Nothings to keep her out. Eleanor wondered if he felt guilty.

Cleo and Eleanor had discussed the problem and had come up with a plan. She was ready to put that plan into play. She picked up the phone and called Cynthia. "Cynthia, this is Eleanor. Some of my friends are coming over to play games this afternoon and we'd like very much for you to join us."

"How lovely! I'd be delighted. What time? Should I bring something? Is it casual?" Cynthia's earnestness was so keen Eleanor almost wished that her invitation was sincere.

"Just come to my house around four. Wear whatever you like. We're not a formal group. See you tomorrow." Eleanor hung up with a sigh and turned her thoughts to snacks and games.

Cleo arrived early to help set up and put the snacks out. When Josephine, Pearl, and Dede arrived everything was ready. They opened the wine and the good times began to roll. Cynthia came promptly at four wearing slacks and a sweater set with her ever-present pearls and her hair carefully styled and held in place by a powerful holding agent. The coffee group wore jeans and Cleo was even in her velvet workout suit. Cynthia brought a tray of freshly baked chocolate chip cookies.

"Come in Cynthia, how nice of you to bake!" Eleanor took the cookies and put them in the kitchen.

"Are we going to play bridge?" she asked hopefully. "You know I just love to play bridge."

"That's not our game," Cleo said between bites of cookie. "We're going to play Headbanz. Have you ever played it?"

"No, I can't say that I have," Cynthia furrowed her brow in thought. "Is that a card game?"

"Sort of . . . it involves cards but don't worry, it's easy. Even kids can play it," Dede said.

"Cynthia, do you want a glass of wine?" asked Eleanor.

Cynthia looked at her watch. "It isn't even five o'clock. Will and I never drink before five, but if you all are having wine, so will I." Eleanor gave her a glass of white and they moved to the dining room table to start the game. Each of the ladies put a headband around their head. Eleanor had to bite her tongue to keep from giggling when she saw the others, but Cleo burst out laughing and could not stop. Soon they were all laughing and snorting while Cynthia looked on in dismay. When the laughing finally stopped, Cynthia said, "I don't think this head thing is going to work with my hair." Cleo stood up and put the band around Cynthia's perfectly coifed do smashing it and rearranging it until the band was in place.

"Perfect," Dede concluded as they proceeded in all seriousness to draw a card from the deck and put it on their headband without looking of course.

"This game always reminds me of that Quentin Tarantino movie *Inglorious Basterds*. You know that scene where they are in a German bar with cards on their heads. Before that I had no idea King Kong was a metaphor for black men and the fear white men have of losing their women to them," Eleanor said.

"You know what they say, 'Once you go black, you never go back,'" Josephine stated.

"Whatever are you talking about?" asked Cynthia. "Wasn't King Kong a horror movie about a giant gorilla?"

"Exactly, although I couldn't really say, since I've never had a black man," Dede said. Josephine watched as Cynthia's eyes widened in horror as she understood the gist of their conversation.

"I don't think it's true," Pearl said. "I'm sure there are white men who are just as big and some black men who aren't big at all."

"Perhaps we should do some research," Josephine proposed.

"I've also heard that size doesn't matter. It's all about how the tool is used," Cleo said.

"Enough, let's get on with the game," ordered Eleanor, flipping over the timer and pointing to Dede whose card revealed a key.

"Do I have legs?"

"No"

"Am I an animal?"

"No"

"Am I alive?"

"No"

"Am I a vegetable?"

"No"

"Am I a tool?"

"Yes"

"Oh my, am I a penis?" Hysterical laughter erupted from the ladies at the table.

"Time's up," Eleanor declared. "Does anyone want more wine?"

"I'm taking another chip," Dede said as she peeked at her card. "A key . . . I'm not even going to go there."

Everyone filled their glasses, and the game continued with more ridiculous comments and even more laughter. At one point, Cynthia spit out her wine and snorted when Dede said she only opened up when she was wet. Cynthia's card was an umbrella. Eleanor calmly passed her a napkin and the game went on even though Cynthia was mortified.

"Let's take a break, and have some pie," Cleo said. They wandered into Eleanor's kitchen in search of treats.

"Don't you have to make dinner for your husbands?" asked Cynthia looking at the clock. The others looked at her as if she were not making sense.

"Not tonight," said Pearl, "it's Cary's night to cook."

"You take turns?" Cynthia was surprised.

"I don't have a husband so I'm having pie for dinner," bragged Eleanor.

"I'm sure Mark can fend for himself," Dede declared.

"Richard's not helpless. He does all of the cooking at our house. When I married him I told him I wasn't going to cook."

"Do you do all the cooking, Cynthia?" Cleo spoke sadly as if she were asking if Cynthia had lost her first-born child.

"Oh yes, and all the cleaning too. I don't think Will knows how to cook anything," Cynthia said.

"He can't make a sandwich?" asked Josephine.

"Well, I'm sure he could, he's just never had to do that. I'm happy to do it for him," she confessed. The others simply looked at her with a mix of pity and disbelief. "Are you girls *feminists*?"

"Of course we are, aren't you?" asked Dede.

"I love men and I don't believe in bashing them," Cynthia said.

"I don't want to speak for all of us, but feminists don't hate men by any means. A feminist is someone who wants equality for men *and* women," Josephine countered.

"I think the term has been misunderstood," Eleanor added. "I love men too and don't have any problem supporting equality. It would be foolish not to in my opinion. Men have just as much to gain as women when the playing field is leveled. Just think of the pressure most men feel that could be eased if women shared an equal part in carrying the load."

"But men are so strong and capable," Cynthia argued.

"So are we," said Pearl.

"What shall we play next?" asked Cleo as she popped the last bite of pie in her mouth.

When the doorbell rang at six thirty, the ladies were in the middle of a lively game of Masterpiece.

Eleanor had scoured her house looking for costumes so they could dress as the characters portrayed on the game cards,

so when she answered the door wearing a smoking jacket and a
mustache, Will Chase was somewhat taken aback.

"Eleanor? Is my wife here?" he asked.

"We're playing a game; do you need her?" she asked.

"Oh, I'm so sorry, Will I didn't realize it was so very late.
Please excuse me, Eleanor. It was fun. Thank you so much
for inviting me." Cynthia took off her beret and left Eleanor's
lorgnette on the table as she rushed to leave with Will. "See
you soon, girls."

After Eleanor closed the door she heard Will ask in
disapproval, "Have you been drinking, Cynthia?"

Eleanor returned to her guests. "I guess this game is over."
They cleared the mess and put away the costumes.

"She really isn't so bad," Cleo said, "maybe just a little
uptight."

"I feel sorry for her," Josephine said. "She doesn't realize
she is a slave to a man of privilege."

"It isn't our job to free her," Pearl said. "Do you think she
hates us now that she sees who we really are?"

"You mean *feminists*?" said Cleo in mock horror.

"We'll have to wait to see if she continues to intrude in
Eleanor's life," Josephine said.

"I enjoyed myself," said Eleanor, "but I think it's you I like."

"You forgot to take off your mustache," Dede giggled.

The following morning Angus called Eleanor earlier than usual.
"Eleanor, have you seen Cynthia lately?" he asked without even
a good morning.

"Not since yesterday. Is everything all right? You seem
concerned."

"Will called this morning. It seems she's run away from home. She took the car and some of her clothes. Will said she never came to bed last night and when he woke up, he couldn't find her. I think he was more concerned that she wasn't there to make his breakfast." Angus actually sounded as if he were disgusted.

"He's sure she took her clothes? Maybe she just went to the grocery store," Eleanor said.

"He's pretty sure she's gone off somewhere. It's not like her to leave before she has his coffee ready when he wakes up. Did anything unusual happen last night that might have caused her to bolt?" he asked.

"Nothing unusual happened here. I can't tell you what happened after she left. Will came and got her about six-thirty."

"So she didn't say anything to you about leaving Will or going somewhere?"

"No."

"I'll tell him you don't know anything and haven't seen her. For some reason he thinks you're to blame."

"Honestly? I can't think why." Eleanor replayed the afternoon through her mind. Nothing stood out that she could remember but she wasn't surprised that someone as tightly wound as Cynthia would eventually break. "I'll call the coffee group and see if they noticed anything."

Eleanor called each of her friends, but no one remembered hearing Cynthia mention a trip or express a desire to run away. Eleanor took a brisk walk to clear her head and ended up at Suzanna's on her return trip. She was surprised to see Art at the table with the Do Nothings. They invited her to join them and she was surprised again when the topic of their conversation was the upcoming county fair and nothing about the missing Cynthia.

"So has Cynthia been located then?" Eleanor couldn't help asking.

"I know where she is," Art said confidently. "If there's nothing else I've learned by chasing Nazis it's that those who run away usually run home. I'm sure Cynthia is on her way back to her friends. They probably already have a bridge game planned."

"Has anyone called her friends to make sure?" Eleanor asked.

"Will has to keep his own wife. She's not my concern." The words left Eleanor cold. She thought Art was a kind and charming man. She was disappointed to hear him speak so callously about his son's wife.

"Is he supposed to keep her in a pumpkin shell?" she asked with a hint of snarky in her voice. The Do Nothings looked at her as if she just said something cruel.

"You have to understand, Eleanor. Cynthia's going through the change of life and she's been difficult to live with lately. Sometimes she becomes unhinged. Frankly, it's a relief to have her out of the house." Art was digging a deeper hole.

"I see. You and Will have had to take care of her while she's been in this fragile state and now you need a rest. Is that it? I'm sure you've been cooking for her and cleaning up after yourself. I bet you even ironed that perfectly pressed shirt you're wearing along with her things as well. I need to go home now before I become unhinged. I hope Will remembers to pick you up since Cynthia isn't here to drive you home." With that Eleanor got up and left the Do Nothings speechless, but a little less enamored with Artemas Chase.

On Eleanor's walk up the hill she stopped at Angus' house and knocked loudly on his door. She was really in a snit and while she stood waiting for him to answer wondered if she should just go home and keep her thoughts to herself and not risk an emotional outburst.

"Hi Ellie, come in. I've got news to share about Johnny Vargas." Evidently Angus wasn't worried about Cynthia Chase's disappearance either.

"What?" Eleanor asked as she stepped into Angus' perfect man cave of leather couch and bearskin rug.

"I played poker with some of my old friends on the force last night. You remember Andy McGraw. I showed him and the other guys the postcard I got saying Johnny was murdered and he told me about the bloody shirt the cleaning lady found in Rob Wakefield's closet. They all agree that it's sufficient cause to open an investigation. They also think it's wise to keep it quiet considering who is being investigated. You know what this means?"

"What?"

"We've got the backing of the local police to investigate Johnny's death as a murder. He also said they put a rush on forensics to identify the DNA on the shirt so we should know something for sure very soon."

"What do you hope they find from the DNA?" Eleanor asked.

"If we're lucky, it will tell us whose blood is on the shirt. If it's just Rob's blood, that won't prove anything, but if there is even a trace of Johnny's blood on Rob's shirt, he'll be in deep."

"How will you know whose blood it is without a sample of Rob or Johnny's DNA?"

"The housekeeper brought in some things she got from Rob's bathroom. I found a towel Johnny left with my fishing gear. He hooked his finger and bled on it, so now we just wait."

"Well, it's not as exciting as a stakeout or breaking into someone's house for evidence, but it is a break. Did I tell you Junie came by to return a cookbook? I thought she was going to tell me something, but Cynthia interrupted, and Junie left without saying anything. She seemed so sad. Whatever we find out won't bring Johnny back."

"No, but it will bring him justice."

"Right now, that's just a word. I don't think that's going to help Junie."

When Eleanor reached her house, she left her shoes on the porch and went into her office. She turned on the gas fireplace—more for atmosphere than heat—and sat at her desk and began to write. It had been a long time since Feathers critiqued her work, so it was surprising to hear him utter, "It was a dark and stormy night," in Walter's voice. It took her back to an earlier time when men ruled the earth and women waited on them and hungered for their approval.

Born a Woman

I was born a woman.
"It's a girl," they cried,
before they said, "She's white, or she's black, or she's mine,"
sealing my fate as wife, mother, and less than divine.
I was born a woman
in a world where misogyny hides and man
decides the choices that should be mine.
I was born a woman
Possessed

Oppressed

Repressed

Undressed

Pampered at best

put to the test and finally blessed.

I was born a woman

Whose struggle has made her strong opened her eyes to see the

hate that portrayed her as vile and wrong who demands fairness

as her fate

I was born a woman

Whose strength before was unheard of

A being whose power is love.

Eleanor felt anger drain out of her like ink flowing from a fountain pen. She stretched her achy fingers and looked at the clock. It always amazed her that time could elapse so quickly while she crafted her thoughts into words. She rolled her neck as she wandered into the kitchen to look for something to eat.

The cookbook Junie returned was still lying on the counter. Eleanor wondered what recipes Junie had used to please Johnny before his death. She wondered what Johnny had eaten as his last meal. She picked up the cookbook and hastily put it on a shelf along with her collection thinking her musings were dark and macabre. Then she poured herself a glass of red wine, put cheddar and crackers on a plate, and hunted for some happy music to lift her spirits. No sooner had she put on Johnny Nash's *I Can See Clearly Now* and danced around the living room than the doorbell rang. Eleanor put down her wine and opened the door to find Angus carrying a large pizza and wearing a sexy grin.

"I like your moves," he said as he raised and lowered his bushy brows. "Would you like to share a pizza with me?" Eleanor opened the door wide enough to let Angus inside where he shared some moves of his own along with the pizza.

"I don't have to save the world. At least I don't have to save it every day," Eleanor thought as she lay in bed pondering the world's problems. Today she just wanted to do nothing. She wondered if she was ready to become one of the Do Nothings. The fate of Cynthia and the disinterest it garnered disturbed her to no end. She needed to move. A walk was definitely in order.

Eleanor looked up at the blue sky. Her feet automatically moved across the flat wet sand. She didn't seem to hear the mewling of the gulls or the rhythm of the breaking waves. She had become blind and deaf to the sights and sounds around her the way a person no longer notices those things too familiar. Eleanor was in her head and her heart was filled with guilt.

A kind person would have reached out to a woman like Cynthia who was stuck in an earlier time with a husband and father-in-law who did not appreciate her. They had moved far from her friends and family to retire near a cold and sandy beach where no one seemed to play bridge. Eleanor had been mean—if not in her actions—in her words and thoughts. She felt the need to investigate Cynthia's disappearance to prove that Eleanor Penrose was a decent human being who was not responsible for pushing someone from their home.

"Eleanor Penrose is a decent human being. Eleanor Penrose is a decent human being," she chanted under her breath until she reached the door of Suzanna's. Peering in the window she could see Art sitting with the Do Nothings and she wondered if they would welcome her this morning after yesterday's rant. She needed to know about Cynthia, so she pushed on, mustering her resolve to be a decent human being.

"Good morning," she greeted them warmly.

"Good morning," Art stood politely as if nothing had happened to change their relationship. "Please join us."

"I really just wanted to know if Cynthia is all right," Eleanor said, "and apologize for flying off the handle yesterday."

"You have no need. You were right. I have been what you might call a jerk. Unfortunately, Will and I have taken Cynthia for granted and used her change of life as an excuse to treat her unkindly. I'm sorry you saw me in an unflattering way, Eleanor but I have to thank you for calling my failings to my attention. If you hadn't, Will and I might have gone on reinforcing our bad behavior with each other. Please forgive me."

Eleanor was surprised. She didn't expect this but maintained her cool. "You should save your apology for Cynthia. Did you find her?"

"Yes, I believe Will is in contact with her friends who expect her to arrive sometime tomorrow. She is punishing Will by not communicating with him, but I'll say no more on the subject."

"What a relief!" Eleanor said, "I'll be on my way then." Mattie was strangely quiet, but Sybil and Mavis uttered their goodbyes as Eleanor left. She trudged up the hill and stopped at the hidey-hole to see if Angus had left anything in the tree's cavity. It was something Eleanor started when Bootsy

Greenwood stayed at the house with her Granny Scattergoods
before Angus moved there. Now Granny was dead and Bootsy
seldom visited but Angus kept up the tradition, and every
now and then Eleanor slipped a treat in the secret hiding spot.
Inside was an envelope. Eleanor opened it and read the letter
that was inside.

Darling,

You've pierced my soul. You don't realize how fascinating you are
and how dangerously attractive you've become to me. You influence
me for the better. You are the one object of my desire. When I
am with you I feel that I am home. I love you without question,
without reason, without reckoning. My love has made me selfish
I know. I am forgetful of everything but seeing you again yet I am
half agony half hope. Am I too late? I love none but you but if you
do not believe it if you do not trust it, I must convince you of it.
Leave your lover, leave for me.

Forever and always,

Your true love

Eleanor did not recognize the handwriting. She was sure
Angus hadn't written it. It was very romantic, Angus was
romantic, but it wasn't his style. As she stood in the road
pondering who might have left something like this in their
hidey-hole Angus came out of his house.

"What are you doing, Ellie?" he asked as he approached.
"Are you leaving me a dinner invitation?"

"No, I'm reading the love letter you wrote," she teased.

"Really? Let me see." Angus took the letter and read it
quickly. "Well, I wish I *had* written it, but I didn't. Why would
I ask you to leave your lover when your lover is me? Is there
something you're not telling me?"

"Of course not. Who else knows about our secret hidey-hole?" Eleanor was still thinking of possible admirers.

"Maybe it's not for you," he suggested. "The handwriting looks feminine so maybe it's for me."

Eleanor grabbed the letter. She did not like the possibility of some other woman writing a letter asking

Angus to leave her. "I'm sure it's for me."

"Let me see it again." Angus took the letter back and studied it carefully. "It's definitely a woman who wrote this. I bet it's Nancy Wilson. I think she has a thing for me. It's definitely for me." Then he walked back into his house and shut the door taking the letter with him.

Eleanor was left standing in the road. Nancy Wilson was Eleanor's friend, and she was married. It was definitely not Nancy. She sighed and began the climb to her house chanting her mantra, "Eleanor Penrose is a decent human being."

Nancy Wilson lived next door to Angus McBride. She and her husband of fifty years enjoyed retirement on the Oregon coast and had forged many friendships over the years. They both loved to golf and were relatively healthy and they both loved Angus and Eleanor. Nancy wasn't surprised when Angus popped over with a golfing magazine and some other pieces of mail that the post office had mistakenly put in his box. She left the mail on a table by the door not paying much attention to it. When Dennis came home from a visit to the dentist, he eagerly picked up the golfing magazine but didn't notice the envelope that fell to the floor. It was the same envelope that Angus had laid on his coffee table earlier and became mixed with his daily mail. It was the envelope that contained the love letter that

Nancy later found on the floor. She opened it and began to read: Darling, You've pierced my soul . . .

Nancy's mind began to race. She looked at the envelope to see if there was some indication of who it was written to or from, but there was nothing. Did Dennis have a secret someone? Was there another woman who felt this way about him? Someone who could write with such passion? Had Dennis really been at the dentist or was that what he told her so he could be with his true love? She wanted to march right into the living room where he was happily humming as he read his golfing magazine and confront him with this note, but she was afraid. They had been together a long time. Maybe she had let things get stale and uninteresting in their marriage.

She carefully folded the note, put it back in the envelope and slipped it into the pocket of the coat that hung on the hook by the door. She would think about it later. Of course, later Dennis took the coat that hung by the door over to Angus' house because Angus had left it in Dennis' car weeks ago when they had played poker with some mutual friends. When Nancy finally worked up enough courage to confront Dennis, the letter was missing along with the coat. She determined to be nicer to him, just in case.

Eleanor needed a day at the beauty shop. It was so easy to neglect the things she used to do as a matter of routine. Now she spent more time plucking her chin hairs than shaving her legs. The energy it took to trim her nails and paint them was more than she could muster sometimes. She drove to Curl Up and Dye to get a haircut and a pedicure. A little pampering was in order.

The shop was buzzing with gossip and laughter. Sometimes the chatter bothered Eleanor but today it seemed right. She remembered to keep her ears open for clues about Johnny Vargas and wondered if the topic was too old to be of interest now.

"What will it be, Eleanor? Are you ready to color your hair and take ten years off your appearance?" asked Jessica Honeycutt. "Or I could just shave it," she teased as she ran her hands through Eleanor's thick silver waves.

"Just do the usual," Eleanor ordered, "a trim and shampoo." Eleanor was old enough to know what she wanted and what looked good on her oval-shaped face. No good could come of experimenting at this late date.

Luna Grant was getting her nails done and bragging about her grandchildren's athletic abilities. "Harvey is playing summer baseball and he's an ace pitcher. Someday he'll be in the major leagues. The family travels all over the state to watch him compete. It takes up every weekend." In Luna's mind it was better to make bragging sound like a complaint.

"I saw her with Eric Fowler at the Red Shed the other night," a disembodied voice claimed. "It's hard to believe she could be so cold. I thought she really loved Johnny, but I guess girls like her can't be without a man for long. As soon as Eric was away at college she took up with Johnny."

"That marriage was doomed from the start. Everybody knew he couldn't keep her in the lifestyle she was used to having. He's not as handsome as Johnny was but at least Eric Fowler has a college degree and will inherit his father's lumber business. It's been in the family since WW ll when his great grandfather came over from Europe. He's not what I would call a catch, but he can pay the bills with money to spare."

"Is the old man still alive? I don't remember seeing his obituary. He must be close to a hundred."

"Oh yes, I heard that they just put him in a home recently. I think he fell and broke his hip."

"Probably won't live long then. When people lose their mobility it's a downward spiral from there."

"He always was a mean son of a gun."

"All the Fowler men are mean. It makes you wonder if it's genetic. I wouldn't go with a man who's cruel no matter how much money he has."

"Eric Fowler is totally smitten with Junie and always has been. Maybe he's different with her."

"He's probably afraid of her father. Everyone else is."

"We'll just have to watch to see how this romance plays out. Are you going to the fair this year?"

"Absolutely, I can't miss it or my kids would have a fit." Eleanor heard other voices she could not identify.

"I have it on good authority that a large group of homeless men are moving into that old apartment building on Tenth Street. No one in the neighborhood is happy about it but I guess there's no law against it."

"How do homeless men afford it?"

"Someone must be paying for them. Evidently, someone bought that old nursing home too and it's become a place for the homeless as well."

"It must be someone with a good heart."

"Maybe, or someone with an agenda. My source told me they're all planning to register to vote."

"Did you see that movie at the Bijou? We saw it last night. It was a riot. I can't think of the name, but you should go."

"Come over to the shampoo area, Eleanor," Jessica ordered. This was Eleanor's favorite part. The sound of water drowned out all voices as Eleanor relaxed and let her mind float away enjoying the physical sensation of Jessica's magic fingers as she massaged her scalp.

"I let my hair get especially dirty so you would have to wash it for a long time," Eleanor purred.

"I know, it's everybody's favorite thing," Jessica murmured as she lathered up and rinsed Eleanor's hair. When Jessica was finished Eleanor moved over to Marie who soaked and scrubbed her tired feet then clipped and painted her toenails a vivid pink. When she left Curl Up and Dye Eleanor felt renewed. She got in her car and drove to Dede's house. There was something fishy going on in Waterton and if Dede didn't already know about it, she should.

Doogie barked ferociously until Dede answered the door and the small Havanese could sniff Eleanor and ascertain her harmlessness. Then he cheerfully went on his way. "Come in, Ava is in the kitchen," Dede led the way.

Ava, Dede's daughter leaned down and gave Eleanor a hug. "I made crack pie, would you like a piece?"

"Did you say crap pie? I think I'll pass."

"No, it's *crack* pie."

"I must have water in my ears. I just came from the hairdressers. What's in it, cocaine?" Eleanor asked as she eyed the pie suspiciously.

"Eleanor, you're hilarious! This pie is mostly sugar, eggs, butter, and cream. It's just called crack pie because after you taste it, you'll be addicted," Ava explained.

"Well then I'll take a bite," Eleanor said and watched Ava put a sliver of the pie on a plate.

"Would you like some coffee to go with that?" asked Dede.

"Yes please," Eleanor said just before she put a forkful in her mouth. "Oh my, this is very rich and delicious. She praised Ava's culinary skills and sipped her coffee almost forgetting the purpose of her visit. "Dede, what do you know about a homeless shelter for men in the old nursing home?"

"The city council approved it. There was just a little resistance from the neighbors but it's on the far side of town and won't impact very many residents," Dede didn't seem concerned.

"And the men that are moving into the old hotel on Tenth Street probably didn't need the city's approval," Eleanor mused. "Did you know all these men are planning to register to vote?"

Dede took a minute to process this information. "Where did you learn of this, Eleanor?"

"I overheard it at Curl Up and Dye. I didn't recognize the voices but something about the entire scenario seemed familiar. Do you remember that town in central Oregon taken over by a commune? They brought in a bunch of street people from the city and tried to register them to vote so they could take over the town. It just seemed strange to me especially after that conversation we had about Howard Wakefield donating money to your opponent." Eleanor watched Dede's face register understanding, concern, and then, anger.

"I'm all over this. Howard Wakefield isn't the only person around here with connections in high places. If he's involved in voter fraud, I'll find out and stop him."

"Great, now Ava, can I get the recipe for your crack pie? I think I'm an addict."

On the drive home Eleanor had an idea. As soon as she walked through the door and after she greeted Feathers, she went in search of a box filled with items from Walter's celebration of life. In it were several sympathy cards with handwritten notes. She scanned through a few quickly then called Angus. He answered on the third ring.

"Hello Angus, can you come over? I've got some information to share with you. Oh, and bring that love letter." Eleanor ordered.

"I'll see if I can find it," he said nonchalantly although he knew exactly where it was considering that he had been studying it when the phone rang. Earlier he had searched high and low for it and could have sworn he left it on the coffee table but oddly enough found it in a coat pocket. He didn't remember putting it there but chalked it up to a senior moment. Angus didn't want Eleanor to know how intrigued he was by the letter or how it had affected him. If it was written to him, it was the most romantic and flattering note he had ever received, including the love letter Trudy Evans had written in eighth grade, but if it was written to Eleanor he knew he had a formidable rival for her affections. Someone who could express themselves in words the way this person could surely had a direct path into Eleanor's heart.

Because she was a poet herself, she would measure his worth against this man's and find him wanting. Angus took the letter and walked to Eleanor's with a worried heart.

"Intruder, intruder, Ellie lock the door!" Feathers cried as Angus walked into the living room. Angus was in no mood to be scolded by a parrot. He scowled at the bird and his lowered brows signaled to Feathers that trouble was afoot. Without another word the fowl flew to his window perch and ignored the humans in the house.

"Let's have it," Angus sighed.

"Did you bring the letter?" Eleanor asked.

Without a word Angus produced the letter. Eleanor took it to the dining table that was laden with cards from friends and family. "I found some samples of writing that might help us at least eliminate some possibilities," she explained as she picked up a card and held it next to the letter. Angus looked over her shoulder curiously. "This card is from Nancy Wilson. She obviously did not write it."

"Obviously," Angus agreed. "You know it could be from Helen Pence. Every time she calls me about the Wednesday night soup kitchen, she uses this breathy voice. I've often wondered if she has a job on the side as a phone sex operator." Eleanor's scornful expression was all he needed to give up on that idea.

They quickly sorted through the cards eliminating Eleanor's female and male friends. "I thought for sure at least one of your friends found me attractive," Angus pouted. Eleanor frowned at him over the top of her glasses.

"None of Walter's friends wrote this note. It must be someone who knows about the hidey-hole, most likely someone in the village. Who have you told?" Eleanor asked.

"No one," Angus said, "Except my poker friends and some guys in the police force. It may have come up while fishing with some other fishermen and I'm sure I told my sister, Fiona and my son Michael." Eleanor continued to frown at Angus in disbelief.

"What?" he asked guiltily. "Don't tell me you haven't told all your friends and family about it. It's a charming little idea."

"Maybe it's a joke," Eleanor proposed. "Maybe it's someone's way of pranking us by putting it in there to keep us guessing and make us crazy."

"It's Howard Wakefield's way of taking our minds off him and putting us at odds with each other so we can't investigate him properly." Angus smiled at the ridiculous thought.

"Really, why should we be concerned? We both care about each other and nothing is going to change that," Eleanor said.

"Right, even if all your friends thought I was the sexiest man alive, I'd only want you," Angus admitted.

"So we should stop all this foolishness and put these cards away," Eleanor said as she began to clear the table.

"I'm hungry, do you want to go down to the Anchor and get a burger?" Angus asked.

"I do," Eleanor said. Those particular words made Angus picture Eleanor in a wedding gown standing beside him at the altar.

Sighing, he said, "Let's go then." Eleanor picked up the box of memories and put it away leaving the love letter on the table as they walked hand in hand to dinner.

Angus gallantly held the door of the Anchor for Eleanor who spied Dennis and Nancy Wilson sitting at a table with a pitcher of beer in front of them. They turned together and waved them over to share their table. Eleanor liked the Wilsons and usually had no qualms about socializing with them, but the chance that one of them could have written a letter declaring their love might make for an uncomfortable evening. She glanced at Angus as if for permission. He nodded and they made their way through the crowded room.

"Well, look what the cat dragged in," said Dennis as he stood to greet them shaking Angus' hand. "Want a beer?"

"Are you buying?" asked Angus as he pulled out a wooden chair for Eleanor.

"You can get the next one." Dennis raised his hand for the waitress who brought two more glasses and took their orders.

"Dennis is cooking tonight," Nancy remarked. Eleanor looked at the couple who seemed to only speak in clichés and knew for a fact neither had the artistry nor the inclination to write that letter.

"Have you heard anything about the disappearance of Cynthia Chase?" asked Nancy.

"The last I heard was that she went back to her old neighborhood to visit her friends. Have you heard something?" Eleanor wondered if Art had lied to get her off his case.

"No, not even that. The last I heard was that she had simply disappeared. It seems odd that she would leave and not tell her husband," Nancy said.

"I don't think it's odd for an unhappy woman to run away from a strange home to return to a place where she might have experienced love and support from her friends," Eleanor said.

"It sounds like you know more than you're saying," Dennis remarked.

"I'm just inferring. From what I know, she wasn't thrilled to be here and missed her bridge club," Eleanor added. "I know I'd miss my friends terribly if I moved away."

"I didn't really know her, but I did hear her say something about being far from her family. I couldn't bear to only see my family a couple times a year," Nancy added.

"I could live anywhere if there's good weather and golfing," Dennis said.

"I'm afraid I'd need some place to fish and Eleanor to cook, of course." Angus said, winking at her.

Eleanor wondered if he was being sweeter than normal or if she was just noticing it more. Was he trying to compete with the anonymous letter writer? Maybe he did believe a man had written it to her. Maybe he believed another woman could have written it to her. The thought made Eleanor smile. Angus noticed and wondered if she was smiling at Dennis. He hadn't considered Dennis as a possibility. If Nancy's handwriting didn't match the letter writer's, it could be because it was Dennis who wrote it to Eleanor. He studied him carefully. Dennis was mostly bald and pretty much only interested in golf and sports. He certainly didn't seem to be the romantic type. Angus and Dennis talked about baseball while Eleanor and Nancy continued their conversation quietly.

"I went to the Oracle and had a reading with Madame Patruska," Nancy admitted. "She told me a change was coming in my life and that travel was in the picture."

"You don't really believe in that, do you?" Eleanor asked with raised brows.

"No, I know it's just for fun, but I *am* planning a trip with my sister. We're going to Paris. Dennis doesn't enjoy traveling. I hope you'll look in on him while I'm gone. You know, make sure he's behaving himself."

"Of course, Angus and I can have him over for dinner. I'm sure Angus will keep an eye out for him if you're worried about him being alone. When are you leaving?"

"We're leaving next week and I'm worried. I think he may have a mistress," Nancy whispered. "Madame Patruska got the travel part right. Maybe she's right about a change too."

Eleanor looked at Dennis and even in her wildest imagination couldn't see him with anyone other than Nancy.

They were perfect together. Nancy obviously wanted to say more but dinner arrived and time for talking ended.

The book club met at Josephine's house to discuss *The Zookeeper's Wife*. Each of the members took turns in a round robin giving a quick, uninterrupted review based on their opinion of the book.

"I loved the book," said Wren. "I'd never thought about how the animals in a zoo might be affected by war, or how a zoo could be used to help shelter Jews from the Germans."

"The fact that the Germans did experiments on these animals to recreate a specific breed was interesting to me," said Mercedes. "Speaking as a veterinarian, animal genetics could prove helpful in curing diseases and eliminating inherited disabilities, especially with the new and advanced technology we have today."

"The whole idea of genetic engineering for the strengthening of the human race makes sense to me. What are we doing when we strive to keep alive the weak and flawed? Is there value in letting only the strong survive? Does our culture of caring weaken and dummy down our species?" asked Cleo.

"That's a slippery slope," Dede said. "Who decides what is weak or flawed? When it's your Granny being put down because she's no longer vital, you may have other ideas. A child with Down's Syndrome might be considered a person with no value or right to live to some, but a gift to others."

"The part of this book that bothered me," said Kim "Was that the protagonists were not Jews. It seems that most of the books we read about the Holocaust demonstrate how virtuous white non-Jews are instead of focusing on the courage of the Jews themselves."

"We did read *The Tattooist of Auschwitz* that told the story of how some Jews survived by using their ingenuity," Josephine reminded the group. "Even after everything they suffered to stay alive, people questioned their intentions and accused them of collaborating with the Germans. The Jews didn't always have the capabilities to help themselves the way the Gentiles did."

"I enjoyed reading about how clever the main characters were in helping all those people escape the ghetto and then hiding them in the zoo. They were definitely courageous and ingenious people, and they were successful and lived to return to the zoo which made me happy in the end," offered Dolly. "It made me wonder if I would have been that brave."

"Exactly," said Pearl, "Looking back on what happened in Europe during that time everything is perfectly clear. We can easily identify the good guys and the villains, so we can say what we would do in that situation, but in reality, it isn't always that way."

"I agree with Pearl," Eleanor stated. "It's easy to blame the German people who lived through that time and did nothing either out of fear, ignorance, or denial, but when you are in the middle of what's going on, it may not be clear to see who the bad guys really are. In movies and books, it's fairly obvious, but it may not have been in real time."

"Many atrocities are happening in the world today and what are we doing about those?" asked Kim.

"I've seen Nazi's marching in the streets and there are those who claim they have the right to do it under our constitution.

Do you believe what happened in World War II couldn't happen again?" asked Josephine.

"Do we know hate crimes aren't happening here already?" asked Dolly.

"Of course, they're happening, but they're happening to minorities: the LBGT community, Blacks, immigrants, some religious groups, and many others. People are bullied all the time, just not on the scale that was seen under Hitler," said Wren.

"What can we do about it really," asked Mercedes, "Other than be outraged and let our political representatives know how we feel?"

"We can speak out when we hear it or see it," said Josephine. "I don't know if I would have had the courage to act like the protagonists in this book, but I know I can stand up for someone verbally."

"That takes courage too," said Cleo. "Remember those men on the bus who stood up for those women wearing hijabs and were stabbed?" There was a long period of silence.

"It must be twenty minutes past the hour," said Pearl.

"Would anyone like dessert?" asked Josephine. "I made Baklava."

Eleanor had called Wanda, Cleo's housekeeper, and made an appointment to discuss expectations and set up a schedule for cleaning. When the doorbell rang, Feathers flew to Eleanor's shoulder and greeted Wanda with a leering, "Well, hello there!"

"Oh, I think I'm going to like working here," Wanda said as she entered Eleanor's space and looked around with the eye of a professional. She took in the exquisite view of the ocean beyond the floor to ceiling windows, the polished hardwood floors and colorful rugs and the tasteful art that hung on the white walls.

"Please come in and have a seat. I've made tea. Would you like a cup?" Eleanor took in Wanda's appearance and demeanor and immediately liked her. She felt warmth emanating from the diminutive woman with the pixie cut brown hair and freckled face.

"Yes please." Wanda sat at the dining room table and took out her notebook and pen. It was her custom to write down the wishes of her clients as well as schedules and payment information. Wanda was computer free.

Eleanor returned with tea and cookies and the two worked out the particulars between sips and nibbles. When Wanda left, Eleanor realized she had not spoken one vulgar word and thought Wanda must have been on her best behavior. She wondered if Cleo had given her a heads-up about Eleanor's stance on the use of crude language. The one thing Eleanor didn't notice was the fact that the mysterious letter was no longer on the table.

On Friday, Eleanor met with her friends at the Boat House. Josephine was sporting a new yellow blouse that coordinated with her lemon quartz earrings and topaz ring. She looked very cool. "The weatherman is forecasting record highs for today and all through the weekend."

"Yes, I heard it was going to be a scorcher," added Pearl, whose long legs poked out from a pair of wildly colorful Bermuda shorts.

"You won't have to worry about the heat, Eleanor," Cleo remarked. "It's always cool at the beach."

"Eleanor, you should have a barbeque and invite us all over so we can be as comfortable as you," Dede said.

"I can do that," Eleanor said. "What shall we barbeque?"

"I'd like to have Howard Wakefield's balls on a kabab," Dede said without emotion. "I'm sure he's trying to unseat me and run the city council through his flunkies."

"Can you do anything to stop him?" Eleanor asked.

"I'm working on it," she answered. "I've made some calls to the Secretary of State and am just waiting for a response. If I don't get one soon, I'm prepared to make a visit to the Capitol."

"For heaven's sake, what's going on?" asked Pearl who fluttered her eyelashes in a most annoying manner.

Dede filled everyone in on the latest evil being perpetrated by Howard Wakefield and how she was no longer afraid of his mafia connections. "I'm sure he's behind this letter someone shoved through my mail slot." Dede pulled out a nondescript envelope and showed them what was written on the single sheet it contained.

Beware! Your secrets are about to be revealed to Waterton residents. There are incriminating photos that will be published if you don't step down from your position and end your campaign.
Quit before everyone knows what you really are.

"What does that mean?" asked Cleo. "Everyone already knows you're Catholic." "Do you have secrets we don't know about?" asked Pearl.

"I'm sure it has to do with Howard Wakefield and his push to take over the city. His talent is finding out a person's weakness and exploiting it. He must think I have a secret, but I bet he doesn't know what it is. He's just bluffing," Dede said.

"What's going on with your eyelashes, Pearl?" asked Josephine who had been totally distracted by what appeared to be large butterflies fluttering on Pearl's eyes.

"It's the Lush Lashes product I was trying. It's finally noticeable. My lashes have grown in thick and long, but now I can't see very well," she explained.

Cleo peered closely at Pearl's eyelashes. "That's amazing, but maybe you should stop using it now so you can see properly." Pearl continued to blink repeatedly. The others continued their conversation without looking at her.

"What are you going to do about the letter?" asked Eleanor.

"I'm going to ignore it and wait for the photos," Dede said. "I can't imagine what they're referring to. Are there any new developments in the Vargas case?"

"Angus said he is just waiting for the DNA test results to come back from the bloody shirt Wanda turned in to the police. If there is any trace of Johnny's blood on the shirt there will be an investigation," Eleanor said.

"I can't prove it, but I just know Johnny was murdered," Cleo said.

"Has anyone heard anything? People are still talking about him, aren't they?" asked Pearl.

No one could look at her without being mesmerized by her enormous lashes. "Can you drive with those?" asked Dede.

"Only if I tilt my head back and open my eyes as wide as I can," she explained.

"You know Wanda has lash extensions," informed Cleo. "She told me the only reason she works is so she can afford them."

"Is there something wrong with having normal eyelashes?" asked Eleanor.

"Probably not," Cleo said, "Although Wanda claims she received a very romantic letter because of her extensions. She thinks the letter is from Howard Wakefield because she found it in her notebook after work one morning. She was going to show it to me but said she must have left it at his house." "I can't imagine Howard Wakefield writing anything except an eviction letter," said Dede.

"Speaking of letters," said Josephine, "What do you think of this one?

Dear Just Josie,

I shop at a small grocery store in my neighborhood. Lately, the lady who owns it has shown signs that concern me. She is an older woman who is usually kind and, on the ball, but yesterday she asked me three times if I wanted to pay with my credit card or use cash. Then she gave me change for a fifty when I gave her only a twenty-dollar bill. It may be that she was distracted, and I could chalk it up to that if it only happened that one time, but it happened again today. She asked me about my husband who recently had knee injury. I told her he was fine, but she asked me about him again before I left the store. I'm very fond of this woman but I don't know how to handle this. She lives alone and I don't know if she has family living somewhere else or how to contact them. I'm not even sure I should interfere, but I worry that some people might take advantage of her if she is suffering from some mental impairment. What should I do?

Concerned Customer

"Well, she should definitely talk to the shop owner about it," said Pearl.

"I agree," said Eleanor. "The woman may have had a stroke and need medical attention."

"She should ask her how she is feeling and tell her about her concerns, then offer to take her to the doctor," said Dede.

"If she won't do that, then she should ask about her family and see if the woman would at least ask them for help with the store until she can get back to normal," said Cleo. "At lot depends on how far gone this woman is. She may realize that something is wrong and jump at the opportunity to get help, especially if she is alone. I know I don't always go to the doctor until Steve tells me he thinks I need to. It definitely helps to have another person's perspective."

"All excellent ideas," said Josephine. "I'll work out something, but I think I may need to get in touch with this person immediately. She might need medical attention right away."

"I may need medical attention soon, too," said Dede. "A couple of months ago when I was leaving the grocery store, I got to my car, opened the door, and there was Sofia, Johnny Vargas' sister, sitting in the front seat writing a postcard. She looked up at me and said, 'Oh' and I said double 'Oh'. It seems I'm not the only one with a white car. Anyway, I found my car parked on the other side of her."

"That's not so weird," said Cleo. "I used to lose my car all the time. Now I always park in the same area, so I don't even have to think about where my car is parked."

"Everyone does things like that. It doesn't mean we're losing our minds," said Josephine. "Although I'm sure it's a fear we all have at our age."

"I know someone I used to work with who suddenly couldn't remember how to get out of his car," said Pearl.

They all agreed that was a grave concern, and then the coffee group dispersed after planning a Saturday evening barbeque at Eleanor's and hoping none of them would forget where they parked their cars. Eleanor hurried home to prepare a lavish feast of crab cakes with red beet and horseradish remoulade for Angus. After all, her eyelashes seemed quite ordinary.

"Delicious," Angus declared as he wiped his graying mustache with Eleanor's rose-colored napkin. "Those have to be the moistest crab cakes I've ever eaten." Eleanor did not tell him her secret of using potatoes instead of breadcrumbs. She simply smiled and thanked him for the compliment.

"I'm afraid I'm too full for dessert," he said as he stretched his long legs and pushed his chair away from the table. "I do have some interesting information to share though." His change of tone caught Eleanor's ear and she stopped midstride on her way to the kitchen to listen for more. "The DNA sample from the bloody shirt showed three different blood types."

"What does that mean?" Eleanor asked. "Was one of them from Johnny?"

"Yes, one was from Johnny and one from Rob Wakefield. The other is unknown, but we suspect it may belong to Eric Fowler."

"What happens now?"

"The police will get a warrant to search the Wakefield residence for more clues. They'll bring Rob in for questioning and, depending on what they find, they'll either let him go or arrest him for Johnny's murder."

"How could he possibly explain Johnny's blood on his shirt?" Eleanor asked as she wondered how he would wiggle out of this one.

"They got in a fight. Everybody knows that's true. To make a murder charge stick the police will have to make sure he doesn't have an alibi for the night Johnny disappeared. If they can get a witness who saw him wearing that particular shirt the day Johnny went missing, or even put him in the vicinity of Johnny's boat it'll help, but without a body or weapon, it will be difficult to prove."

"Will they try to get Eric to flip on him?" asked Eleanor who had been watching a lot of crime dramas lately.

Angus smiled, "I'm sure they'll try. We'll just have to wait to see if the other blood sample belongs to Eric or somebody else."

"Who else? Howard Wakefield wouldn't get his hands dirty that way." Eleanor speculated. "He'd simply pay him to go away or threaten to tell his darkest secret."

"You're forgetting that Johnny wasn't the kind of man to be bought. If anything, he would have paid a lesser man to get rid of Johnny. Eric Fowler's that kind of man. He might have thought he'd get Junie back too, which appears to be true." Angus had narrowed it down, in his mind, to Rob and Eric.

"Junie wouldn't be involved," Eleanor said. "If she didn't want to be married anymore, she could just leave him and go home."

"Unless Daddy said no," Angus speculated. "She might have felt discouraged by what was happening. Wakefield made it hard for Johnny to get a job. We don't know if he was interfering in other ways."

"What do you mean?" Eleanor asked.

"Think about that letter we found and how it made us question our commitment to each other. What if he did that to Junie? What if he made her believe Johnny was fooling around on the side? She's young and vulnerable to lies."

Eleanor frowned. "I can't imagine Junie killing Johnny," she said, "and what a horrible thing for a father to do to his daughter."

"Welcome to my world, Eleanor. Sadly, I've seen worse—much worse."

Eleanor sat on his lap and held him tight as if she could make the bad memories fade away. She kissed his dimpled cheek and whispered in his ear, "I love you, Angus." And for a short time, the old memories receded to make room for new ones. It was only the second time Angus could remember Eleanor saying those words.

When the kissing was done, and the angel food cake and strawberries eaten Eleanor snuggled next to Angus on the couch while they listened to the waves breaking on the shore. Their constant rhythm was like music entering through the open sliding doors, a promise that some things on this earth were never ending, changing but never ending.

"Where's that letter?" Angus asked suddenly.

"I'm not sure. Don't you have it?" Eleanor tried to remember where she had seen it last.

"No, I brought it over here so we could compare it with the cards you had from Walter's memorial."

"Hmmm, I left it on the table. I don't remember seeing it but maybe I put it away with the other cards in the office." Eleanor rose to get it. "Why do you want it?"

"Something strange happened the other day. Dennis returned a coat that I left in his car weeks ago and I found the letter in the pocket. Then you called and I brought the letter over here. For the life of me, I cannot explain how the letter got in that coat pocket. I thought Dennis might have written it to you. We only compared the handwriting on the card and Nancy most likely wrote that. It didn't match but it could have been Dennis who wrote the letter."

"Would you recognize his writing?" asked Eleanor.

"No. That's why I brought this note he left on my door once asking me to water his African violets."

Eleanor found the idea of Angus tending to Dennis' plants amusing. She pressed her lips together to keep from laughing and went in search of the missing letter. When she returned, she simply shrugged, "It's not here. Are you sure you don't have it? Maybe it's in that coat pocket."

Angus wasn't amused. "Do you find Dennis attractive?" he asked casually.

"That depends," Eleanor paused.

Angus turned to look her in the eye. "Depends on what?" he asked.

"If he wrote that letter."

Eleanor liked to walk in the morning before the wind kicked up. Sometimes the wind blew so hard in the afternoons that the sand pelted her legs and she felt like a stone building being sandblasted. Today the sun was shining, and the beach looked inviting but crowded with flatlanders.

Flatlander was a term the locals used to describe people from the valley. She chose to take the trail that led away from the beach to the east. As she walked, the scent of pine trees filled the air and Eleanor experienced a sense of euphoria. On some days, happiness welled up without reason. She breathed in the briny air and felt glad to be alive and part of the world that surrounded her. Ahead and off to the left was a tall spruce tree that had been struck by lightning years ago. It carried a long scar like a badge of honor, declaring its ability to survive the worst nature could throw at it. The alder that once stood close in the spruce's embrace hadn't fared as well. The lightning had travelled down to its roots and blown the earth away along with the grass and daffodils that grew there. The tree died but for a couple of years it stood propped up by the nearby spruce.

Eleanor remembered it as she looked at the rotten log it had become. It made her think of Walter. For years, she and Walter stood together like those two trees, separate but together, until he grew ill. Then it was Eleanor who propped him up. She was the strong one. She was the spruce.

Thoughts flowed in and out of her mind like rain through a leaky roof. She had no power to stop them until a figure appeared on the trail coming her way.

"Good morning, Eleanor." Andrew Chase greeted her like an old friend.

"It *is* a good morning," Eleanor agreed, dramatically sweeping her arms outward and tripping over a root that crossed the trail. Andrew instinctively caught her in his arms and stopped her from falling on her face.

"Are you all right?" he asked as he steadied her.

"Yes, I'm fine, just a little embarrassed. I'm not usually so clumsy. How is Cynthia? Do you know when she's planning to come back?" Eleanor was eager to put her near catastrophe behind her.

"She misses her friends. It was never her plan to move here. My father pushed the idea and I thought it would be a chance to start a new life in a new place. I didn't realize how unhappy it would make Cynthia."

"Will you move back?"

"We haven't decided yet. Dad has some unfinished business here. Perhaps when that's completed we'll go back. I must say I love it here. Everything is fresh and beautiful. The people are friendly and unaffected and there is an endless list of things to do and places to see. I'll be sad to leave."

"I'm sorry Cynthia was so unhappy, but she really didn't give us much of a chance to get to know her," Eleanor said, with only a twinge of guilt at the small white lie.

"Don't blame yourself, Eleanor. Cynthia isn't an easy person to please." Eleanor nodded and continued on her way with a simple wave. Her thoughts turned to her part in making Cynthia feel unwelcome, so immersed in her guilt that she didn't notice Angus suddenly beside her.

"Angus," she gasped in surprise, "where did you come from?"

"I stopped by your house hoping to catch you before you left for your walk. When I didn't see you on the beach, I figured you might be on the trail," he explained. "I've been following you for a while."

"Did you see Andrew Chase?"

"I rounded the corner in time to see you fall into his arms," Angus said. "Is he the guy who wrote the letter?"

Eleanor stopped in her tracks and looked into Angus' sullen face. "Are you serious?" she scolded. "That man is married and years younger than I am. He was assisting an old lady who tripped on that tree root back there."

Angus knew he was being a jerk, but sometimes his insecurities overrode his good sense. He shook his head and took Eleanor's hand in his and they continued to walk. "I'm sorry. It shocked me to see you in his arms. You know I can be jealous Eleanor. If you married me things would be different."

"No they wouldn't," she said. "You'd still be an old fool only I'd be married to you. It certainly doesn't help your case."

Angus was silenced by her rebuff. She was right and he was pushing her away by his overprotective behavior. He decided to change his strategy. "I came looking for you to tell you about the latest development in Johnny's case."

"What's happened?" Eleanor asked.

"A warrant to search the Wakefield residence has been issued. They're bringing Rob Wakefield in for questioning today and they want me to consult in the case. I'll be gone most of the day and may not be able to help you prepare for your barbeque this evening."

Eleanor bit her lip. She felt a mixture of delight and disappointment. "I'm glad the police are pursuing this as a murder investigation, Angus, but I'm going to miss you."

Her words delighted him more than he could say. He simply pulled her into his embrace and kissed her long and hard. "I'll try to make it, but that will have to do until then. I've got to go. I just wanted you to know." With that Angus turned around and jogged back the way he had come.

Eleanor walked on and soon was lost in her own thoughts once more, planning the menu for the barbeque and making a mental list of everything that needed to be done. She would go to Waterton's Saturday market to get the fresh fruits and vegetables necessary to make the three salsas for her grilled beef tenderloin. Having made the decision, she picked up the pace and headed home.

By the time her first guests arrived Eleanor had whipped up an avocado and pumpkin seed salsa, tomato and cumin salsa, toasted chili and tomato salsa, prepped the steaks for grilling and potatoes for roasting, tossed an enormous green salad, and set out the makings for gin and tonics. Fortunately, Dede and Pearl offered to bring dessert, and Cleo was providing beer and sodas while Josephine was bringing some surprise appetizers.

"It is sweltering in town," Dede exclaimed.

"Thank goodness for a cool ocean breeze," said Cleo as she poured herself a gin and tonic.

"Where's Angus?" asked Josephine's husband, Richard.

"He's working the Vargas murder case," Eleanor said before sipping her gin and tonic. "They got a warrant to search Rob Wakefield's house because of the bloody T-shirt Wanda found in his closet," Eleanor said.

"So they're searching today?" asked Pearl.

"I wonder what they're looking for?" mused Josephine.

"A weapon, incriminating notes, or emails maybe," suggested Cary. "Good detectives know when they find something out of the ordinary." Pearl's husband watched reruns of the detective-mystery TV series *Monk* between golf games and helping Pearl sell items on eBay.

"There must have been something incriminating on the T-shirt besides Rob's blood," noted Cleo's Steve. "Johnny Vargas' blood was also on the shirt." Eleanor didn't think it was a secret.

"That doesn't mean he killed him. It's going to be difficult to prove murder on the basis of one bloody shirt," Mark said as he brought Dede a drink.

"The fact that it was hidden in Rob's closet doesn't look good for Mr. Wakefield," Cleo said.

"I wonder if Angus will be able to tell us anything if they find something new," said Cary.

"Is Angus coming?" asked Pearl.

"We'll have to wait and see," Eleanor said. "I'm going to put the steaks on the grill."

The others grabbed their drinks and joined her on the deck overlooking the beach. Josephine carried her seven-layer dip and chips to the table and the friends sat enjoying the gentle breeze against the backdrop of ocean and good conversation until Eleanor proclaimed that dinner was ready. Just as everyone dished up what looked to be a delicious repast Angus appeared. He helped himself to a beer and greeted everyone warmly giving away nothing of his inner turmoil.

"So, what's the word?" asked Cary. "Is Rob Wakefield guilty?"

"I really can't talk about it." Angus' said, shutting down that avenue of discussion. Everyone could tell by his lowered brow that the topic was dead.

When the sun dipped low into the western sky, everyone went home to their stuffy houses wondering what secrets Angus knew, but couldn't tell. It grew dark as the sun finally disappeared in the brilliance of fire over water leaving an afterglow of alizarin crimson. Eleanor and Angus stood on her deck until she couldn't stand it any longer.

"Angus, what's wrong? I can tell that something is bothering you."

Angus turned away from the light show in the sky, looked at Eleanor and shook his head. "I can't explain it. Somehow that letter we found in the hidey-hole was in Rob Wakefield's garbage can and now it's evidence in a murder investigation."

Sunday mornings were special to Eleanor. She enjoyed lounging in her nightgown, reading the Sunday newspaper and completing the crossword puzzle while drinking her coffee laced with creamer. Feathers perched on the back of the couch voicing his fowl complaints about a parrot's life was routine fare.

This Sunday morning presented a puzzle she could not solve. How did the mysterious letter get to Rob Wakefield's house? She had given it a great deal of thought and couldn't come up with a way. Last night she had been tired and just a little tipsy. Nothing Angus told her made any sense at all unless there were several letters that said the same thing circulating around the area. Maybe it was someone's idea of a sick joke. This morning she looked at it again with a sober well-rested brain. She tried tracing the letter from hidey-hole to Rob Wakefield and couldn't remember if she or Angus had seen it last. Just as she was pouring another cup of coffee, someone knocked at her door disturbing her thought processes and upsetting Feathers who did not respond well to a break in routine. Angus stood on her porch wearing the same dark scowl he sported the previous night.

"Good morning, Ellie" he said, walking right in without invitation and poured a cup of coffee. "I've been thinking about this letter and we need to trace it from when we first saw it until it showed up at the Wakefield residence."

"Right," Eleanor agreed. "Did you tell the other detectives working the case that you had knowledge of this letter?"

"Geez Ellie, you sound like an attorney for the prosecution. I told them I had seen a letter like it. I wasn't sure it could be our letter. When they dust it for prints, we'll find out for sure. Our prints will be all over it." This evidence seemed to be of great concern.

"So what? The letter by itself doesn't prove anything," Eleanor stated emphatically. "They can't believe either of us killed Johnny on the basis of our fingerprints on a letter. It's a love letter so it could be from Olivia or some other girl to Rob. He didn't think much of it if you found it in the garbage."

"You don't know how detectives think. They suspect everyone of everything."

"What do you mean exactly?" Eleanor needed examples.

"Let's say the letter was sent to Junie from another man. It might be a motive for her to kill Johnny to be with someone else, highly unlikely but possible. It's more likely the person who sent it to Junie killed Johnny to be with her but either way it leads to a love triangle." Angus paused to consider other possibilities. "If they match the writing to Eric Fowler, he could be a suspect especially if they find his blood on the T-shirt."

"Perhaps the letter was meant for Howard Wakefield. No one knows anything about his love life. What if Rob intercepted the letter from one of his father's mistresses and threw it in the garbage so he wouldn't see it."

"That's possible but has no bearing on the Vargas murder." Angus looked at Eleanor over the rim of his coffee cup.

"You suggested before that Howard Wakefield may have interfered with Junie and Johnny in other ways besides his employment. He may have sent the letter to one of them. Imagine if Junie found that letter among Johnny's things," Eleanor said.

"I don't know. She was already living at the family home. The timing doesn't seem right for that."

"It's possible that someone wrote several of those letters and sent them to various people as some sort of prank to stir up trouble. Have you searched your house for our letter?" Eleanor's tone was accusatory.

"Our letter, is it now?" Angus smiled. "Did you write the letter to me, Eleanor? It has a very poetic sound to it."

"Do you remember what the letter said?" Eleanor raised an eyebrow. "*Leave your lover.* Do you have a lover Angus?"

Angus shook his head as if to clear it. "I need to talk to Dennis Wilson. I'm sure he had that letter. It was in the pocket of my coat, the one he brought over to me. I'm positive I didn't put it there." He drank the rest of his coffee and was halfway out the door before he thought to give Eleanor a quick peck on the cheek. He didn't want her to think he had someone else on the side.

Eleanor answered her phone on the second ring. Cleo sounded strange and at first Eleanor didn't even recognize her voice.

"What is it, Cleo?"

"Something terrible has happened." She was crying. "There's been an accident."

"Tell me, is it Steve?"

"Oh no, it's Wanda. She was driving home from the Wakefield's and her car crashed. They say her brakes failed. She's dead, Eleanor. Wanda is dead."

"That's horrible," Eleanor said.

"Eleanor, can you come over? Steve and his brother are at a baseball game. He's away for the night. I need to talk to someone because I think Wanda was murdered."

"Sure, Cleo, I'll be right over," Eleanor said as she tried to process the information.

"Eleanor, bring your toothbrush. I don't want to be alone tonight," Cleo said. "Oh, could you also stop and get me some Metamucil? I'm desperately in need of fiber."

Eleanor packed an overnight bag, stowed Feathers in the back seat, found a container of Metamucil in her pantry, and drove to Cleo's. As she passed Angus' house she wondered if she should let him know what had happened but decided to wait until she had more information.

When Eleanor reached the road that led to Cleo's house, she could see a barricade and several emergency vehicles parked beyond the turn off. She slowed and made a turn that climbed the steep grade that gave Cleo the awesome view of the valley below. She parked her car away from the house so Cleo could get her car out of the garage. She put the container of Metamucil on top of her car while she rescued Feathers and walked to the front door with her overnight bag. Fortunately, Cleo opened the door first. Eleanor's load made it difficult to ring the bell.

"I've been pacing back and forth. There is nothing I can do, and I feel so sad and helpless," Cleo said as she tried to hug Eleanor who was still holding a big bird cage. Suddenly Ollie, Cleo's white Lhasa Apso got a whiff of Feathers and began to voice his disapproval which set Feathers to flapping and squawking in a very ungentlemanly way.

"Danger, danger," he said. "Jaws and claws!"

Cleo quickly herded Ollie into the laundry room where he continued to bark as though he were being murdered. Eleanor put Feathers in the back bedroom and when things finally settled down the two women sat at Cleo's dining table with cups of tea.

"So, what happened?" Eleanor asked.

"I don't know. It was Wanda's day off, so I don't know why she was even at the Wakefield's. They live at the top of the hill on the other side of the gully and her brakes must have gone out. She didn't stop and slammed into a big truck full of cow chow. I was reading the Sunday paper when I heard the crash, a horrific metal ripping sound. It was so loud and then nothing. I ran outside and looked over the hill and saw her car. By the time I got down there, the driver of the truck was out looking in Wanda's window. He waved me away and shook his head. Her car was crushed like an accordion. I knew there was no way she could have survived. I called 911 and when they got here several of the neighbors had gathered. No one wanted to look in the car. It took them a long time to extricate her body. I didn't stay. It felt ghoulish. I came home and called you."

"I'm sorry Cleo. I know you were fond of her." Eleanor said in an attempt to comfort her.

"I was just getting to know her really. I can't say we were friends yet, but she was a character for sure and someone I wanted to know better, plus she cleaned my house." Cleo paused. "I can't help but think this is related to the Wakefields in some way."

"What is it that makes you think she was murdered?" Eleanor asked.

"She did turn the bloody T-shirt in to the police," Cleo said. "I'm sure Rob wasn't happy about that." "Wouldn't they have just fired her then? Killing her wouldn't make sense unless she knew something more that would incriminate Rob. Do you think she could have been blackmailing them?" Eleanor was reluctant to believe the person she met a few days ago would do something like that.

"I don't know. What if she was and they refused to pay so she turned the T-shirt over to the police and this was how they reacted? They're mean and vengeful," Cleo said. "Maybe they thought she knew more than she did."

"Maybe it was just an accident. Her brakes could have failed because she didn't take care of her car," Eleanor suggested.

"That's possible I guess, but I have a bad feeling about it. Wanda found a love letter in her notebook and thought Howard Wakefield put it there. She had some strong opinions about him."

Eleanor felt the hairs on her neck rise as she made a connection regarding the mysterious letter.

"Did you see the letter?" Eleanor asked.

"No, but I'm sure she was telling the truth. She quoted part of it to me, something about leaving her lover for him."

"Did Wanda have a lover?" Eleanor asked.

"I know her husband is dead and she was living with her daughter, but I couldn't say for sure that there wasn't someone else in her life." Cleo felt a sadness descend upon her as she imagined all the people who knew and loved Wanda coming to grips with their loss.

"I think I may know something about that letter," Eleanor said. Cleo's puzzled expression caused Eleanor to continue. "I found a letter in the hidey-hole. It was very romantic and beautifully written. Angus didn't write it and we were going back and forth trying to find out who it was for and who might have written it. Anyway, somehow the letter disappeared. I think Wanda may have inadvertently picked it up when she visited my house."

"So the letter wasn't for Wanda from Howard Wakefield?" Cleo asked.

"Angus came back from searching Rob's house and told me they found the letter in the wastebasket there and now it's evidence in the murder investigation of Johnny Vargas," Eleanor explained.

"Wow, how do you think it got there?" Cleo asked.

"Wanda must have left it there and someone found it and tossed it in the trash," Eleanor speculated.

"I wonder if the 'someone' who found it thought it was written for them. It's really sort of funny." Cleo smiled. "It's possible that Wanda had gone to the Wakefield's to get the letter, and now Wanda's dead. Do you think it's related to the murder?"

"I don't know how it could be," Eleanor said. "It's just a letter that's traveled around giving people ideas about love and romance. I don't know how many have read it thinking there's someone out there pining for them. I must admit it's a heady feeling."

"So you still don't know who wrote it?" Cleo asked.

"No, but since it was in the hidey-hole, Angus believes it was for him, but I think it was for me."

"How many people know about your secret hiding spot?" Cleo asked.

"Evidently quite a few," Eleanor said remembering Angus' list.

"I think it's time for a glass of wine," said Cleo as she went to the kitchen to open a bottle. "Would you like some cheese and crackers?"

"Sure, but I need to call Angus and tell him about Wanda and the letter before he drives himself crazy trying make a connection to the murder investigation." Eleanor went to the back bedroom to check on Feathers who was sulking in his cage and called Angus. When he didn't answer she left a message.

"Hey Angus, it's Eleanor. I'm with Cleo. We've discovered how the letter got to Rob Wakefield's house and I don't think it's connected to the murder investigation. It seems Wanda, Cleo's housekeeper works for the Wakefields. She was at my house and must have picked up the letter by mistake when she gathered her papers. Unfortunately, Wanda died in a car accident today. I'll talk to you later."

She tried to console the miserable Feathers with gentle words and then they joined Cleo in the kitchen for wine and a crab salad that Cleo threw together. "I still can't get over the feeling that Wanda was killed by the Wakefields," Cleo admitted. "Do you think I'm being paranoid?"

"I don't think you're paranoid, but what would their motive be?" Eleanor asked.

"Would she have to testify about the T-shirt?"

"She already took it to the police and I'm sure their retelling of her account would hold up in court. I'm not a lawyer though so I could be wrong."

"The Wakefields aren't lawyers either and they might have thought they could throw doubt on her story if she wasn't alive to defend it. Howard Wakefield has lots of enemies, maybe Wanda was one of them," Cleo said. "What if they know about my friendship with her and think she told me something? Do you think they would come after me? I think someone fiddled with her brakes."

"Cleo, that's all speculation. You'll make yourself crazy if you continue to think that way," Eleanor said.

"The Wakefields aren't the type to pay attention to who's friends with their housekeeper. They're so concerned about themselves they can't be bothered with us little people. Besides, if her brakes were tampered with, we'll find out. They would have to try a different method with you. Two old women crashing due to faulty brakes would be suspicious, to say the least."

"Let's call the others and make this a party," Cleo suggested. "You can teach me how to play Bridge. I need something to keep my mind off Wanda and the Wakefields." Cleo picked up the phone and called Dede, Pearl, and Josephine. After she informed them of the situation, they arrived within the hour with snacks and more wine.

"Do you really think Rob Wakefield tried to kill Wanda?" asked Pearl.

"She is dead, you know. Her brakes failed after leaving the Wakefield house," Cleo said.

"But why? Why kill her?" asked Dede. "Howard Wakefield is an evil bastard, but I'm not sure he's a killer."

"Don't the police think Rob Wakefield killed Johnny Vargas?" asked Eleanor.

"Just what do you know about that?" asked Dede.

Eleanor explained everything she knew about the bloody shirt and the three different blood types that were found. "What I don't know is what Rob Wakefield told the police when they took him in for questioning."

"So they didn't arrest him or anything?" asked Pearl.

"I don't think they have enough evidence for that," Eleanor said.

"I'm not playing Bridge," Pearl said. "It gives me anxiety and this murder stuff is creepy enough. No wonder you don't want to be alone, Cleo."

"I have something to share," said Dede and went to her bag and pulled out a large envelope. "Here are the pictures that are supposed to have me shaking in fear of exposure."

The ladies gathered around and inspected the two photos. They showed Dede in her car with a strange-looking man with a mustache.

"This is you with Lorenzo," said Josephine, and she began to laugh.

Lorenzo was the blowup man the coffee ladies gave Dede to keep her company while Mark was off hunting. She kept him in her car to ward off anyone who thought they could take advantage of a woman who traveled alone.

"That's hilarious," giggled Cleo and she began to snort, which caused more laughter.

"He doesn't even look like a real man," said Josephine. "Do you think they're inferring you have a boyfriend or that you're a pervert with a blowup doll?"

"If that's all they have on you, there is nothing to worry about," said Pearl.

"Do you have Apples to Apples?" asked Dede who was finished with the entire drama.

Cleo went to her game closet and came back with Clue. "Look what I found," she said.

"Just the ticket," Josephine said. "That will surely keep our minds off of murder and murderers."

"I love that game," said Pearl. "But I haven't played it since I was a child, so I may not remember all the rules."

They quickly set up the game and began to play. In the midst of it Pearl began to hum. Then Eleanor began to sing in her opera voice, "I think Mrs. Peacock did it. She did it. She did it."

"No, no no no, it is a TRAP!" sang Dede with emotion. "Mrs. Peacock is innocent."

"She did it! I know she did it la la la," sang Eleanor.

"It was Mr. Green. He's green with envy. Green is evil. He did it and he is glad," Cleo joined in the Clue opera.

"You are all crazy. You've had too much WINE! Everyone knows it was Professor Plum—dum dum dum," Josephine's clear soprano rang out.

Suddenly, Ollie ran to the door and began to bark. "Oh no, our voices have activated the little dog," said Pearl.

"Intruders, intruders," squawked Feathers, who furiously flapped his wings in his cage.

"They just want to be part of the opera," said Dede. There was a loud clang followed by a thud. The ladies looked at one another with wide eyes.

"Someone's outside," whispered Cleo and she got up, went through the kitchen and out to the garage.

"Wait, Cleo," said Eleanor, who followed quickly behind, grabbing the fireplace poker on her way out. "The rest of you stay put and turn out the lights."

Cleo and Eleanor peered out the garage door windows. "I don't see anything," said Cleo. Eleanor moved to the side door and quietly opened it. They heard a smacking sound followed by something that resembled sneezing. Someone was definitely out there.

Inside, the other ladies sat silently in the dark. Dede stroked Ollie in an attempt to calm him, but no one tried to silence the caged bird. When a scream cut through the night, just like in a horror movie, they all jumped up and ran to the large window overlooking Cleo's driveway. A dark hulking something loped out of view into the shrubbery.

"What was that?" asked Pearl whose fringed eyes were wide with terror. The outdoor lights came on and they saw Cleo outside waving. Eleanor stood beside her with the poker. Josephine ran to the front door and opened it.

"Are you two all right?" she asked.

"What was that?" repeated Pearl.

"It was a bear," Cleo said, "He was in the garbage can. I don't know who was more scared, but I think I need to change my pants." Cleo and Eleanor came back in and decided they needed something a little stronger than wine. When everyone's heart rates had returned to normal, Josephine drove Pearl and Dede home, leaving Eleanor and Cleo to clean up after the bear.

"What's this all over the driveway?" asked Cleo as she observed a frothy orange substance near Eleanor's car. Eleanor studied it closely and began to laugh as she realized what it was.

"It's Metamucil," she said between chuckles. "I don't see any sign of the container so the bear must have taken it."

"It was the flavored kind too," moaned Cleo.

"That certainly answers the age-old question," Eleanor said.

"What's that?" asked Cleo.

"Does a bear shit in the woods?"

Eleanor did not hear from Angus and assumed he was occupied with the investigation. After completing her usual morning routine, she opted to drive into town to visit one of her friends who recently moved into the retirement home. Gladys Reyburg was more than ninety years old but hadn't lost her mind or her sense of humor. What she had lost was her quick step and sharp eyesight. Periodically, Eleanor read to Gladys, visited with her, and sometimes took her to lunch. On this day Eleanor found Gladys strolling amid the well-manicured grounds outside her room smelling the flowers in the company of an older gentleman.

"Eleanor, how lovely to see you." Gladys opened her arms and Eleanor walked into them. "Don't mind this old cane. It seems I can't get any place without it."

"I have one too," said the gentleman, holding up his cane.

"Eleanor, this is Artemas Chase. Art, this is Eleanor Penrose," Gladys said.

"We know each other," Eleanor said.

"Yes, indeed." Art smiled and his eyes twinkled with mischief. "Eleanor and I often have coffee together."

"Of course, you both live out at the beach. Art was just asking me about some of the residents here. He's interested in making friends with the greatest generation," Gladys said. "I believe he's planning to write a book."

"That should make for interesting reading," Eleanor said. "Speaking of reading I thought I'd drop by to see if you wanted to do some, but it *is* a beautiful day, too beautiful for indoor activities and you have company, so I'll just come another time."

When neither Gladys or Art protested Eleanor said her good-byes and did some errands in town. It shouldn't have raised concerns that Art was with Gladys, but for an unknown reason Eleanor was disturbed by it. Gladys was born in Waterton County and knew its history and almost everyone in it. She continued to be active in community endeavors, serving on many boards and volunteering on endless committees. Her mind was razor sharp and held information like a steel trap so when Eleanor wanted to know about something or someone, she went to Gladys to get answers. What was it that Artemas Chase wanted from Gladys Reyburg? He didn't seem the type to idly visit someone living in a retirement home. He wanted to know something, and Eleanor wanted to know what.

Eleanor stopped at the grocery store and picked up some things for dinner. She planned to invite Amy and Taylor and the grandchildren over. In the morning Eleanor intended to quiz Mattie May for answers about Art's intentions. He may have let something slip, and if he did, Mattie would know.

Eleanor's son-in-law, Taylor Ash, was tall and lean. Already Eleanor's grandchildren were beginning to look down on her. For the most part, they were respectful and fun to be with, but tonight was an exception. Amy was into the wine and babbled nonstop about her work while Taylor complained about his job, threatening to quit and become a house husband now that the children were mostly raised. Their time was filled up with work, social events, volunteering, and sporting activities. Eleanor didn't remember surviving that kind of busy, but times had changed and were evolving still.

Eleanor had prepared hearty steak and potatoes with balsamic cranberry pan sauce, cooked cabbage, and lemon-lime meringue pie for dessert. As they sat at the table, it seemed as though the food was an afterthought because no one commented on it.

"When's your next baseball game, Wesley?" she asked innocently.

"Saturday, Gramma, but I don't want you to come," Wesley sulked.

"Why not? You know I love to watch you play," Eleanor said.

"I suck. Even Dad won't come because he's embarrassed by me," Wesley said.

"That's not true," said Elise, "he doesn't come because you're adopted."

"Elise, that's not funny," Amy said as she watched Wesley scowl and cross his arms over his chest.

"He knows I'm teasing," Elise countered.

"Wesley, sometimes your father is very busy because of his job. He can't always make it to your games," Amy explained without conviction.

"I'll try to be at the next one, Wesley," Taylor sighed. "Sorry, Eleanor, I think I'm getting a migraine."

"I'm sorry too, Gramma. I'd really like you to come to my game," Wesley admitted. "Do you know what has 18 legs, spits uncontrollably, and catches flies?"

"No, is it a bug of some kind?" Eleanor asked.

"A baseball team," Wesley smiled.

"Ewww, I hope there isn't any spitting at your game," Addie commented.

"Why was Cinderella taken out of the game?" Elise asked.

"Why?" asked Addie.

"She ran away from the ball," Elise said.

"Do you know why the bicycle couldn't stand up?" asked Addie.

"It didn't have a kickstand," guessed Wesley.

"It was two tired," smiled Addie. The laughter was faint and forced. Something was definitely off this evening.

"I've learned to play *The Entertainer*," said Elise. "I could play it for you after dinner."

"I'd like that very much," Eleanor said.

"I wouldn't," mumbled Taylor, "My head is throbbing."

Eleanor left the table and came back with a pill. "Why don't you take this and go lie down in the guest room, Taylor. A rest might do you good." Surprisingly, he did just that while the others finished their dinner.

Later, Elise went to the Bosendorfer and played *The Entertainer* perfectly. Wesley and Addie performed their own practice pieces and then they walked down to the beach while Amy helped Eleanor clean up in the kitchen.

"Sorry everyone seems out of sorts tonight, Mom. I think we're overextended. There just isn't enough time to squeeze everything into our lives," Amy lamented.

"Maybe it's time to take some things out of your lives," she suggested.

"You may be right. Everything we do seems so important but it's killing us. The girls have dance practice so they can perform at the fair. All of the kids want to enter exhibits in a million different categories. Then they have baseball, softball, summer camp, swimming, and piano lessons. Then there's my committee and volunteer work as well as the boards I serve on and my job. What should we cut?"

"I thought summer was for relaxing. You know: blue sky time, lounging in a hammock in the shade of a big tree, reading beach books, and napping." Eleanor sighed remembering an earlier time.

"That sounds so good," Amy said, "But there's always so much to do."

"Let's cut this pie and eat it out on the deck," Eleanor suggested. "Maybe we can see the kids from there."

The sun was setting over the ocean, turning the distant layers of clouds a beautiful crimson. Eleanor and Amy watched the three children digging in the sand, collecting rocks and shells. They seemed oblivious to the exquisite artistry that surrounded them so intent on their own ambitions. Amy gasped when she saw the flash of green as the sun slipped down and darkness began to fall.

"I've never seen that before," she said in awe. Eleanor said nothing. She knew the benefits of sitting still and watching.

"Alone at last," Eleanor said to Feathers as she stroked his sleek gray plumage. "How nice to have company who doesn't talk back!" Eleanor was always happy when her family came to visit, and usually exhausted when they left. "I think I'm feeling my age tonight." Feathers swayed back and forth and nodded his head as if in agreement. The doorbell shattered their moment of peace and sent Feathers flying to check it out.

"Scallywags and intruders," he cried.

"I could smell pie," Angus said as soon as Eleanor opened the door.

"Please come in and help yourself." Eleanor's invitation was unnecessary as Angus walked in and continued to the kitchen where he dished up a huge piece of the lemon-lime meringue pie.

"Did you eat dinner?" Eleanor asked, wondering what mad skill enabled him to detect pie.

"I grabbed a burrito from the deli on the way home," he said between bites. It didn't take him long to finish off the dessert, pour three fingers of Crown Royal into a glass and make himself comfortable on the couch.

In dismay, Eleanor seated herself on the opposite couch instead of snuggling next to him. This was a different Angus. This was a husband. She looked at him long and hard until he felt her steamy gaze sear into his very being. "Hard day at the office?" she finally asked.

"I'm sorry Eleanor, I'm tired I guess. How was your day?" he asked as an afterthought.

"I'm tired too. Can you tell me anything about Wanda's accident?" Eleanor thought he might have heard something from his friends on the force. She would like to be able to tell Cleo that Wanda wasn't murdered.

"Wanda? You mean the Wakefield's housekeeper?" he asked.

"Yes, I heard her brakes gave out. Could they have been tampered with? Cleo thinks the Wakefields may have done her in," Eleanor elaborated.

"She's the link to the letter. Rob Wakefield was brought in for questioning. He said he found the letter outside on the driveway where Wanda parks her car. She must have dropped it. When he saw what it was he tossed it in the garbage. I believe him. It was covered with so many prints forensics couldn't get any clear ones. The letter isn't connected to the murder investigation."

"Did he say anything interesting that you can share?" Eleanor probed.

"Of course, he says someone planted the bloody T-shirt in his closet and he has an alibi for the night Johnny went missing," Angus said. "He's probably lying, but we'll find out the truth when we check out his alibi."

"What is his alibi?"

"He claims he was with Olivia and Eric Fowler at the Red Shed," Angus said.

"So what happens next?"

"We'll have to bring Eric and Olivia in for questioning and probably get a warrant for Eric's place so we can check his DNA against the third blood type on the T-shirt."

"Investigating takes a great deal of time and patience," Eleanor said thoughtfully.

Angus looked at her and had a sudden epiphany. He was rude and thoughtless and totally distracted by this investigation. His intense focus on one thing, the thing that made him an excellent detective, also made him an absent friend and a lackluster lover. He knew it. It was what ruined his marriage to Margo and most likely kept Eleanor from committing to him. He stood and sat down next to Eleanor putting his arm around her and drawing her close. He felt her stiffen.

"I'm sorry, Eleanor. I haven't been very attentive lately." Angus nuzzled her neck and kissed her behind her ear, but Eleanor was not in the mood to be thrown a bone and pushed him away.

"I understand, Angus," she began, "I'm the same way when I'm in the zone for writing. I don't want anything or anyone interrupting my flow. I appreciate the fact that you came over to share information about the case, but you haven't told me if Wanda's death was caused by someone tampering with her brakes or if it was an unfortunate accident."

"Oh, you don't know. Wanda didn't die in the accident. She's in Waterton County Hospital's ICU. It looks like her brake line could have been tampered with, but her car was so damaged it was hard to make a clear determination. When the doctors give the OK we'll question her too." Angus watched Eleanor's jaw drop in amazement. "I didn't realize you were so connected to her." Eleanor was speechless. She simply leaned into Angus and planted a big kiss on his willing lips.

Eleanor called Cleo as soon as Angus left despite the lateness of the hour. The two planned to meet at the hospital the following afternoon in hope of discovering more about Wanda's situation. That night,

Eleanor dreamed about speeding down a steep hill. When she tried to slow down her car didn't respond. She pumped the brakes, but nothing happened. Her car went from one side of the road to the other teetering over a deep ravine before she corrected it and almost hit the bank. Finally, she covered her eyes and crashed into Wanda at the bottom of the hill who then climbed out of her smashed car covered in blood. Eleanor ran from the scene screaming. Suddenly Cleo was there with a large bear covered in orange gel and the three ran into the woods with Wanda slowly and awkwardly giving chase like a zombie. The bear led them to its den where they hid in fear until Wanda Zombie lost interest and wandered away. Eleanor looked around the den and noticed Taylor sleeping next to three bear cubs who climbed over him and nuzzled him with their cute teddy bear noses while he swatted them away and continued his slumber.

Eleanor woke early and exhausted from her nighttime exertions and set out for a brisk morning walk on the beach. Like many mornings when the weather was hot in the valley, the marine air brought fog to the coastal regions. On this day, Sand Beach was enveloped in a thick moist layer that dimmed the day and muffled the sound of the sea and everything else. Eleanor walked on the gray sand along a gray ocean and contemplated her life. She could tolerate Angus' obsession with the murder investigation. Eleanor enjoyed solitude because she was comfortable with her own company. It was during these times when she was most creative. Ideas swirled through her mind and solutions were often resolved as she let her thoughts flow.

As much as she loved the attention Angus lavished on her at times it could be suffocating. It hadn't occurred to her until now, but she was good at balancing her alone time with social time and thought perhaps she had been shorting her friends and family in favor of Angus. Dinner with Amy and the grandchildren last night reinforced that thought. It had been different and at times uncomfortable because they hadn't spent as much time together. She wasn't positive that was why, but she certainly didn't want a repeat of it. She vowed to be at Wesley's next baseball game to cheer him on even if he sat in the dugout. Her grandchildren needed her just as much as Angus did. Disconnecting with them was not an option.

Eleanor stopped at Suzanna's and was happy to see no sign of Artemas Chase at the Do Nothing's table. "Do you mind if I join you for a cup of coffee," she asked as she slipped off her jacket.

"Please, we've missed you lately," Sybil said kindly.

"Yes, where have you been keeping yourself?" asked Mavis. "I bet Angus has been taking up all your time. It seems like once a man gets in the door, friends fly out the window."

Mattie sat quietly biting her lip. She sensed they were talking about her and Artemas and she had to admit there might be truth to it. He did come to her house regularly for a meal or to watch television. She even drove him into Waterton on occasion to catch a movie or go for Chinese. A few times he just wanted a ride into town to do errands. He wasn't always open about his activities and she'd dropped him off and later picked him up at a prearranged time and place. She was curious and had her own theories about the man, but didn't probe too deeply because she was afraid he might pull away and she enjoyed his company.

"Where is Art?" asked Eleanor as if she had read their thoughts.

"He claims he's under the weather this morning," Mattie said.

"Hungover most likely. Just what did you give the man last night?" asked Mavis.

"Maybe he doesn't have the stamina he used to," suggested Sybil. "After a long night satisfying you, he needs a day to recover."

"Oh stop it. You're just jealous that you don't have a gentleman like him to spend time with you," Mattie countered.

"No, that's not it," corrected Mavis. "We're jealous because now you're too busy to spend time with your dear friends. Last week you cancelled our fun night to spend it with him."

"We haven't really been able to have a real girl talk since he came into the picture," complained Sybil.

"So what do you know about him Mattie?" Eleanor quizzed. "What's he up to?"

"I don't know what you mean?" Mattie seemed suddenly defensive. "Do you think he's an axe murderer?"

"I saw him talking to Gladys Reyburg at the Riverside Retirement Home the other day. She's my source of information when I need to learn about people and places in the area. What's his interest?"

"So Happy Butt has finally moved into a home has she?" Mattie said meanly.

"Ouch, Mattie, Gladys is a wonderful person. That remark is beneath you," scolded Mavis.

"Happy Butt? I don't get it?" Eleanor shrugged.

"Glad Ass, Happy Butt, you don't want to get it," Sybil said. "Mattie and Gladys haven't always seen eye to eye, but that's a story for another day."

"You're not worried that Gladys is moving in on your man are you Mattie?" asked Mavis.

"Ladies, you're friends. Let's not forget that. No man is worth losing what you have here," Eleanor stated. "It wasn't long ago when you were bragging about not having men in your lives and how wonderful that was. Remember?"

"It was wonderful until this man waltzed in here and took over our table and monopolized our friend," Mavis said.

"Do you think he's up to no good?" asked Sybil.

"I don't have a clue. I was hoping you ladies might have information. Gladys thought he might be writing a book," Eleanor said.

Mattie leaned in and whispered, "He is a Nazi hunter, don't forget."

"A retired one," Mavis said. "I suppose he could write an interesting account of his life after the war. It would beat having to listen to him talk about it every time we see him. Getting it out of his system might be cathartic."

Mattie pressed her lips together. It was a gesture that didn't go unnoticed by Eleanor who wondered what she wasn't telling.

Eleanor met Cleo for lunch at the Blue Lagoon. "I can't believe Wanda got out of that mangled mess of metal alive. I was sure she was dead," Cleo said as she nibbled on her taco salad.

"The truck driver who hit her must have thought the same thing. Getting her out of the car would have been a challenge for the firemen. I just hope her injuries aren't insurmountable. She's not an old woman but she isn't young either."

"We may not be allowed to see her," Cleo said.

"We'll leave our good wishes and she'll know we tried," Eleanor said.

"Do you think they'll let us see her before the police?" Cleo asked.

"I don't know why not. It's not like we're going to coach her on what to tell or not tell them. Of course, if we were the Wakefields it might be different," Eleanor said.

"How does the hospital make that determination?" Cleo asked.

"Maybe they have a list of who isn't allowed to see her. Family and close friends might be okay and mean employers who tamper with a patient's brakes are not."

"Eleanor you are not making any sense at all. I'm almost positive they won't let any of us in to see her based on your flawed logic. Do you think Wanda is in danger?"

"No, I don't, but I'm illogical so don't take my word for it."

By the time they arrived at Waterton County Hospital they had resigned themselves to the fact that they wouldn't be allowed to see Wanda, so they were pleasantly surprised when they were told she was out of ICU and in a private room on the second floor. Nothing however prepared them for her appearance.

Wanda lay in bed with several tubes connected to her. Her face was covered with bandages and the only parts they could see were swollen and discolored. Her left arm and leg were in casts. She looked miserable.

"Is that you Wanda?" Cleo approached cautiously.

"Who the fuck wants to know," she muttered between her puffy lips.

"Yep, it's Wanda all right," Cleo said. "I recognize her foul mouth."

"Good grief, Wanda, what happened?" Eleanor moved close to hear Wanda better.

"I don't remember a friggin' thing. I went back to the Wakefield's to get my notebook. I'd left it in the kitchen and there was a letter in it that I wanted to reread. It was such a lovely letter. Coming down the steep part of the hill I realized my brakes weren't working. That's all I remember . . . the fear and panic, and I knew I was going to die."

"It sounds like your brain is still working. I'm sure you'll be up and about in no time." Cleo tried to be positive but looking at Wanda made it difficult.

"Are my extensions still on?" she asked. "The fucking bastards won't let me have a mirror." Eleanor leaned close to see if she could detect any eyelashes amid the damaged tissue, then simply nodded.

"Can you find that letter? I really want to read it again. It reminds me of my late husband." Wanda's eyes closed and she sighed deeply, "Oscar . . . "

"We can do that," Eleanor said.

"I think we'd better let you rest," Cleo said, but Wanda was out for the count.

In the elevator, Cleo looked at Eleanor and said, "She looked horrible."

"Yes, she did, but she's alive," Eleanor said.

"Did you really see her extensions?" Cleo asked.

"I'm not sure. I think it might have been stitches. Are you going home now?"

"No," said Cleo, "I'm taking my car to the Service Center to have the brakes checked."

"Let's go to the Red Shed," Eleanor suggested as the coffee group sat at their usual table enjoying their usual breakfasts at the Boat House.

"Why? That place is a pickup joint for singles and sexual deviants," Josephine said.

"Wait a minute now, I go there sometimes to play video poker and smoke cigarettes in the back room," Pearl reminded them.

"I think Rob Wakefield and Eric Fowler hang out there," Eleanor said. "I bet we could learn something if we listened closely. They claim they were there the night Johnny disappeared."

"I'll go with you," Dede offered.

"I'm all in too," said Cleo.

"Why don't we take Angus? You know for protection?" asked Josephine.

"No one would talk if they saw Angus hanging around," Eleanor said. "Besides, he won't take me there. He says it's not a nice place."

Pearl hesitated. "Is this a stakeout?"

"Yes, Pearl, only there will be video poker, drinks, and a bathroom," Dede said.

"Now you're talking," Pearl said. "Are we going tonight?"

"I have dinner with Angus tonight," Eleanor said.

"Saturday night is more likely to be when those party animals are at the Red Shed," Cleo said. "I can go Saturday."

"Let's meet at my house and go together," suggested Dede.

"What time?" asked Pearl.

"Is eight too early?" asked Josephine. "You know when the action starts, Pearl."

"We should meet at nine," Pearl said. And the plan was set in motion.

Eleanor planned a simple dinner of fiery hot Texas T-bone with chipotle smashed potatoes and hot and sweet pepper sauté. She'd made it for Angus before and it was a success. If she were being honest, she would have said everything she served him was a success because he always ate whatever she put in front of him, even the infamous vegan Tex-Mex skillet dinner. When Angus arrived with a bottle of cab and a bouquet of pink carnations, Eleanor was just preparing to flambé the steak pan.

"Let me do that," he said as he put down his gifts, picked up the bottle of bourbon and lit it. As Angus and Eleanor watched the fire, he retrieved a serving platter from the shelf that Eleanor could never reach without her step stool. Without a word he transferred the steaks to the dish and poured the pan juices over them while Eleanor sautéed the bell peppers. He put the flowers in a vase and poured himself a drink. They worked together like gears in a fine watch and then, while the steaks rested, enjoyed their drinks on the deck.

"Is there anything new in the investigation?" Eleanor asked.

"They did bring Eric Fowler and Olivia Martin in for questioning," Angus said. "They gave conflicting stories so it's obvious they haven't coordinated anything."

"Do tell," Eleanor probed.

"Olivia said she was with Eric that night, but Eric said he was with Rob," Angus said.

"So Olivia is in love with Eric and wants to . . . " Eleanor started.

" . . . provide him with an alibi," finished Angus, nodding his head. "Eric, on the other hand, sees his friend in trouble . . . "

" . . . and wants to give him an alibi." Eleanor nodded. "When they were questioned did they say they weren't all together?"

"Olivia said she was with Eric all night and didn't see Rob at all," Angus said.

"They're lying," they said in unison.

"Let's eat," Eleanor said.

"That was delicious," Angus said as he pushed away from the table. "I'll help you clean up but then I have to go. Will Chase and I are going fishing in the morning and we want to get an early start." What he didn't say was that he had a file he wanted to study, one that included the mysterious letter. Even though it couldn't be connected to the case, they didn't know who had written it to whom and Angus found that fact extraordinarily vexing. He needed to read it again. The truth was he enjoyed reading it when he thought it was for him, but he feared it was for Eleanor.

"So you're saying . . . " Eleanor began.

" . . . no room or time for dessert," Angus finished.

When the dishes were washed and put away, Angus pecked Eleanor on the cheek and left for home. "Goodbye, loser," squawked Feathers as the door closed behind him. Eleanor sighed. It wasn't marriage that turned romance stale. It was time.

The following day Eleanor drove into Waterton early to have dinner with Mark and Dede. "What's happening with the issue of voter fraud?" asked Eleanor as they sat at Dede's dining table.

"Don't worry," Dede said, "The Secretary of State is investigating my concerns and has reassured me that those men will not be allowed to vote in Waterton if she finds anything suspicious."

"Does that mean Howard Wakefield will be investigated too?" Eleanor asked.

"He's as slippery as a greased pig," Mark said. "He hasn't had to be responsible for anything in his entire life. He's got a ton of money to pay for a slew of lawyers. If anyone criticizes him, he slaps a lawsuit on them to intimidate them. Most people can't afford to fight him in court. He must have enemies up the ying-yang."

"We'll see." Dede got up to bring dessert and the telephone rang. "Can you get that Mark?"

Mark checked the caller ID and returned to the table letting the answering machine pick it up. "Who was it?" asked Dede as she placed a pineapple upside-down cake in front of them.

"It was Helen Pence," he said matter of fact. "You know I can't talk to her."

"I know you say she uses a sexy porn voice when she calls here but I've never heard it," Dede said.

"That's because she only talks that way to me!" Mark shivered in disgust and his face turned red with embarrassment. Dede shrugged her shoulders and Eleanor held her tongue. Evidently Helen Pence had a side she only revealed to men. Nothing good could come from telling Dede that Angus also hesitated to take her calls for the same reason.

When nine o'clock came so did Josephine, Pearl, and Cleo. "I told Mark we were going to a special meeting, which he assumed was book club, so I didn't technically lie, but he'd worry if I told him we were going to the Red Shed to stakeout a couple of hoodlums," Dede explained. It was evident she didn't like lying to Mark, but it was for his own good. They piled into Josephine's SUV and drove to the Red Shed.

As soon as they walked into the place Eleanor spotted Rob Wakefield with Olivia Martin standing at the bar. Olivia wore a low-cut top and tight white jeans that revealed her firm, youthful body. Her blonde hair, which she flipped periodically, cascaded down her back in waves. Eleanor thought cute instead of beautiful while Cleo was thinking she looked like the barroom skank, and Josephine diagnosed her as a daughter with daddy issues. Pearl simply disappeared into the back room to play video poker and smoke a forbidden cigarette. The ladies took a seat at an empty table and ordered drinks.

"I've never been in here," said Josephine, who looked around curiously. "I'm disturbed that Pearl feels at home here."

"Don't you approve of the décor?" asked Dede.

"It's typical Waterton country," Cleo added as she nibbled on some peanuts and threw the shells on the floor.

"Remember that night at Cleo's when we saw a bear?" asked Josephine. "When we pulled up to Dede's house that night we saw two men lurking around her house. I think one of them looks a lot like Rob Wakefield."

"I forgot all about that," said Dede as she eyed Rob suspiciously.

"I can't hear what they're saying," Eleanor said. "I'm moving to the bar." The others did nothing to stop her.

Eleanor made herself comfortable on a stool next to Rob just as Eric Fowler walked through the door. It was obvious he had already had a few drinks under his belt. He stood next to Olivia and threw his arm over her shoulder. Eleanor didn't think they even noticed her, but she kept herself partially turned away from them to try and be inconspicuous.

"Hello Sweetheart," Eric said. "Can I buy you a drink?" Olivia leaned into him and nodded. Eleanor could feel the anger emanating from Rob Wakefield like heat from the hinges of hell.

"Where's Junie, Eric?" Rob asked as he rolled a stick of Black Jack gum and popped it into his mouth throwing the blue wrapper on the floor.

"She's got a headache," Eric said. "She's always got a headache." He wouldn't admit that Junie didn't want to see him anymore and hadn't for some time.

"I've got a headache too," Rob said. "The police think I had something to do with Johnny Vargas' disappearance. What did you tell them? You know I told them I was here with you two the night Johnny died. I hope you backed me up."

"You know I've got your back, man," Eric said.

"For all I know," Rob sneered, "You could have planted that bloody shirt in my room."

"Why would I do that?" Eric sincerely seemed offended.

"You got your eyes all over my girl. Maybe you're thinking you want her back. Get me in trouble and out of the way."

"I don't need to get you out of the way to get Olivia back. All I have to do is crook my finger and she's mine," Eric bragged as if Olivia were not standing next to him. "Just the way I did with Junie."

"Oh yeah, maybe you got rid of Johnny to get Junie back," Rob taunted. "She wouldn't be with you if he was still in the picture."

"And maybe you did it because you knew that was the only way you could have Olivia," Eric growled.

This was more than Rob could bear because he knew it to be true. He took a swing at Eric and before anyone could stop it there was a barroom brawl and Eleanor was in the middle of it. Fists flew, chairs toppled, and glasses broke. When the dust cleared Josephine and Cleo picked Eleanor off the floor and Dede went to get Pearl who had just won two hundred dollars playing her favorite numbers in Keno.

Fortunately, Mark had already gone upstairs to bed when they got back to Dede's where they iced Eleanor's face and probed her for other injuries. "I must have caught Rob's elbow when he swung at Eric," Eleanor said. "I think I'd better go home before my eye swells shut."

"Are you sure you can drive?" asked Josephine who had been the designated driver.

"I never finished my drink," Eleanor said. "I'll be fine. I just want to go home and go to bed."

"Did we learn anything at the stakeout?" asked Pearl. "Did anyone confess?"

"I think the only thing those two are guilty of is an overabundance of testosterone," said Eleanor.

Eleanor slept fitfully. She had iced her swollen eye, taken ibuprofen, and gone to bed, but her sleep was filled with strange, colorful dreams. In one, Angus appeared at her door wearing a blue plaid shirt and jeans, the exact same outfit that she was wearing. He was in her kitchen handing her the ingredients for Thai chicken curry before she even thought to ask for them. Her friends came for dinner and complimented Angus on the dinner he had prepared. It was as if they had become one person finishing each other's sentences, aping mannerisms, and saying the same things at the same time. She didn't know where she ended, and he began.

In another dream, Angus sat at her desk in her office writing poetry. The telephone rang and her publisher told him his latest book had just sold a million copies. Instead of feeling happy for her friend, Eleanor felt displaced and jealous watching from the corner of the room as Angus became more vibrant and she slowly faded away. She woke up and took more ibuprofen and went back to bed, only to toss and turn until the sun came up.

Feathers watched as Eleanor made coffee. He eyed her curiously and chided, "Bad girl, bad girl," evidently judging her for having stayed out late and returning with a black eye from a barroom brawl. She was applying more ice when the doorbell rang. It was way too early for company and Eleanor thought about hiding when she saw Angus at the door but summoned her courage and went to let him in. He deserved everything he saw for invading a person's privacy this early in the morning.

Angus's eyes opened wide when he saw the black and blue swollen slit that was once Eleanor's bright sparkling eye. "Good lord, what happened to you?" he blurted.

Eleanor squinted at him with her good eye and noticed that he too was sporting a painful looking black eye as well as some abrasions on his cheek. "Barroom brawl, how about you?" she muttered as she turned to go back to the kitchen for coffee. After her latest dream she wasn't surprised that she couldn't even be original in her injuries.

"First tell me how this happened," Angus ordered to know as he turned her face toward him and peered carefully at her damaged eye. He obviously didn't believe her barroom brawl story.

Eleanor toyed with the idea of telling him she ran into a door, but that seemed trite. "I ran into Rob Wakefield's elbow when he was taking a swing at Eric Fowler at the Red Shed." Eleanor poured two cups of coffee as if the news were an everyday occurrence.

"Quit being funny Ellie and tell me the truth." Angus could be very bossy it seemed.

"That *is* the truth unless you'd rather believe Feathers threw a fit and it hit me in the eye," Eleanor said.

"What were you doing at the Red Shed? That place is a sleazy pick-up dive." Angus was nonplussed. He thought he knew this woman, but she continued to surprise him.

"The coffee group was on a stakeout trying to glean information about Rob and Eric's whereabouts on the night Johnny Vargas disappeared." Eleanor suddenly needed to sit down. She took her coffee into the living room and sat on the couch. Angus followed and sat beside her. He couldn't take his eyes off the shiner.

"Quit staring," Eleanor snapped. "You don't look all that great either. What happened to you? I didn't see you at the Red Shed so don't tell me you were in that fight."

"Did you learn anything?" Angus persisted with his line of questioning while suppressing a smile. Evidently the idea of Eleanor and her cronies at the Red Shed was funny.

"Eric is covering for Rob, but Rob thinks Eric set him up. I think they're both innocent because they each think the other is guilty. They are so full of manly hormones it's amazing they didn't' kill each other over Olivia Martin." Eleanor took a sip of her coffee and waited patiently for Angus to tell his story.

"Will Chase and I went fishing yesterday. I invited him in for a beer afterward and he saw the love letter we found in the hidey-hole," Angus began.

"Was he the one who wrote it?" Eleanor interrupted. She imagined Angus punching Will for trying to steal his woman and experienced a jolt of happy vindication.

Angus shook his head. "I was studying the information in Johnny's file and had left the letter on the coffee table. Will recognized Cynthia's handwriting and inferred the worst, thinking we were involved in an affair, so he punched me. It was perfectly understandable. I would have done the same thing if the roles were reversed."

"Cynthia wrote the letter for *you*?" Eleanor felt deflated. "I didn't think she even knew you?"

"Well, she's seen me," Angus said with all the arrogance of a man used to adoration from the opposite sex.

"And that caused you to pierce her soul? I don't believe it. Did you square it with Will or is he still angry?" Eleanor asked.

"I explained to him that I was madly in love with you, Ellie. I can't help it if I'm irresistible to women, but I didn't do anything to lead Cynthia on in any way and nothing happened between us. He seemed to believe me and went home to confront her."

Angus stroked Eleanor's neck and nuzzled her ear, but she wasn't in a romantic mood. "Do you have any ibuprofen?" Angus asked giving up on hanky-panky.

"It's in the bathroom medicine cabinet." Eleanor was not waiting on Angus. She found his attitude aggravating and the solution to the mysterious letter unacceptable.

When Angus returned, he brought more ice for Eleanor's eye and the Sunday paper. As he settled down next to her, he offered graciously to assist her with the crossword puzzle. With just a slight jolt, she realized that doing things as a team wasn't the same as becoming the same person and relaxed.

"I'll read the clues and you can tell me the answers. With two good eyes between us, we should be able to get this done."

Eleanor took time to reflect. She donned a large pair of sunglasses and walked on her foggy beach. There were many

questions about a variety of issues that needed answers. When
Angus said Will was going home to confront Cynthia about
the love letter did that mean she was home, or did it mean he
would call her. No one had heard from Cynthia since she left
unexpectedly, and they only had Art and Will's word that they
had been in contact with her at all. What if she were dead,
murdered even, by her oppressive husband or unsympathetic
father-in-law? Maybe she'd run off the road and was trapped
in her car in a gully in some remote area slowly dying of thirst?
The possibilities were endless. There was no way Eleanor could
know. Then there was the question of why Cynthia would
write a love letter to Angus in the first place.

There was no way she could feel the passion for Angus that
the letter implied. Eleanor toyed with the idea that Cynthia
could have fallen in love with *her*. That made more sense but
certainly didn't fit with Cynthia's way of thinking. Surely, she
would never in a million years accept love between two women
as an option, yet there it was: Will recognized her handwriting.
She had knowledge of the hidey-hole and easy access to it.
Eleanor admitted to herself that she was surprised at Cynthia's
talent having written such a beautiful expression of love.

Her mind turned to Johnny Vargas and his murder. If
neither Eric Fowler nor Rob Wakefield killed him, who did?
Howard Wakefield came to mind. If he had done it would he
have planted the incriminating shirt in his son's closet? Not
likely. Who else had access to the Wakefield house? Did Junie
murder her own husband? What would her motive be and why
would she plant a bloody shirt in Rob's closet? What about
Wanda? What did Eleanor really know about her? Maybe she
wasn't an innocent housekeeper after all but someone who had

a grudge against the Wakefields and set Rob up to get revenge on them.

Perhaps she was the one who sent the note to Angus suggesting Johnny was the victim of foul play. Maybe he wasn't even murdered, and it was all an unfortunate accident. Did it mean anything that Wanda thought Howard Wakefield had sent the letter to her? Did they have a past together? She wondered if Cleo knew anything about Wanda and if the police had already questioned her. Olivia Martin might even play a role in this convoluted love story. She loved Eric Fowler. That much was clear, so why did she hang out with Rob Wakefield, and would she plant false evidence against him to get him out of her life? What would she gain by that? It wouldn't cause Eric to fall out of love with Junie and return to her. It would make more sense to plant a bloody shirt in Junie's closet. If Junie went to jail Eric would be hers again.

Then there was the mysterious Artemas Chase and his visit to Riverside Retirement Home. Mattie knew something but wasn't telling. Eleanor distinctly remembered the way she pressed her lips together so she wouldn't tell her secret. What had she said? There was something, a clue she gave that eluded Eleanor now. She shook her head and realized she had completed her entire walk without noticing her surroundings. Fortunately, the tide was going out and she was in no danger of a sneaker wave knocking her down in her unfocused state. How foolish to allow her mind to block out the roar of the surf, cries of the gulls, and the dangers of the ocean. Eleanor plodded up the hill. There would be no stopping at Suzanna's for coffee with the Do Nothings today. She didn't want to explain her black eye or have to conjure up a believable cover story.

As she walked past Angus' house she wondered again about where their relationship was going and if she liked its evolution or not. If there were boundaries that needed to be set could she tell him without bruising his fragile pride? She remembered his sweet caring nature of yesterday and decided to stop to make sure he was okay. Angus answered her knock wearing sunglasses. When they saw each other, they both burst out laughing. "Come in," Angus said.

Eleanor stepped through the doorway and took off her glasses so she could see in the dimness. "Why are you wearing sunglasses inside?"

"I saw you coming and put them on just to open the door," he answered taking his shades off and revealing a beauty of purple and blue, his cheek already scabbing over.

"It looks worse than last night," Eleanor said.

"Yours doesn't look much better," he said peering closely into her eye. "The white of your eye is blood red."

"We are a sorry couple, I'm afraid," Eleanor sighed.

"I'm not sorry," Angus said. "I know the author of the mysterious love letter and I have a fresh pot of coffee. Are you interested?"

"In your love life or the coffee?" Eleanor asked.

"Aren't you interested in both?" Angus raised one brow.

"Oh yes," Eleanor said and followed him into his kitchen to get a cup.

"I also know more about the Vargas case."

"Yes . . . " Eleanor patiently waited while Angus drew out the suspense and slowly poured the coffee.

"The third person's blood on Rob's T-shirt turned out to match Eric Fowler's DNA."

"So what does that prove exactly?" Eleanor asked.

"It's possible all three were involved in a violent altercation. Most of the blood belonged to Johnny."

"How did your guys manage to get Eric's DNA?"

"Tricks of the trade," Angus said. "They had him in for questioning, turned up the heat, and collected his sweat for testing."

"Can forensics determine the age of the blood? Maybe it was really old." Eleanor asked. "You said they were always beating up on Johnny."

"Forensics can determine the age of the bloodstain by the decomposition of the cellular structure of the DNA. They use some fairly sophisticated technology these days, Ellie. The bloodstains are all relatively fresh, at least within a couple of months, so they aren't old and fall within the timeline of Johnny's disappearance."

"What will happen now?" she asked.

"A warrant will be issued to search Eric Fowler's residence and we'll see what turns up."

"Are either of them going to be put in jail?" asked Eleanor.

"Not until there's sufficient evidence to put them there," he answered.

"It sounds like there's nothing to do until the search is complete. Have the police questioned Wanda yet?"

"Someone took her statement, but I don't believe anything new has come from it," Angus said.

"You know Wanda thought Howard Wakefield gave that letter to her. She might be in love with him."

"It's a clear bet he isn't in love with her. I just heard he's engaged to some supermodel," Angus said. "Let's see how Rob handles this news. He can't be happy that he might have to share his inheritance because of his dad's midlife crisis."

"I'm going home to take nap," Eleanor said.

"Do you want company?" Angus asked with a twinkle in his blackened eye.

"Not today," she answered.

"As you wish," was all he said. Eleanor wondered if he already knew he had stepped over her boundaries.

Eleanor was sure no one would disturb her as she entered her office and sat at the desk. Feathers flew in to check things out and say hello then perched by the window to look out at the trees. Peace and quiet and a little blue sky beginning to break through the fog was all she needed for inspiration.

I am
I am
Invisible
I need no magic cape to make me so.
I wear it
A crown of graying hair
Lines upon my aging face
I am
Matter
Yet it doesn't seem I do.
I hear it I need special care
I take up time and space.
I am
Old
Although it wasn't always so
I bear it To many I'm as vaporous as air
They look but put me in my place.

I am
Wisdom
With no place for it to go
I'd share it
With others if they'd dare
To honor age along with youth and grace.
I am
Left
To wonder who will lift me up or let me go
Beware They only lift me there
To toss me in the waste and leave no trace.

When she emerged from her creative lair, time had elapsed, and Eleanor felt renewed. She made a tuna sandwich and conversed with her feathered friend. "What do you think, Feathers? Should we visit Madame Patruska to see what she has to say about bloody things?" Feathers looked at her first with one yellow eye and then another and flew to his window perch without comment. He obviously did not believe in such things.

When Eleanor entered the Oracle she felt an abandoned air. Easy listening music played softly and the heavy scent of eucalyptus filled her nostrils. Madame Patruska appeared from behind a black beaded curtain and welcomed her with a slight bow that set her bangles and beads clinking. "Good afternoon. Mow hay I be of service to you?" she asked. Eleanor wondered if she remembered her from her earlier visit.

"I'd like a tarot reading," Eleanor said, without knowing why she had asked for that. It popped out of her mouth because it was on a poster she spied in the distance. All she really wanted was information about Junie Vargas and how blood would begin and end her suffering. Madame Patruska simply nodded and pointed to the beaded doorway. Eleanor sat at the table covered with a black star-studded cloth and faced the seer. Madame Patruska carefully revealed a deck of cards wrapped in black silk, shuffled them, and spread them out face down in front of Eleanor.

"Before you choose your 10 cards you should have a question in mind." Madame Patruska invited Eleanor to pick her cards.

Eleanor thought about her question. What did the words mean that Junie's suffering would begin and end with blood? But her mind wandered and instead she asked if she was strong enough to maintain her unique identity in the face of a closer and changing relationship with Angus.

Eleanor selected her cards and Madame Patruska laid them out in a pattern and began to read them.

"The cage of pups, I mean the page of cups," Madame Patruska said as she turned the first card, "signifies the birth of something new, perhaps a new feeling in a relationship and a renewal of the capacity to love that starts with love of self after a time of hurt and withdrawal. This is a fragile thing and can vanish if not nurtured."

Eleanor was amazed as each card seemed to relate to her question and provide her with a clear and meaningful path to its answer. She suddenly realized that pride and fear stood in the way of creating a loving relationship, but through compromise and her own strength she could choose to give up control and face her fear that Angus might try to own her or cast his shadow over her. It was a confusing time for her, but she needed to look deeply inside herself to find what she truly wanted. Perhaps she was more than a poet and Angus could be the catalyst that brought her new endeavors.

Madame Patruska sat quietly observing Eleanor as she processed the reading of her cards. She did not try to supply answers or predict a fixed fate but allowed Eleanor's subconscious mind to work out her own solutions. Madame Patruska is a therapist with a different vehicle for accessing the inner workings of the mind, Eleanor thought. She couldn't wait to tell Josephine.

"Thank you, Madame Patruska," Eleanor said sincerely as she rose to go.

"You are welcome," she replied. "The answer to the other question was never about you. It is a diversion and wears the face of someone else's deceit. He is a fart smeller. I mean a smart feller." "What do you mean?" Eleanor was puzzled. She never asked her other question out loud.

"The reason you came here was to discover something about someone else. I'm right, aren't I?" Madame Patruska asked.

"Yes, but how did you know that?" Eleanor asked.

Madame Patruska shrugged. "Sometimes I thick up on pings, a hesitation, shifty look of the eyes. I can only tell you that what you believe to be true is not true." With that she stood and led Eleanor to the door.

Eleanor pondered the entire experience as she drove home. She opened herself to her real feelings about Angus. She loved him, that was a given. She wanted him in her life, that much was true. The rest would have to be the compromise part and the strength to let him know exactly where her boundaries were. Eleanor was strong. She would never disappear or be overshadowed by a man. Angus had needs too and if she really loved him she had to consider those as well. Eleanor decided a serious talk about their mutual needs and desires was long overdue.

The strange ending to the visit was something else altogether. Madame Patruska didn't even know what her first question was so she couldn't give an answer to it. It *was* about someone other than herself, but that whole episode was ridiculous, and Eleanor decided not to give it any credence. "What you believe to be true is not true," could mean almost anything. Junie's suffering, beginning and ending with blood, held no belief for Eleanor. She didn't have a clue.

Angus called to invite Eleanor out for an early dinner and a movie in Waterton. He picked her up and they sat in a booth at Pacific House and enjoyed the happy hour menu. Eleanor sipped her martini with extra olives while Angus made love to his Crown Royal. As she looked across the table at him, she tried to see him the way others would; a handsome man with an air of confidence and strength. No wonder Cynthia had written a love letter to him. Angus gazed back at her and she was suddenly self-conscience of her black eye which she had tried to cover with concealer and shadow. His battle scars only seemed to enhance his masculinity. Why was it that as women aged they seemed to fade away while men grew older and gained respect and power? She thought it must have something to do with money, but that couldn't be the only thing. Eleanor had more money than Angus. She was sure of it. Maybe it had to do with height. Angus was tall by any standard and Eleanor was average.

No sooner had she thought about powerful men than Howard Wakefield walked into the restaurant with an exotic looking young woman on his arm. Eleanor watched as heads turned in their direction. Every man there, including Angus, stared at the tall, voluptuous beauty as she tossed her long blonde hair and pranced through the restaurant like a high-strung race horse on her aging escort's arm. Even though Howard Wakefield was an attractive man, it was obvious they were mismatched in age and vigor. He was short, thin, and well- groomed wearing an expensive suit and surrounded by an aura of money and influence. They found a table on the other side of the restaurant and when Eleanor turned her attention back to Angus she was pleased to see that he met her eyes. He sighed and shook his head.

"Gold-digger?" he asked.

"I thought you said his fiancée was a model. She doesn't look like a prospector to me," Eleanor teased.

"I'm glad I don't have money. I'm certain you love me for other reasons," he said. His brows rose and fell suggestively.

"I do love you," Eleanor said.

Angus took her hand and kissed her palm. Whatever gave her reason to think romance had left this relationship flew out the door. Just as they were finishing their dinner, there was a disturbance at the Wakefield table. Evidently Rob and Olivia had joined them unnoticed and there was a problem with the fiancée's order. Everyone in the restaurant could hear her shrill complaint even if they couldn't make out the words. Something about the meal was not up to her standards. The server was apologizing and soon the chef came from the kitchen to soothe the irate customer. When the staff finally left, it was Rob's voice that everyone heard raised in anger toward his father. "You old fool," were the only words Eleanor could clearly make out before Rob threw down his napkin and stormed out the door with Olivia in tow.

"It seems neither the Wakefields nor the Fowlers can have a pleasant meal without spoiling everyone else's experience," Angus said.

"There does seem to be a pattern. I'd hate to see what their family dinners are like at home." Eleanor remembered her last family dinner and regretted her words, realizing no family was perfect.

"We'd better get out of here or we'll miss our movie." Angus and Eleanor only had to walk across the street to get to the Bijou where they found Cleo and Steve sitting in the back row along with Dede and Mark. The comedy was twice as funny because of them. There was a great deal of laughing and even some snorting. It seems everything is better in the company of friends.

"No one sees much of Howard Wakefield," Dede commented at coffee. "He must spend most of his time out of town."

"Wanda said he's rarely at his house on the hill," Cleo confirmed.

"I don't remember seeing him at Junie's wedding. He didn't walk her down the aisle. Was he even there?" asked Eleanor.

"I saw him walking around during the reception inspecting everything and I even heard him scolding the caterers because the coffee was too hot," Pearl remembered.

"He was probably afraid of a lawsuit," said Eleanor.

"I'd like to sue him," Cleo said. "I took my car into his Service Center to get my brakes checked and they told me my transmission needed to be replaced. Steve said that was crazy, so he took it to a trusted friend of his for a second opinion. He told Steve the transmission was ready to fall out because all the bolts had been loosened."

"That's terrible!" exclaimed Dede who was ready to believe anything of Howard Wakefield including promoting shady work practices.

"What are you going to do about it?" asked Pearl.

"I can't prove it was done at the Service Center so I'm not doing anything, but I won't be going there again, that's for sure," Cleo stated venomously.

"You know they searched Eric Fowler's house and found a bloody T-shirt stuffed under his mattress," Dede said.

"Do you think Rob and Eric killed Johnny?" asked Eleanor. "After that brawl at the Red Shed I'm inclined to think they're innocent."

"Why do you say that?" asked Cleo.

"They both accused each other of doing it," Eleanor said.

"Maybe they were putting on a show to make people believe that very thing," said Josephine. "They did argue in a public place where they had plenty of witnesses."

"The bloody T-shirts could have been planted," offered Pearl.

"Are you suggesting they're both trying to frame each other?" Dede asked. "That's almost funny."

"It sounds like something they would do." Eleanor laughed. "They have no idea what friendship is about, courting the same girl and fighting over her in bars. Where is their code of ethics? I wonder if they are still friends."

"What if they did kill Johnny together? Eric then plants his bloody shirt in Rob's closet and after Rob is brought in for questioning, Rob plants his shirt under Eric's mattress. They both have access to each other's houses. It's the perfect plan for two idiots who think alike." Dede smiled.

"Then they used each other for their alibi," Eleanor said, "but when they were questioned separately their alibis didn't ring true. Eric said he was with Rob, and Olivia said she was with Eric all night and didn't see Rob."

"So they didn't have enough smarts to create an alibi together that would work for them," Josephine said. "I didn't think they were that stupid."

"Do you know if there were other witnesses at the Red Shed who might have seen them?" asked Cleo.

"I'm sure they were all at the Red Shed later that evening, but Johnny was probably killed earlier. Remember he'd gone fishing and was late for dinner," Eleanor said.

"Without a body we have to assume he was killed in the early evening. We didn't get to the Red Shed until after nine the night of the stakeout and Eric came after that. I bet they don't go much before that," assumed Pearl. "Maybe we should go back and ask questions."

The mere thought of going back to the Red Shed made Eleanor's eye ache. "I'm sure the police have already covered that. They're not making any arrests yet so they must not have a solid case."

"Listen to this letter to 'Just Josie,'" said Josephine as she pulled it out of her bag.

Dear Josie,

I am a young fun-loving girl who has two guys in my life. One of them says he loves me. He is cute and has lots of money, but I can't help myself when the other guy calls or comes in and out of my life. This other guy is smart and really handsome. He sometimes goes with other girls, but he always comes back to me when things don't work out. I don't know what to do. Should I keep seeing the one who loves me or hope the other guy will quit fooling around with other girls?

Torn between two lovers

"That could be from Olivia Martin," said Cleo. "She was all over Rob Wakefield at the Red Shed until Eric walked in and then she was all starry-eyed over him."

"What are you going to tell her?" asked Pearl.

"She should definitely kick Eric to the curb," Eleanor said. "He'll never change."

"Yes, but she doesn't love Rob," Dede added. "As much as I hate to say it, Rob Wakefield doesn't deserve to be treated that way."

"What do they see in her anyway?" asked Cleo. "She's cute, but there are lots of cute girls in Waterton."

"She's fun-loving and probably free with her favors," said Eleanor.

"It seems like she's definitely available to Eric whenever, but why would Rob put up with that?" asked Pearl.

"Love has no reason. He must love her," said Josephine. "This is my response:

Dear Torn,

I am struck by the descriptions of these two men: "cute, lots of money, smart, really handsome." There is not one word about your feelings for them. Do you love either one? I think you need to take inventory of your values and what you want for yourself. The descriptions sound like they are coming from a girl in junior high school. As an adult you need to take responsibility for yourself and your future. Why would you even consider a man who has to have more than one woman at a time? This is a man who will probably never change, and you would have a lifetime of wondering if he had other partners.

There are more than two men in this world. Step back. You aren't ready for a relationship. You need to do some inner work. Find a good counselor to help you gain insight into yourself."

Just Josie

"Perfect!" said Cleo.

"I couldn't have said it better myself," said Pearl.

"What happened to those outrageous eyelashes?" asked Dede as she peered closely at Pearl's face.

"I stopped using the product and now they're falling out," Pearl admitted. "They made seeing impossible and the fluttering annoyed Cary."

"We saw Howard Wakefield at dinner the other night. He was with his fiancée," Eleanor reported. "She's quite young and beautiful with thick eyelashes."

"I saw her too," said Pearl. "She was at the jewelry store scoping out diamonds. I didn't know who she was but overheard another customer say she was Howard's city woman, and he was keeping her at the Best Western."

"Does that mean he has a country woman?" asked Cleo.

"It wouldn't surprise me if he had several women. It seems some females are attracted to power and wealth no matter where they live," Dede said. "I wonder why she isn't staying at his house?"

"I'm sure Rob doesn't approve of her, and maybe Junie doesn't either," Eleanor related the episode at dinner. "Maybe Howard Wakefield cares about what his children think."

"I think she must be difficult. She crowded in front of this other customer and demanded to try on a ring as if she were more important than anyone else in the store," Pearl continued.

"She was with a strapping young man too. Someone said he was her brother, but he didn't act like her brother."

"What do you mean by that?" asked Dede.

"He held the door for her and put his hand on her lower back to guide her the way a lover would," Pearl said. "My brothers don't do that. Maybe he's at the Best Western too."

"What were you doing in the jewelry store?" asked Josephine who was always interested in everyone's jewels.

"Just getting a new battery for my watch," Pearl said. "Anyway, I could tell by the way she talked to the salesclerk that she has a black soul."

"Then she will be a perfect match for Howard Wakefield," Dede huffed.

"Is there more trouble with him at city hall?" asked Eleanor.

"Just the same old power plays," Dede explained. "Edward Fowler was at the last council meeting and very critical of everything I've done so far. Somehow, he managed to turn the council meeting into his personal rally. He even had the gall to find fault with the new highway project that won an award from the Chamber of Commerce and put the blame on me."

"You must have developed a tough skin by now," Cleo said.

"It's a wonder I have any ass left after they chewed off so much at the last meeting," said Dede. "There seem to be several men who think they are entitled to have this massage parlor in town. They are loud and cheer whenever he makes a comment. I've never seen any of them before. I'm sure they are the ones Wakefield brought in to do his bidding. I've never used my gavel to call for order so much. It certainly makes for an interesting meeting."

"Did I tell you that Angus found out Cynthia Chase wrote that mysterious letter?" Eleanor asked.

"Is that how he got the black eye?" asked Cleo. "I didn't want to pry the other night when I noticed it after the movie."

"I thought he did it to make you feel better about your shiner," commented Dede.

"Will saw the letter at Angus' house and recognized Cynthia's handwriting. He punched Angus before he could explain that there was nothing going on between them," Eleanor said.

"That doesn't sound like the Cynthia I met. She seemed so prim and proper. I can't imagine her doing something so forward," Pearl said.

"She didn't sign it," said Josephine, "So maybe she was acting out her hidden feelings and didn't think she would be found out."

"I haven't seen or heard from her since she left town. I wonder if she's all right," Eleanor said, worry creeping into her voice.

She didn't have to worry long because when Eleanor got home, she received a call from a very contrite Cynthia Chase.

"Oh Eleanor, Will called and told me about the altercation with Angus and I am so very sorry. I didn't write that letter to Angus. I wrote it to *you* hoping Angus would see it, get jealous, and propose marriage to you. You know how men are. They always seem to want something more if they know others value it. Please accept my apology. I truly am sorry," Cynthia lamented.

"No worries, Cynthia. Angus has a black eye but it's very attractive on him and he was flattered when he thought the letter was for him. I must say it has caused quite a stir around here. The letter was so passionate. I was impressed with the depth of feeling it conveyed." Eleanor didn't go into detail about how the letter had been passed around involving several people in the mystery.

"I didn't write it," Cynthia confessed. "A college beau wrote it to me. It was the most romantic note I've ever received so I kept it. His name was Oscar Dinklage. I often wonder what happened to him and how my life would be different if I'd left my lover for him. Anyway, I just copied it and put it in your hidey-hole. Angus told Will about your charming way of communicating with each other. I'm sorry it backfired."

"Don't give it another thought," Eleanor said happily. It would give her great pleasure to burst Angus' bubble when she told him the truth of it all. She imagined them laughing together over it at dinner tonight. She would bake an apple pie for him to take the sting out of his bruised ego. "I'm not interested in marrying, Cynthia. Angus and I are happy as we are."

There was a long silence on the other end while Cynthia processed the information that there were women who chose an unmarried state. She wondered if she had misread Eleanor and Angus' romantic involvement. Maybe one of them was gay. Eleanor *did* spend a great deal of time with her girlfriends. What if Angus had ideas about Will? Fishing could be a pretense to pull him into an unsavory relationship and she had left Will alone and vulnerable. She would have to watch carefully for clues when she returned home and she would have to get home as soon as possible.

"I should start packing and come home," Cynthia said. "I've been away too long." After Eleanor hung up, she began to bake her pie, smiling and humming as she worked.

Angus arrived promptly at six with a bouquet of roses and a box of chocolates. He wanted to ease the hurt he was sure Eleanor felt knowing Cynthia had written the love letter to him. When she opened the door, he was filled with an overwhelming love for her as he gazed upon her black eye and smelled the aroma of fresh apple pie. He leaned in and kissed her. It was a sweet lingering kiss that was meant to tell her she was the one he cared for even as another woman offered herself to him. He was surprised at the ardor Eleanor exhibited as she returned his kiss. Maybe the letter had made her realize her true feelings for him. She had said she loved him at the restaurant the other night. It made him happy.

"What's for dinner?" he asked as he released her.

"London broil with buttered potatoes and caramelized zucchini and mushrooms," Eleanor said, heading back to the kitchen with her flowers and candy. Angus poured two fingers of Crown Royal and peeked in the oven as Eleanor took out the meat and put it on the counter to rest.

"Your eye looks better," he said smiling.

"So does yours." Eleanor looked into Angus' dimpled face. He looked so happy. She was suddenly reluctant to tell him about Cynthia's confession. What if it made him sad and spoiled the entire evening? She would tell him before he left.

"Did I tell you they found a bloody T-shirt at Eric Fowler's house?" he asked.

"Dede told me. What do you make of it?"

"I'm not sure. It's too neat and tidy. Forensics will have to test it to see if Johnny's blood is on it. I suspect it will be, along with a little of Eric's as well as Rob's," Angus said.

"Are you thinking the shirts were planted?" Eleanor asked.

"Yes, even though I don't want to," Angus said.

"Do you think Junie did it?" Eleanor asked.

Angus sighed. "Yes, I think she planted the shirts. They probably belonged to Johnny, but I can't believe Junie is capable of murder."

"Maybe she isn't but thinks Rob and Eric are and planted evidence to make sure they'd get caught," Eleanor suggested.

"She's going to have to be brought in for more questioning," Angus said sadly. "Who else had access to both Eric and Rob's homes?"

"Olivia Martin," Eleanor said as she handed Angus a carving knife.

"What possible motive would she have to set up both her boyfriends?" Angus pondered while he cut the steak into thin slices.

"Maybe she wants them both out of her life?" Eleanor offered knowing how unlikely that sounded.

"I don't think Eric and Rob did it either, but If Junie planted the T-shirts to punish them for the way they treated Johnny, I understand that. It would also explain why she hung out with Eric—to gain access to his room to plant it."

"Could she get in trouble for that?" asked Eleanor.

"I'm sure the law would be lenient with her considering what she's been through," Angus said.

"But where did she get the blood?" asked Eleanor.

"I don't know," Angus said. "Maybe Johnny wasn't very good at doing the laundry."

They sat at the dining room table and ate their dinner. "That's not all they found of interest at Eric Fowler's house," Angus said.

"What else?"

"Hidden in a fake book in the library, they found a collection of Nazi pins and medals," Angus said.

"Really? I never would have guessed Eric or his family would be Nazi sympathizers," Eleanor said.

"There's no law against collecting that kind of stuff, but it makes you wonder what kind of people they are," Angus said.

"They must have done a thorough search if they found it in a library," Eleanor commented. "Did they look through every book?"

"They were looking for the unusual and are trained to see things like false books that contain secrets. I'm not sure the Fowlers ever went in their library or even read those books. Sometimes people like that have libraries just for show," Angus said. "Have you read all the books on your shelves?"

"No, but I think I'd know if there was a false book filled with Nazi memorabilia among them," Eleanor said.

"Delicious, Ellie. You never disappoint me. Have you ever made a bad meal?" Angus asked wiping his mustache with his napkin.

Eleanor wanted to lie. She really wanted him to think she was a food magician. "I think you'd say that about anything I put in front of you."

"Why don't you put yourself in front of me?" he said. "I'd like a tasty dessert."

"Are you still hungry?" she asked purposely obtuse.

"Not for pie," he said pulling her onto his lap. Later when he *was* hungry for pie, Eleanor decided it was important for him to know the truth about Cynthia.

"Guess who called me today?" she asked innocently.

"Who?" Angus put a big bite of apple pie in his mouth.

"Cynthia Chase." Eleanor had his attention. "She wanted to set things straight."

"Yes . . . " he prodded, "Did she admit to writing the letter?"

"She did and she's sorry about it. It was supposed to be a letter to me from an anonymous man that would make you so jealous you'd ask me to marry you. Evidently Cynthia thinks we need to be married."

"Did it work? Do you think we should be married?" Angus didn't seem bothered in the least by the revelation.

"I don't think you understand, Angus," Eleanor said. "The letter was for *me*. *You* were supposed to be jealous."

"Right, but you were jealous, weren't you? Didn't it make you want me because you thought someone else was interested in me?"

Eleanor laughed because he was right. She wondered if he'd twisted the whole thing from the beginning knowing the letter was never intended for him. "I've always wanted *you*," she said, "It's marriage I don't want."

Eleanor needed a new outfit to wear to Pearl's gala exhibition at the Bayside Art Center. Josephine and Dede were both putting mosaics that they'd created at Pearl's studio on display as well and Eleanor was eager to see it all. She drove into

Waterton and entered Deep Bay Fashions hoping to find something summery and yet not too casual.

"Hello Eleanor, may I help you find something?" asked Mabel who owned the shop.

Eleanor was always thankful for the small-town courtesy and service she received here. There were never long lines at the cash register when it came time to pay and Mabel had often let her take items home to try on and bring back if she wasn't satisfied.

"I'm looking for a summer dress suitable for an art exhibition," Eleanor said.

"I just got these dresses in this morning. I know you like blue and there was one in here that made me think of you as soon as I saw it." Mabel rushed to a rack of clothes and searched for it.

"Bring me this dress in a smaller size," came a demanding voice from the fitting room. Eleanor took the dress in Mabel's hand as she rushed to help her other customer. Eleanor stepped into the room next to the voice to try on the turquois floral dress. She was disturbed to hear the way the other customer spoke to Mabel.

"I can't wear that cheap thing; take it away. It's inconceivable that this town doesn't have a decent seamstress to do alterations. I've never bought anything off the rack!"

"You are a perfect size six. The dress doesn't need alterations and looks wonderful on you just as it is," Mabel said.

"No, I wear a size four. Give that one to me and get out." There was more muttering from the room next to Eleanor as she tried on her dress and decided it was perfect for her evening.

"I'll take this one, Mabel. It's exactly what I was looking for." Eleanor stepped out of the dressing room with her dress and was preparing to pay Mabel when she was interrupted by the customer's new demand.

"I can't get this one zipped up. I need assistance now!"

Mabel rolled her eyes, "I'm sorry, Eleanor. Will you excuse me for a minute?" Mabel disappeared but Eleanor could still hear the conversation and wondered who this person thought she was to be so impatient and impolite. Surely it wasn't anyone she knew. She didn't recognize the voice, so maybe it was a tourist or someone who was having a fashion emergency.

"The dress is simply too small. There's no way to zip it without tearing the fabric," Mabel said.

"I always wear a four. Just let me . . . " Eleanor heard a ripping sound. "I knew this was cheap material. Just get out of here!"

Mabel returned, her face red with anger and frustration. "Thank you for waiting, Eleanor."

While she was completing Eleanor's purchase, the voice revealed herself as she blew out of the dressing room, threw the torn dress at Mabel, and left the store. Eleanor recognized the exotic fiancée of Howard Wakefield and felt sorry for Mabel who now had a ruined dress and no sale.

"I'll take this little sweater too," Eleanor added in an attempt to make Mabel's day a little more profitable. "It's a perfect match for the dress and it could be chilly this evening. If I were you, I'd send the bill for that dress to Howard Wakefield." Mabel smiled.

Angus didn't necessarily enjoy art exhibitions, but he did like looking at Eleanor in her summer finery. Bruce Springsteen had it right when he sang about girls in their summer dresses. He enjoyed Eleanor on his arm, the way she looked at him when he showed up in his dressy clothes, and her unexpected quips and witty banter. Absolutely delightful, and he certainly enjoyed the company of friends who gathered there, and the feeling of belonging to Eleanor's group always brought him joy. The evening of Pearl's mosaic extravaganza was no exception. Angus showed up smelling of Old Spice in khaki slacks and a brown sports jacket. Eleanor wore her new outfit and looked beautiful, to Angus' eyes at least.

"Will there be dancing?" he asked when he saw the swish of chiffon.

"Only if you want to go to The Landing afterward." Eleanor liked the way Angus danced.

"We'll see. You look lovely, by the way." Eleanor simply nodded.

The Bayside Art Center was decked out for the event. Walking into it was like being in church. The lights were dim, and candles glowed from the darkest corners while colorful masterpieces of glass hung in the windows taking advantage of the evening light. Vibrant reds, emerald greens, yellows, and blues cast a mesmerizing, rainbow-like jewels in the sun. Pearl's work was breathtaking. Many of the pieces belonged to her students who learned from the master, but most of them belonged to her and were a testament to her skillful hands and critical eye. After the first awe-inspiring moments passed, Angus went for wine and Eleanor sought out Pearl to congratulate her on the display.

"These are very impressive, Pearl, and the way the pieces are presented makes the entire exhibit feel sacred," Eleanor said.

"I just hope some of them sell," Pearl stated. "That's the true mark of success."

"Which one is yours, Dede?"

"Mine isn't in the windows because it's not on glass. The one with the white frame and girl with the heart is mine."

"Mine is that bowling ball covered in various shades of green gems," Josephine added.

"I don't do glass, believe me when I tell you, it's dangerous. Honestly, I tried, but ended up with Band-Aids on every finger. I'll stick to paint, thank you," confessed Cleo.

"I understand," said Eleanor who knew her talent was writing.

Angus returned with wine and complimented Pearl on her creativity. "I especially like the one with the fish. I think it's just the right size to put in my downstairs door. Then I can at least look at a fish when I'm not actually catching one."

"I like that, too," Dede remarked. "It reminds me of something I've seen before, but I can't remember what."

They nibbled on crackers and cheese and decided to walk to The Landing when the exhibit closed for a late dinner. Angus put the fish mosaic in his car. It reminded him of Johnny Vargas, for some reason. Perhaps because it resembled the postcard he had received with the message about Johnny being murdered. The rainbow trout among the green grass and stones was something Angus would never get tired of seeing.

As they walked to The Landing they chatted and laughed until Cary stepped in dog poop. "Aww, shit," he yelled.

"That's disgusting," said Pearl, "Maybe you should just leave that shoe outside."

"What if someone takes it?" he asked. But realizing how unlikely that would be, left it in a corner just outside the door.

The Landing wasn't a fancy restaurant and mainly catered to the Bayside locals, serving up home-cooked meals like chicken and dumplings and hamburgers and fries. They pushed some tables together and ordered drinks.

"Look, I see Dolly from book club over there." Cleo jumped up and went to chat with her.

"Don't tell me this is Geraoke night!" exclaimed Dede, who remembered Dolly saying she and some old friends often met at the Landing for karaoke.

"Yes, it *is* karaoke night!" exclaimed Mark. "I can hardly wait to sing my rendition of *Hamburger in Paradise*." The others looked around and noticed the equipment being set up and realized they had stumbled upon one of Bayside's best-kept secrets.

"Keep the drinks coming," Cary said. "This could be a night to remember."

"Or a night to forget," said Josephine.

As it turned out, the men in the group were more courageous and talented in the singing department than the ladies. It was that or as Eleanor said, "They had more to drink than we did."

Mark did sing *Hamburger in Paradise* and dared Angus to join him in *Margaritaville*, another of Jimmy Buffet's tunes. Everyone was impressed at Richard's baritone as he sang *Don't Let it Show* a la Alan Parsons. The ladies took to the floor en masse and cranked out *I Will Survive*, which they did just barely but with a great deal of enthusiasm and clever dance moves.

Steve refused to make a fool of himself, but Cary dedicated his rendition of Elton John's *Your Song* to Pearl and it made her cry. After their performances they stuck around to listen to Dolly and her geriatric group singing several oldies but goodies and then they headed for home. Cary found the fact that his shoe with the doggie residue was still by the door bittersweet. "If only someone had taken it I might have bought a new pair. Now I'll just have to clean these."

"I admit it," Angus confessed on the ride home. "That was fun. I think we should go to geraoke night every week."

"You're just saying that because you can sing," Eleanor said laughing.

"Thank you, thank you very much." Angus' attempt at impersonating Elvis cracked Eleanor up which started a laugh fest that lasted at least a half mile.

Eleanor completed her walk on the beach and stopped in at Suzanna's to visit the Do Nothings. Mavis and Sybil sat at their usual table, but Mattie and Artemas were missing.

"Good morning," welcomed Sybil. "Isn't it a beautiful day?"

"Yes, may I join you?" asked Eleanor.

"Oh, please do, we are so bored with each other. We need an infusion of community information," complained Mavis.

"She means gossip," Sybil interpreted.

"Where's Mattie?" asked Eleanor.

"She's stood us up again and worse, it's for a man!" Mavis exclaimed.

"Artemas asked her to go into Waterton for some mysterious reason she can't reveal," Sybil said. "It's just like high school when you'd make plans with your friends and then they canceled because they got a date with a boy. I thought we were so over that period in our lives. How can we expect men to put us first when we don't do it for each other?"

"That's a good question. I never thought of it like that," Mavis said.

"Did you have plans to do something with Mattie?" asked Eleanor.

"No, but if we did she would have canceled them," Sybil continued.

"You have no idea what she and Art are up to in Waterton?" asked Eleanor.

"No, it's a secret. I know she's taken him to the courthouse to do research and you told us he was at Riverside asking Gladys Reyburg questions, but we really don't know what's going on," Mavis said. "Do you know?"

"No, but maybe we should find out. I do know that Cynthia Chase is out of town, Will Chase is fishing with Angus, and Artemas Chase is in Waterton with Mattie. That means no one is home at the Chase residence."

"Yes," said Mavis.

"Are you suggesting that we break into their house and do a little snooping?" asked Sybil with a sly smile.

Mavis gasped, "How exciting! We'd better get moving. There's no telling when Mattie will get back."

The three raced out the door as fast as senior citizens could race and climbed in Sybil's car. When they arrived at the Chase house, Eleanor got out and did a complete walk around scoping out the area. She loved a good snoop. "There's no one here," she said as she met the others on the front porch. "The last time I was here the door wasn't even locked."

"Well today the door isn't even closed," whispered Mavis who was totally into the adventure. "It isn't breaking and entering if the door is open." In they went on tiptoe. They wandered through the massive living room and marveled at the vaulted ceiling and the magnificent view of the ocean.

"The kitchen is totally updated and very neat and tidy for two men," Sybil noticed. Eleanor showed them the secret room behind the bookcase, and they all entered it. She had been in the house before.

"Just what are we looking for?" asked Mavis.

"Anything that might give us a clue to what Art is up to," said Eleanor as she hit the light switch.

"There doesn't seem to be anything in here," said Sybil who poked around behind some old picture frames. Eleanor found a few boxes and was rifling through a file, paper in hand, when she heard a strange sound.

"Did you hear that?" she whispered.

"Yes," said Sybil. "It sounds like an animal of some sort."

"Let's get out of here," whispered Mavis who stumbled out in a panic.

"Wait," said Eleanor, "I think the sound is coming from the downstairs bedroom. What if a raccoon came in through the open door?" She walked very quietly toward the noise with the two older women following close behind. The bedroom door was ajar, and Eleanor peeked in and saw two naked people lying on the bed in a love embrace. They were both deeply asleep and snoring. Eleanor backed away and headed for the door. Sybil followed with her hand over her mouth trying to stifle her laughter. Mavis continued to stare at the figures because she couldn't make out what she was seeing. When things became clear, she hurried out of the house almost knocking the leaders down in her rush to escape. No one spoke until they were well away from the scene.

"I don't think I will ever get that image out of my mind," said Sybil.

"I'll have to scrape out my eyes with a rusty spoon," said Mavis.

"At least we know what Mattie and Art are up to these days," chuckled Eleanor.

"That was Mattie?" exclaimed Mavis. "I can't believe it." Sybil and Eleanor laughed so hard Sybil split her pants.

Eleanor literally collapsed from hysterical laughter-induced exhaustion. She lay on the couch until she fell asleep and woke up and laughed some more. Every time she recalled the image of Mattie in the arms of her lover it brought a smile to her face. Mattie had to be almost 90 and yet she was living her life to the fullest.

Eleanor wondered where she parked her car when she and Art were trysting. Neither of them could walk far and her Lincoln Town car was known by everyone in and around Sand Beach. Mattie may have made excuses to her friends to be alone with Art, but that didn't explain why he was questioning Gladys Reyburg at Riverside Retirement Home. Eleanor freshened up and drove to town to visit Gladys.

Riverside had two different levels of care, independent and assisted living. Gladys was in the first and had her own little apartment with a living space, small kitchen, bathroom, and one bedroom. Her rooms were connected to the larger building that held a workout room, library, theater, dining room, and other amenities such as a pool, hair salon, and several common areas. Gladys' room was on the ground floor and was quite lovely. A large patio door filled the rooms with light and provided Gladys with a private outdoor space where she tended to her flowers. She was expecting Eleanor and welcomed her warmly with a hug.

"Did you bring something to read today?" Gladys asked. "I think I would just like it if you read the local newspaper."

"Perfect." Eleanor read the *Fish Wrapper* from front to back and they discussed the news as they went.

"I certainly enjoy reading *Just Josie*. That's an excellent addition and she gives sensible advice which I agree with so far, but I worry because Waterton County is so small that everyone will know who's asking and who she's advising. That latest letter about two lovers has to be Olivia Martin."

"These letters come from all over the state, Gladys. I'm sure there's an Olivia Martin in every city," Eleanor said.

Gladys yawned and said, "Well, that's good to know." Eleanor would have to ask her about Artemas before she dozed off.

"Gladys, do you remember Artemas Chase?" Eleanor asked.

"Certainly, I never forget a name. He's the polite gentleman who was visiting our resident veterans. I don't think he actually said he was writing a book, but I got that impression because of the questions he was asking. He's been here several times you know."

"What kind of questions did he ask you?" Eleanor asked.

"Are you writing a book, too?" Gladys was quick to ask.

"I'm curious about him. He's made friends with some of the Do Nothings and I want to make sure he's not trying to take advantage of them."

"He was especially interested in men who came here after World War ll and asked if I knew any who were still living and where he might find them. There really aren't many of those old soldiers still alive. I gave him a few names. There are a couple of regular guys who settled here after the war. Henry Ott was one but he's dead and then there's Peter Fowler, Edward's grandfather. He just moved in here because he broke his hip and is in the assisted living side. I was never fond of Peter. There was something that oozed from him that seemed mean-spirited and petty. He always thought he was getting the short end of the stick and sought revenge for every imagined slight. I avoid him and I urged Artemas to do the same."

"Did Artemas say he wanted to interview anyone in particular?" Eleanor probed.

"I don't know. If he was really doing something about veterans, he wouldn't want to know about Peter Fowler, but now that I think of it, he was interested in Peter more than the others. I've seen him here since so maybe he *is* interviewing Peter. You know he was also talking to Greta Mahar. You remember her, she was a seamstress for many years and now she's downsized and living here."

"Do you think we could ask her about what Artemas was interested in?" Eleanor asked.

"Certainly, Greta is a Holocaust survivor, so maybe he wanted to know about that," Gladys mentioned.

Eleanor followed Gladys to a nearby room and rapped loudly on the door. It was answered by a small, hunched woman with white hair and thick spectacles. "Hello, Gladys. I see you brought a new friend to visit. Please come in." Greta's warmth was genuine as Gladys introduced Eleanor and explained her interest in Artemas Chase.

"He was interested in my time at the camp, but I don't like to talk about it anymore. It makes me have bad dreams now, but I did tell him about that awful Fowler man who moved in here. I'm sure he noticed my tattoo and he stares at me whenever I see him. It's not a nice stare either. It's more like the gaze of a dead fish, cold and blue. He and his son give me an uneasy feeling, nothing more," Greta said.

"Did Artemas ask you about this man?"

"I don't remember if he asked or if it just came up. I told him he reminded me of soldiers in the camp. It's the way he looks down his nose at me as if I'm something smelly he brought in on his shoe, and his son even called me a *kike* once when I passed him in the hall." She paused before adding, "I'd offer you something, but I don't have anything in my cupboards to eat," Greta apologized.

"That's all right. We can't stay anyway," Eleanor said. "It was lovely meeting you."

"Before we go," Gladys began, "Tell me what you did with all those lovely fabrics you had in your house before you moved. I know how much you love to sew and you had such a fabulous collection."

Greta smiled and went to the small kitchen and opened each cupboard. Inside were yards and yards of beautiful material in every type, texture, and color. "I still love to sew."

Eleanor was shown the sewing machine setup in Greta's bedroom and was given a tour of her current works in progress. She quilted blankets for the homeless and each one was a work of art, masterfully pieced and sewn together with an eye to color and design.

After they left Greta, Eleanor walked Gladys back to her room. "I see you're tired, Gladys, so I'll be off. Thank you for a lovely afternoon." Eleanor hugged Gladys again and left for the store to buy some ice cream.

As she drove home, she realized she had skipped lunch. The "udderly" chocolate mudslide ice cream was calling to her from the backseat. She sped up the hill, noticed Angus was still not home from fishing, and pulled into her garage. Not even bothering to get a bowl, Eleanor spooned the creamy concoction directly from the carton into her mouth. Feathers watched and scolded her, "Bad girl, bad girl. I love you, Ellie."

It wasn't until later that she discovered the sheet of paper that Sybil had slipped under her front door.

I found this in the backseat after I left you.

At first Eleanor didn't understand what she was looking at. It showed images of Nazi pins and medals. Then she remembered she had this paper in her hand in the secret room when they heard the snoring. In her startled state Eleanor must have held onto it but then left it in Sybil's car. The pieces fell together like a puzzle when there are only a few left. Mattie had tried to tell her when she said Artemas is a Nazi hunter. He wasn't retired at all. He was still hunting, and Eleanor wondered if he was hunting Peter Fowler.

She desperately wanted to tell Angus about this new information. It might not be connected to the Vargas case, but it was an interesting development. Eleanor wondered what would happen to Peter Fowler if Artemas captured him at this late time in his life. Would there be a trial? Would he be extradited to wherever he came from and punished? What would the Fowlers do if all this came out? She could see the headlines in the *Fish Wrapper*: Local Man Found to be War Criminal. She wondered just what crimes he had committed. The shame would be overwhelming and might give Peter

Fowler a heart attack if indeed he had a heart. It might even have an impact on Edward's mill. She studied pictures of the pins and medals. Some were red and blue with swastikas on them. Others were stamped with German words. Why would someone keep these where anyone could find them, especially if they *were* Nazi sympathizers? Maybe they were proud of it. Maybe they still felt the same way they felt during the war. Maybe they still practiced hate and bigotry. Eleanor had heard rumors of Nazi groups reviving but didn't believe they could be here in this small community.

Eleanor picked up the phone and called Mattie May. "Mattie, it's Eleanor. I'd like to see you. Is now a good time?"

"Eleanor, how nice to hear your voice," Mattie said. "Artemas is coming for dinner later so a short visit would be lovely. Come on over."

Not wanting to waste any time, Eleanor drove to the sweet cottage that Mattie called home. It was a gray shingled house with white trim set back in the trees with just a peekaboo view of the ocean. The wide porch complete with two white Adirondack chairs made up for the limited vista. Eleanor rang the bell and sighed deeply as she waited for Mattie to open her door. "Eleanor, I don't remember the last time you were here," Mattie said as she welcomed her into the cozy front room. "Would you like some iced tea?"

"That sounds lovely," Eleanor said.

Mattie disappeared into the kitchen and returned with two glasses. "Let's sit on the porch. It's such a beautiful day." Eleanor settled in to one of the porch chairs with her iced tea and felt the warm breeze against her face. Mattie sat next to her and smiled. "What's on your mind?"

"Artemas Chase." Eleanor didn't mince words. She flashed back to the image of Mattie in his arms and suddenly felt like a meddling relative. "I think he's still hunting Nazis. Do you know who?"

Mattie's eyes widened. "I knew you were curious, and I really wanted to tell you but he's sworn me to secrecy. Believe me Eleanor I can't tell you anything. His entire search depends on the element of surprise."

"What if I told you I know Peter Fowler was keeping Nazi memorabilia in his home? What if I already know that Artemas has been talking to Peter at the Riverside Retirement Home? Could you tell me that Peter Fowler is the Nazi that Artemas is after?"

Mattie took a long drink from her glass and licked her lips. "I'm not at liberty to tell you a thing, Eleanor. Why do you want to know? How could this be any concern to you?"

Eleanor pondered this for a moment. There wasn't any reason for her to know. Maybe she was just a nosy old lady whose curiosity got her into trouble. Maybe she was concerned about her friend getting hurt. Maybe she thought that everything was connected to everything and there was a clue to Johnny Vargas' death here. It was a stretch, but Eleanor decided to take it.

"Eric Fowler is a person of interest in the disappearance of Johnny Vargas. I just think there could be a connection. Has Artemas said anything about Eric?" Eleanor asked.

Mattie was silent for a long time. "Eric loves his grandfather. I know it's strange to think that someone as ornery as Eric could care for anyone, but I understand that both Eric and Edward visit him often. Artemas did say that they both have hot tempers and chased him off once when he was visiting Peter, but that's all I know."

Eleanor could tell that Mattie wasn't going to say more and decided to change the subject, "Your friends miss you, Mattie. We're all concerned about you and don't want anyone to hurt you."

"I know, but I've never felt as alive as when I'm with Artemas. He never talks about his aches and pains or complains about how lonely he is. He just goes on living as if he isn't an old man, and I'm not an old woman when I'm with him. I'm just me. I know it won't last. He'll leave when he finishes his work here, but I'm going to squeeze out every last ounce of joy I can while I can. If old age has given me anything worthwhile, it's fearlessness." Eleanor simply nodded.

As she drove by the Chase house, she noticed a green SUV parked outside. Cynthia was home.

"It's an emergency," Cleo claimed. "I desperately need to learn to play bridge."

"Why?" asked Josephine, "You're almost 70 and you haven't needed it so far."

"My friends from Portland are coming for the fair. Every year they come to the beach, bring me lunch and wine and go to the fair. It's great. They like my art. It's something I can't explain. As soon as I met them I felt like we had been forever friends," Cleo said.

"So what does bridge have to do with it?" asked Pearl suspiciously.

"They play bridge and they want to play bridge with me."

"This can't be happening," Eleanor murmured. "It's like this bridge thing is a disease and it's spreading. Cynthia is back and I invited her over to play bridge. I was hoping you would come and play with us."

"Count me out," said Pearl decisively.

"I'll play," said Josephine, "I enjoy the game."

"When are you doing this?" asked Dede who usually had some meeting to attend.

"Let's do it tonight," Eleanor said. "We can teach Cleo and make Cynthia happy all at the same time." "It just so happens that I am free tonight," said Dede.

"Well, I'm not going to be left out," said Pearl. And that was how six giggle goofs ended up at Eleanor's with the intent to play bridge.

Eleanor baked Parmesan puffs and set out nuts and chocolates. Josephine brought shrimp dip to spread on cucumber rounds; Pearl whipped up crispy chicken wontons with mustard sauce; and Cleo and Dede arrived with strawberry pizza and Kahlua truffles.

"I hope this bridge playing doesn't get in the way of my eating and drinking," said Cleo as she gazed upon the lavish spread and poured herself a glass of the red sunset sangria Eleanor just finished pouring into a punch bowl.

"It does look delicious," Josephine added as she popped a puff into her mouth.

Cynthia rang the bell and was greeted warmly by all the members of the coffee group. It may have been that they were glad to see her or perhaps they felt a tinge of guilt about their harsh judgment of her, but they raved over the tray of brownies she added to the feast and poured her a generous cup of sangria.

"Where were you?" asked Dede.

"Well, after spending time with you, I missed my friends so much I just decided to visit them. The closest ones are in Idaho, around Coeur d'Alene. We've moved so much it's difficult to keep making friends I know I'll have to leave. Maybe this will be home for a while now that Will's retired."

"Did you get your bridge fix?" asked Cleo.

Cynthia smiled. "There's never enough bridge."

"I bet Will was happy to see you," Eleanor said.

Cynthia nodded. "Absence does make the heart grow fonder."

"Sometimes it makes the heart go wander," muttered Dede under her breath while thinking of the massage parlor Harold Wakefield planned to build.

"Well, let's get this game started. I don't want Will to get lonely without me." Cynthia sat at the card table. The other ladies sat down too, and Eleanor dealt the cards. Pearl and Dede opted out but hovered over Cleo to teach her the rules of the game. When Eleanor took the bid Cleo complained vehemently, "I don't want to be the dummy hand! It just seems rude." No one took the game seriously except Cynthia who bit her tongue until it bled while the others laughed and hooted over every little thing. The final straw came when Cleo was dealt a hand full of honors and she and Eleanor made a grand slam. Cynthia couldn't believe people who played so flippantly could pull off a grand slam. She seldom had a grand slam and she had been playing for years. It was just unheard of and so unfair.

"I really should go home," she said. "Will and I haven't had much time together and there are so many of you here, you won't miss me. Congratulations on your grand slam. I don't think you realize what a coup it is. Please excuse me." With that, she picked up her brownies and left with Eleanor trailing behind urging her to stay.

"I guess we aren't serious enough for her," said Josephine after closing the door.

"No, she isn't a good fit for this group," added Pearl.

"Maybe she's just a poor loser," said Cleo, who was still basking in her rare victory.

"Or she got tired of turning tricks," laughed Dede.

"What do you think of bridge, Cleo?" asked Eleanor.

"I think it's a lot like marriage," she said. "It starts with hearts and diamonds and ends up with partners looking for clubs and spades." No one argued with that.

Back home after finishing her daily walk, Eleanor had just kicked off her shoes when she heard the telephone ringing. "Hello, Eleanor. This is Gladys Reyburg."

"Hi Gladys. Is there something wrong?" Eleanor detected a worrisome sound in Gladys' usually upbeat tone.

"Yes, there's something that's bothering me, and I'd like to bounce it off you, but I don't feel comfortable discussing it over the phone. Do you think you could come to Riverside?"

"Of course, I just need a few minutes to shower and change my clothes. I can be there within the hour."

"Thank you, Eleanor. I'll see you soon." Eleanor's curiosity was piqued. She finished cleaning up in record time and drove into Waterton.

Gladys sat on the red floral couch reading a magazine in the lobby waiting for Eleanor. When she spotted her coming through the front door she rose and without a word of greeting led her back to her room, but not without first looking in both directions to be sure they were not being watched. Eleanor wondered if this paranoia was a sign that dementia had finally taken hold of Gladys' magnificent brain.

Once inside, Gladys closed and locked the door. "Gee whiz, Gladys, what's up?"

"Sit down Eleanor. I think I've stumbled on a serial killer who is systematically killing off people in this place."

"Tell me about it." Eleanor had known Gladys for years and was willing to hear her out no matter how ridiculous it sounded or how old Gladys had become.

"This month, six residents have been hauled away and haven't come back. I know these people are old and some of them are sick, but I've checked those numbers against the ones from last month when I first came here and only two people died that month."

"Is that all?" Eleanor asked. "That doesn't sound so unusual to me."

"You were the one asking about Artemas Chase. That's what set my mind to questioning his visits here and what I discovered is disturbing. I marked his visits to me on this calendar in blue and checked the guest log to see when he visited someone else in green. Then I marked the deaths in red."

Eleanor peered carefully at the calendar, furrowing her brow as she noted that each of those six deaths occurred on the day following one of his visits.

"What do you think is happening?" Eleanor asked.

"That's not all," Gladys continued. "Three of the residents who died were Hispanic, one was Jewish, and the other two had dementia."

Eleanor scratched an itch she didn't have. "Do you think Artemas Chase is killing these people?"

"I don't know. I just find it strange," Gladys admitted. "None of the dead have been white."

"Are the victims the people he's come to visit?" Eleanor asked.

"I don't think so, because I'm still alive and he's visited me three times, Greta's still with us, and I know he's also visited Peter Fowler and he's still alive. I just saw him this morning with Eric and his father, Edward."

"Are you afraid, Gladys?" Eleanor asked.

"Yes, I am. I think something is going on here that feels off."

"Have you told anyone else about your suspicions?"

"I'm afraid they'll think I'm batty. When I look at your face, I'm afraid *you* think I'm batty."

"No, I have to admit I've had my suspicions about Artemas Chase too. I'm sorry if I've passed them along to you, but I really don't think he's a murderer." Eleanor paused to process this new information. "Let's find out who else he visited while he was here. Maybe we can also find out how these residents died."

"Great! The game's afoot!" Gladys said with enthusiasm.

"Can you ask around without drawing attention to yourself?" Eleanor didn't think Gladys was in any real danger. There were things she knew about Artemas Chase she wasn't telling Gladys. If people were dying here, Artemas wasn't killing them.

"Oh, yes." Gladys seemed excited to have a mission.

"Gladys, be careful. Hang out where there are lots of people and lock your door behind you when you come into your room. I'll do some investigating too and get back to you as soon as I can." With that Eleanor gave Gladys a hug and left. She saw Eric and Edward Fowler in the parking lot getting into a black Jaguar but didn't notice that for once she wasn't invisible.

Artemas Chase sat at Mattie's dining room table and looked at Eleanor. "I think you are still hunting Nazis, Art. I've pieced together a few facts and think maybe there's someone at Riverside Retirement Home you are tracking. Who is Peter Fowler?" Eleanor held nothing back and watched with interest as Artemas absorbed this bit of information. Other than a slight widening of the eyes, Art maintained a perfectly neutral expression. He leaned in with his weight on one elbow and began his history lesson.

"During the late 1930s and early 1940s the Nazi's implemented a state euthanasia program called Action T4. It began earlier, of course, with the involuntary sterilization of people carrying what were considered to be hereditary defects and even antisocial behavior such as epilepsy, schizophrenia, Huntington's chorea, and imbecility along with chronic alcoholism and social deviances. The German people needed to be cleansed to strengthen the race. It was called a merciful death and expanded to include those with physical deformities, mental illnesses, and then racial enemies. The Reich Committee for the Scientific Registering of Hereditary and Congenital Illnesses was established to register sick children or newborns that were deemed defective. Cuts in funding to state mental hospitals and the squalor created by that caused many to support the effort to rid society of those who were deemed unworthy of life," Artemas said.

"That sounds familiar," noted Eleanor. "We have so many homeless living on the streets now because the mental institutions have been closed due to lack of funding. I'm sure there are people today who would support ridding society of them."

"Yes, and the Nazi movement is gaining popularity again," Artemas said.

"It's like a cycle that repeats when our population becomes too large," Mattie added.

"Too large or too weak," Artemas continued. "As early as 1920 there was an extreme German eugenics movement that interpreted Darwinism to justify eradicating harmful genes, but from 1939, this Reich Committee selected children to be killed based on serious hereditary diseases. They used deceit when dealing with the parents and claimed to be moving these children to places where they would receive special treatment but killed them after a couple of weeks by lethal injections and recorded their deaths as pneumonia. Many of their brains were kept for research. As time went on older children and adolescents were included and impairments were expanded to include juvenile delinquents and Jews and finally adults with dementia and other ailments. The death panels received lists from all hospitals, nursing homes, old-age homes, and sanatoriums. If a patient met the required conditions they were removed and killed. The hospitals thought they were releasing information used to identify those capable of working for the state and often overstated their incapacity to protect them. If institutions refused to comply T4 doctors were sent to make their own lists. Hundreds of thousands were killed. Artemis' paused before taking a breath and adding, "I believe there is a man living in this area who was involved in these killings even after Hitler shut them down. I can't say if it is Peter Fowler."

"Are you aware that Nazi memorabilia was found in his family home?" Eleanor asked.

"Yes, Mattie told me." Artemas' face registered nothing.

"Gladys Reyburg believes residents at Riverside are being murdered. She's documented your visits and determined that after each visit someone at Riverside was found dead the following day," Eleanor stated.

Artemas was obviously disturbed by this information. His white brows descended like angry gulls, giving his face a stern and serious expression. "I won't be returning to Riverside. Please reassure Gladys that I am not a murderer, but I need your promise that you will not mention this discussion to anyone. It is critical that no one knows what we have discussed here today."

"I won't tell a soul," promised Mattie.

"I can only promise to keep silent until Gladys has completed her own investigation," Eleanor said. "She may be in danger."

"Is she Jewish, black, Hispanic, demented, or deformed?" Artemas asked.

"No," answered Eleanor.

"Then she has nothing to fear," Artemas said. "My investigation is nearly complete."

Eleanor left, but with an uneasy feeling. As she walked home her thoughts returned to things Artemas had revealed. Without saying anything he had led Eleanor to believe that

Peter Fowler was a war criminal. Much of what he told her was old news put into a new context. Eleanor remembered the genetic experiments done on those held in concentration camps during WWll but hadn't thought about genetic cleansing and how it could be used in today's world. Now people willingly gave their DNA samples to companies that offered to give them the names of family members in return. To complete their family trees, they had sacrificed genetic information that could possibly be used against them in the event the government became determined to create a healthier human race. The thought was chilling.

Eleanor spent several hours in her office researching the euthanasia centers. It had no purpose other than to depress her. Her attempts to write left her dry and she abandoned the room to open a bottle of wine and turn on Sam Smith's *In the Lonely Hours*. When the doorbell rang, she answered thinking it might be Angus, but was completely caught off guard to see Eric Fowler and Rob Wakefield standing on her porch.

"Hello Mrs. Penrose," Eric said.

"Eric, Rob, what brings you two out here?" Eleanor did not want either of them to pick up on the fear she felt. Neither did she want them in her house. She stood in the doorway without inviting them inside.

"We just wanted to check on you and make sure you didn't have any long-lasting complications from your accident at the Red Shed," Rob stated.

"I didn't think you noticed I was involved in that brawl," Eleanor said.

"At the time, I'm afraid we were inebriated and didn't act appropriately. I'm sorry about the entire episode, Mrs. Penrose," Rob said. "We should have helped you and at least apologized sooner."

"It looks like you've recovered," Eric added. "I don't see any scars."

"Oh yes, I'm fine. Thank you for your concern." Eleanor was reminded of the insincere Eddie Haskell from the fifty's television program, *Leave It to Beaver* and wondered what they really wanted. She waited for it.

"I think I saw you at Riverside today," Eric said and waited for her to offer something.

"I have many old friends there," Eleanor said.

"Do you also know someone named Art Chase?" Rob asked. Eleanor began to feel uncomfortable. She shifted her weight from one foot to the other while she contemplated an answer.

"I don't believe I know anyone at Riverside by that name," she said.

Rob and Eric exchanged a look that Eleanor could not read. She was relieved to see Angus walking up the hill toward her house and waved at him. The two young men turned and when they recognized him their faces fell. "Angus, surely you know these two. They stopped by to check on my good health. Isn't that kind?" Eleanor smiled.

If Angus were a beast he would have growled, but his bulk and dangerously lowered brows was more than enough to send the two hoodlums scurrying back to their car where Edward Fowler sat waiting.

They had tangled with Angus before and had no appetite for it.

"Glad to see you looking well," Rob sputtered before they got in and Edward drove off. Angus watched until they were out of sight.

"What did they want?" Angus asked.

"I don't know for sure, but I'm really glad to see you!" Eleanor threw her arms around his middle and squeezed him tight. "Come in, I don't have anything to eat but I can offer you a drink."

After Eleanor poured Angus his favorite Crown Royal, she told him everything she knew about Artemas and Peter Fowler, including the images of the Nazi medals and pins she found in the secret room. She shared Gladys' observations and fears and let Angus draw his own conclusions.

"Those goons won't be back here tonight," he said. "I'll ask Andy McGraw to swing by later and check on you. I think Gladys may need my support tonight."

Then he surprised her by kissing her goodnight and warning her to close her windows and lock her doors before he left her alone.

Eleanor's anxiety increased as the night wore on. Why did Angus leave her alone? He couldn't be sure those thugs wouldn't come back. She didn't know what they wanted from her but assumed it had something to do with Artemas. Perhaps they felt threatened by the old Nazi hunter. Maybe they were on to him, but what did she know that would be of interest to them? She locked her doors, checked the windows, and told herself she was a big girl who could look out for herself. She rigged some pots and pans from her kitchen to her door, just in case, took a long soak in the tub, and went to bed.

Angus headed directly to Riverside Retirement Home where he had a long chat with Gladys Reyburg, and then stationed himself in a chair outside her door to spend the night guarding one of Waterton's most valuable treasures.

In the morning, Angus woke stiff from his night sitting in a chair. He must have dozed off. Slowly he stretched his long legs and checked Gladys' door. It was early but Gladys was awake and opened her door when she heard him tapping.

"Is everything all right?" Gladys asked.

"I didn't see anything suspicious, but I have to admit, I didn't stray far from your door. Did you sleep?" Angus asked.

Gladys smiled. "Like a baby," she said. "I think you might want to go home and catch a few hours of sleep yourself. That chair is a poor excuse for a bed."

"I think I'll do that." Angus hugged Gladys and headed out of the building while Gladys headed to the dining room for an early breakfast. It wasn't until later that afternoon that a rumor spread throughout the building that Peter Fowler had disappeared during the night. The residents speculated that he had been taken to the hospital. Others said his grandson had sprung him and taken him to some far away tropical paradise, and a few believed he had simply walked out of the place on his own power. A thorough search turned up nothing. Whatever it was, there were no clues left behind and no one had seen a thing. He was gone as if by magic.

When Gladys called to tell Eleanor about his disappearance, she wasn't surprised. "I can't tell you how reassuring it was to have Angus here. He talked with me at great length about my concerns and never once made me feel like a foolish old woman. Then he spent the night outside my door like a loyal watch dog. I hope you know what a good man he is. He's a keeper, Eleanor."

"I do know, Gladys, and I'm glad he was there for you. Do you feel safer now that Peter Fowler is gone?" asked Eleanor.

"Well, if you remember, my original concern was Artemas Chase. I still intend to keep track of the deaths here and see if they coincide with his visits."

"Artemas told me he has no intention of visiting again, but good luck with your research, Gladys. I'll talk with you again soon."

Artemas said his investigation was nearly complete and Eleanor knew the Counterintelligence Corps had ways of making people disappear. There was no need to tell Gladys about her theories. Artemas had asked for confidence and she would honor that. Peter Fowler wasn't someone she would miss, but there might be others who would.

On a foggy Saturday morning Eleanor drove to Waterton to watch Wesley play baseball. She arrived early and found a seat on the bleachers behind home plate where a team of four-year old kids were playing T-ball.

The petite girl at bat took a mighty swing and the ball flew higher than anyone imagined surprising even her teammates who in their excitement took to the field and ran the bases along with her. The spectators laughed uproariously.

"Now that's what I like to see," said the woman sitting next to her. "That's what I call team support!"

The man next to her shook his head. Eleanor didn't know if he found it funny or just sad, but when the next batter hit the ball and took his time leaning the bat carefully against the stand before taking to the bases, he stood up and began to yell, "Run, you idiot!" Several others looked at him in disgust.

"They're only four," said the woman. "You need to relax and enjoy their play."

"They'll never learn if you don't teach them. You can't just let them think everything they do is cute." The man stood up and left. Fortunately, the T-ball players were finished with their game and left with their parents who offered the hope of ice cream and celebrations. A few older boys appeared on the scene and began throwing balls back and forth to warm up their muscles. It wasn't long before Eleanor spotted Wesley as he joined his teammates on the field. He looked tall and handsome in his red jersey and white pants. Amy found Eleanor and sat next to her.

"Where are Taylor and the girls?" Eleanor asked.

"Elise had a sleepover and Addie is at a birthday party. Taylor's catching up on some work."

"I guess we'll have to yell extra loud then," Eleanor said.

It wasn't long after the game started that Angus joined them and squeezed beside Eleanor on a bench that was already full. "I'm glad you could make it," Eleanor said. "Oh, Wesley is up to bat."

They yelled words of support and cheered loudly when he got a base hit. Amy took a video and sent it to Taylor from her phone. The next batter advanced Wesley to second and the crowd continued to clap and cheer. Suddenly Wesley was on third base but the player on first forgot to tag up after a foul ball and was called out. Eleanor's heart ached for that kid whose father ran down to the dugout and began to berate the boy who hung his head in shame.

"Do you kiss your wife with that mouth?" another father asked the angry one when he heard the harsh language he was using.

"Yeah, and I kiss your wife with it too," he replied, clearly angling for a fight. The other man would not be baited and only shook his head.

"I'm not sure I understand the purpose of yelling at someone who knows they erred and already feels defeated," Eleanor said sadly, but forgot all about it as Wesley sped to home plate to score the first run of the game. The fans were on their feet and Wesley was grinning proudly as his teammates slapped him on the back and high fived him as he returned to the dugout.

"Wesley's doing a great job. I thought he wasn't any good," Angus whispered.

Amy eyed him sadly, "He thinks that, but it isn't true. You know how kids are. They focus on the flaws instead of the positives."

"That's just perfectionists," Angus said. "Not all kids think they have to be perfect."

"It helps if they have good role models," Eleanor said. "I'm sorry if I expected you to be perfect, Amy."

"I don't expect perfection!" Amy exclaimed defensively.

"I never said you did, dear. I said I did and I'm sorry." Eleanor knew it was true and it was the thing she regretted most. It was so easy to find the one little flaw when everything else was good. She intended to make up for it with her grandchildren and for the most part she had, but she'd never admitted it to Amy. By the time her second daughter had come along she had given up on perfection and lowered her expectations considerably. Everything Erin accomplished surprised and astounded her. Both of her children turned out to be what Eleanor liked to call magnificent human beings, but

Amy was more of a human doing—always busy trying to save the world while Erin enjoyed a more laidback life.

Wesley continued to surprise and awe even himself as the game progressed. Halfway through Taylor showed up and watched his son with pride as he stood near the bleachers. At one point Wesley spotted his father and waved happily from the outfield after catching a fly ball. When the game was over, they all gathered around a happy Wesley.

"What a great game you had, Buddy!" Angus said. "Let's go for ice cream. I'll treat."

"And your team won!" said Taylor.

"We did?" asked Wesley who hadn't noticed the score.

Angus and Eleanor sat on her deck and watched the waves roll in on a perfect summer day. "Isn't life great?" asked Eleanor as she looked at all the beauty that surrounded her. "I just don't want this to end."

"What don't you want to end?" Angus asked, "The weather, summer, or just this particular moment?"

"Life, I don't want this life to end. I know everything ends, but I love my life, my friends, you. I've lived a wonderful life and I don't want anything to change."

Angus turned his attention away from the ocean and looked into Eleanor's eyes. "Don't think about the future then, just live in the now."

"I guess I'm tempting fate by counting my blessings." Eleanor said. "I read a poem once where a man who cherished an orange threw it high in the air as though he didn't value it. He didn't want anyone to know what a great thing he had so he pretended it didn't matter to him so they wouldn't try to take it away." Angus took Eleanor in his arms and held her. He had no answer to her worry. Everything changed. That's just the way life was, but he intended to hold tight as long as he could to what he cherished.

Eleanor picked Bootsy Greenwood up at the bus station. Her parents were grateful to send their 11-year-old daughter to Sand Beach for a few days during the summer because they were very busy people and Bootsy was delighted to visit her bosom friend. Bootsy's Granny Scattergoods had lived in Sand Beach until she died and now Angus lived in her house. Every summer Bootsy had visited her Granny and now she visited Eleanor. It was for Bootsy that Eleanor created the hidey-hole. They shared a love of books, baking, and an interest in all things having to do with Sand Beach. Her visit was a gift to them both.

"How was the bus ride?" Eleanor asked as they rode to Sand Beach.

"Well, it was mostly uneventful except for the bank robber who got on the bus with a suitcase full of money. I knew he was trouble because he had a mustache with a curl and his eyes were always shifting from one side to the other. I can't be sure, but I think he had a gun under his coat. When he got off the bus there was another criminal looking man waiting for him in a blue Volvo. Maybe you saw him. His eyes bulged strangely, and his lips were swollen as if they were bee stung. He drove away in a hurry."

"I see," said Eleanor without blinking an eye. She was used to Bootsy's vivid imagination. "Are you hungry? Is there something special you would like for dinner?"

"I was hoping we could roast hotdogs on the beach," Bootsy said hopefully.

"Perfect, we can get some at the grocery in Sand Beach. Mrs. Kelly always has hotdogs." Eleanor had stocked up on baking ingredients and many of Bootsy's favorite foods. Hotdogs had not been on her list.

Driving into the village was always a breathtaking event and when Bootsy spied the ocean for the first time she cried out in delight. Eleanor was used to the view and sadly took its awesome beauty for granted most of the time, but today she saw it again through Bootsy's eyes and almost braked as they rounded the corner.

Once inside Eleanor's house, Bootsy took no time rekindling her friendship with Feathers who allowed her to carry him around while she stroked his back and cooed to him in baby talk. Bootsy put her things away in the guest room and changed her clothes while Eleanor packed a basket with items necessary for roasting hotdogs on the beach.

They staked out their spot near a large log and began a search for driftwood for fire building. When they had amassed a huge pile, they began in earnest to seek out the largest agate or the least broken seashell. It was a perfect day on the beach with few people and no wind. As the sun dropped lower the temperature fell too. They lit their fire and stuck the hotdogs on sticks and began to roast their dinner while sitting comfortably on a blanket with their backs against a log.

"Are you ever afraid, Eleanor?" Bootsy asked as she gazed into the fire.

"Afraid? How do you mean?" Eleanor needed clarification.

"You live all by yourself. Sometimes when I'm home alone I hear things that scare me," Bootsy said.

"Sure. One time I heard a knocking on the wall outside. There was no one home but Feathers and me. I was sure someone was out on the deck and it was dark, so I turned on the outside light but there was no one there. I kept hearing it so I finally plucked up my courage and went out on the deck and saw that the wind was blowing a rocking chair and it was hitting the house."

"Did you think it was a ghost?" Bootsy asked.

"No, I don't believe in ghosts," Eleanor said as she put her hotdog in a bun.

"My Mom told me about a ghost she saw once when she worked in a restaurant. She had to go downstairs to get something they stored in the basement and she saw the shadow of a man walking two Scottie dogs, but when she rounded the corner, no one was there. She said the hairs on her neck stood up and she got goosebumps. Later she mentioned it to someone else who worked there and they said that was just one of the ghosts that lived down there and lots of other people had seen them too."

"I've never seen a ghost," Eleanor said, "But there is a creepy story people tell about the tunnel that goes to the other side of the point."

Bootsy shivered. "Is it like the story of Bandage Man?" Bandage Man had haunted her ever since Eleanor had given her the book, *Oregon's Ghosts and Monsters.* It was a tale about an injured logger wrapped in bandages who haunted a stretch of the coast highway. He jumped in the back of pickup trucks, ate people's dogs, and left stinky bits of his bandages behind.

"No, I'm sure it's just a story someone made up to keep their children out of the tunnel after dark," Eleanor said.

"Tell me," Bootsy said.

"There's not much to tell really, it's just about four young kids who were on the beach at night when they saw a glow coming from the tunnel." Eleanor looked toward the tunnel that ran through the point to a more secluded beach. Bootsy looked that way too expecting to see something eerie emanating from the entrance but there was nothing out of the ordinary.

"Of course, they went to investigate thinking there was someone in the tunnel with a light of some kind. One of them was too afraid to go in so she stayed outside to wait for them. When they got inside, it was dark but as they tripped over the rocks, they noticed the tunnel branched off in a way they'd never seen before."

"The tunnel doesn't branch off," corrected Bootsy, "It just goes to the other side."

"Well on this night they saw a light that led them in another direction, and they followed it deeper and deeper until it disappeared leaving them in total darkness. They didn't know what to do because they couldn't see where to go. They tried going back the way they came but they had taken so many different paths they couldn't find their way out."

"Did they get out?" Bootsy looked worried.

"The girl that stayed outside waited until the tide came in through the tunnel. She called and called for them, but they never came out."

"Never? You mean they never found them?" Bootsy was horrified.

"No, but some people say they've seen a glow coming from the tunnel and they've heard children crying for help when they go near it," Eleanor finished.

"What do you think happened to them?" Bootsy asked.

"Some people say they just went to the other side of the tunnel and were trapped by the incoming tide and washed out to sea, but I think grownups simply want their children to stay out of the tunnel because they might get trapped there or hit by falling rocks, so they made up a scary story," Eleanor explained.

"Oh, I see. That's like the story my Uncle Jason told my cousins and me about the Nail Monster. He said there was a monster that lived upstairs in his house. He showed us the skin he pulled from its head and it was really ugly. I know he made it up to keep us from going upstairs and getting into his stuff. The skin was really an old Halloween mask. I know because I found it later. It was a very scary story and I believed it for a long time. Sometimes he even made hammering noises to keep me terrified, but now that I'm older that doesn't work on me anymore."

"I see," said Eleanor. They sat in silence eating their hotdogs, enjoying the warmth of the fire and listening for calls of distress coming from the tunnel over the sounds of the ocean's surf. They didn't see Angus as he walked up behind them and when he spoke, they both jumped. Bootsy even let out a terrified scream.

"I didn't think I was that scary," Angus said as he sat close to Eleanor.

"I thought you were Bandage Man," gasped Bootsy.

"I promise not to eat your dog if you feed me one of those." Angus pointed to the hotdogs. Eleanor and Bootsy laughed and were only too happy to share their beach picnic with Angus.

"I feel a little safer now that you're here," said Bootsy. "Eleanor was telling me scary stories."

"That's very naughty of you, Eleanor. Bootsy will have nightmares. I may have to spend the night too to protect her," he said as his eyebrows went up and down.

"Now that is a scary thought," said Eleanor.

"Not as scary as the Troll of Horny Chessman," Angus said as he loaded his hotdog on a stick.

"I've heard about him," said Bootsy." Isn't he just a big bear?"

"Maybe, but some campers think he's Big Foot or Sasquatch," Angus said. "I had my own experience with him when I was camping just north of here. I went for a hike and when I came back my tent was torn apart and my food was gone. Whatever it was left big footprints and a big mess behind. People up north call him the Troll of Horny Chessman."

"He doesn't come this far south," Eleanor said as she put a marshmallow on her stick and began roasting it. "I've never heard of Sasquatch being seen on the beach."

"He would leave footprints in the sand," Bootsy added.

"His footprints would quickly wash away though," Angus said.

"Have you ever seen Bigfoot?" Bootsy asked.

"No, but I did see a ghost once," Angus said. Eleanor gave him a sideways glance, but it didn't deter him. "When I was younger, I came up from California to work in the forests around Medford. It was a summer job and a bunch of guys I knew rented a house together. We didn't know why the rent was so cheap and just thought it was because the house was old, but we found out later no one wanted to live there because it was haunted. Things started out innocently enough, lights flickered, strange noises were heard, and items disappeared and turned up in strange places—all easily explained away by sane people. Then we had an infestation of flies and discovered they were coming in from the fireplace so we searched it thinking some animals fell in and died but we couldn't find anything so we sealed the opening up with duct tape. The last straw for me happened late one night when we were coming home and saw a face looking out the upstairs window of my bedroom. We all saw it. It was a little girl. We searched the house from top to bottom but never found anything. We moved out that very night. It wasn't long after that I heard the story about a little girl who lived in that house who disappeared. Her family searched for her for weeks and didn't find her until they had an infestation of flies and discovered her rotting corpse in the chimney."

"Yuk," said Bootsy as she shivered and wriggled closer to Eleanor who had scooted into Angus' embrace. "How did a little girl get in the chimney?" asked Eleanor.

"She climbed a tree and dropped from a limb," Angus said taking advantage of Eleanor's fear to hold her tight.

"I think you made that up," accused Eleanor suddenly standing and brushing the sand from her pants.

"It's time for us to go home but before we go, we need to put out this fire." Angus took a bucket he brought just for that purpose and went to fetch water while Eleanor and Bootsy stirred the embers. With the fire out and everything packed they walked up the hill to Eleanor's, but Bootsy couldn't stop looking back to see if there was a light coming from the dark tunnel.

Despite their evening of scary tales, both Eleanor and Bootsy slept without being haunted by nightmares and woke the next morning ready to experience a new adventure. Eleanor looked out the window and declared it a perfect day for a hike on Bayocean spit. They ate a big breakfast of pancakes and bacon, packed water, trail mix and two apples in their backpacks and drove to the spit that separated the ocean from Waterton Bay. It was a two-mile hike to the end of the spit where a rock jetty had been built in 1965 to offset the north jetty that was built in 1917 and caused the erosion of the spit in 1952.

Eleanor and Bootsy walked at a leisurely pace enjoying the sun and watching for birds and other wildlife along the way. Fishing boats floated on the bay and Eleanor remembered days spent with Walter as they fished those waters together long ago.

"Look, Eleanor, two deer!" Bootsy exclaimed. They watched as the deer meandered across the trail and into the brush. "Is it true that there was an entire city here once?"

"Hard to believe isn't it?" Eleanor said, "But it's true. It was a vacation resort with several homes, a hotel, post office, grocery store, a natatorium, and a paved road."

"What's a natatorium?" asked Bootsy.

"It was a huge swimming pool with artificial waves that simulated the surf."

"What happened to it? Where is the town?" Bootsy asked.

"It all fell into the ocean. You can't build on sand and expect the ocean to respect that," Eleanor explained.

"We learned about erosion in school," Bootsy said.

"It was there that the ocean broke through the spit and made the part we're on now an island." Eleanor pointed to a spot behind them.

Bootsy looked back in awe. "How did it get fixed?"

"People built another jetty and slowly the ocean deposited sand again, but I wouldn't build a house on it now."

"People are silly," Bootsy said. "Sometimes they just believe things even when they know it can't be true. I used to believe in Santa Claus because it made me happy and the people who built their houses out here wanted to believe sand was a safe place because it made them happy, but their houses fell into the ocean."

"If I remember correctly, you believed in fairies, unicorns, miracles, and magic not so long ago. Do you still?" Eleanor asked as she looked into Bootsy's serious face.

"No, not anymore," she sighed. "I've prayed for a miracle to make my Grandma Alice remember me, but she doesn't." Her answer made Eleanor sad. Bootsy was too young to be cynical.

They stopped to pick some wild blackberries on the way home. Their plan was to invite Angus over for dinner and get him to fix up an old bicycle in Eleanor's garage so they could ride down the beach to Camp Cheerful. Bootsy only had three days at Sand Beach and wanted to make the most of them. Even Bootsy knew Angus could not resist a blackberry pie.

Angus stood with his hands on his hips and looked at the bicycle. It had a flat tire, but other than that it was perfect for Bootsy to ride down the beach. Eleanor's bike was in good shape even though it had been years since she had ridden it. He had checked the brakes and pumped up the tires, now he just needed to patch the inner tube on Bootsy's and then enjoy his reward.

Eleanor and Bootsy were in the kitchen preparing a homemade pizza with Canadian bacon and pineapple and a fresh vegetable salad. Bootsy poured grape juice in one of Eleanor's wine glasses and sipped it as they worked mimicking Eleanor with her pinot noir.

"I'll go tell Angus the pizza will be ready soon," Bootsy said. She entered the garage just in time to see Angus mount the bike and ride it out onto the lane. The sight of him on a small bike with his long legs made her laugh.

"I wouldn't want to ride this vintage bike up Eleanor's hill," he said as he circled back inside. "It doesn't have any gears, but the seat sure is comfortable."

Bootsy studied the bike carefully. "Wouldn't it be neat if you could put a motor on it?"

"Some old things are better left alone," Angus said. "If you start messing with something like that it could blow up on you."

"My parents won't let me have a hoverboard because their batteries explode," Bootsy lamented.

"Maybe in time they'll work the kinks out and you can get one." Angus got off the bike. "Do you want to give it a spin?"

"Absolutely!" Bootsy climbed on and rode out of the garage and down the lane. "Oh, dinner's ready," she shouted over her shoulder.

After the pizza and pie, the three sat down to watch *The Wizard of Oz*. Tomorrow they would ride their bikes to Camp Cheerful along the sandy beach road and then Eleanor would drive Bootsy back to her parents because there is no place like home. Bootsy would be sad to leave but even she knew what Benjamin Franklin said about company and fish was true: after three days they began to stink.

Eleanor took possession of the letter and made a copy for Wanda. It might give her a little pleasure and reason to recover sooner. It wasn't wrong to let Wanda go on believing something that wasn't true if Eleanor could justify it. Cleo planned to go with her to visit Wanda who was recovering at her daughter's house just up the hill from Cleo.

"I've never been to Wanda's house before. She told me she lives in the basement, but I don't see how she could possibly maneuver stairs with her broken leg," Cleo commented.

"I guess we'll soon find out," said Eleanor as they knocked on the double red doors. A younger version of Wanda opened the door and smiled.

"You must be Mom's friends. I'm Gretchen and I'm so glad to meet you. Please come in. Mom is in the living room watching one of her shows." Gretchen led them into a large open space that encompassed a great room with a river rock fireplace, dining area, and kitchen. The vaulted ceiling was held up by heavy beams and most of the walls were made of a light-colored wood giving the space a log cabin feeling.

Large windows to the east provided a view of the coast range and allowed morning light to enter. Wanda sat on a reclining chair with her leg elevated and her broken arm resting on a pillow. Her face still showed evidence of injuries not yet healed but the swelling was gone, and she looked more like herself. Actually, she looked like a queen sitting on her throne. The hair sticking up in spikey disarray on her head resembled a crown of sorts.

"You look great!" Cleo exclaimed. "How do you feel?"

"With my fingers," said Wanda. "How do you feel?" Wanda was feeling a little feisty.

"We brought you some things that might help in your recovery." Eleanor offered a bag filled with a variety of items she and Cleo had put together.

"Just put it over there." Wanda didn't seem interested in the bag. "Gretchen, would you mind bringing me and my friends some lemonade?"

"Of course." Gretchen moved into the kitchen area.

"Did you bring the letter?" whispered Wanda. Obviously, she didn't want Gretchen to know about it.

"It's in the bag," said Cleo.

"Well get it out. I can't wait to read it again. Did you read it?"

"No," Cleo said truthfully.

"Then read it to me. I still can't see very well out of this one eye." Eleanor rummaged around in the bag and pulled out the envelope that contained the copy of Cynthia's letter.

"Oh, are those See's chocolates?" Wanda asked. "Put those over here by me." Eleanor did as instructed. It was clear that Wanda was making the most of her disabilities. Cleo took the letter out of its envelope and read it out loud.

Darling,

You've pierced my soul. You don't realize how fascinating you are and how dangerously attractive you've become to me. You influence me for the better. You are the one object of my desire. When I am with you, I feel that I am home. I love you without question, without reason, without reckoning. My love has made me selfish I know. I am forgetful of everything but seeing you again, yet I am half agony half hope. Am I too late? I love none but you but if you do not believe it, if you do not trust it, I must convince you of it. Leave your lover, leave for me.

Forever and always,

Your true love

"Wow, that's powerful. Who do you think wrote it?"

"Oh, I know who wrote it. It was my husband, Oscar Dinklage. The mystery is how Howard Wakefield got hold of it. You know my husband used to be a successful journalist until Howard Wakefield took exception to an exposé he wrote about one of his business ventures. Wakefield slapped a lawsuit on him for libel. The suit drug on for years until the courts threw it out, but it cost the paper thousands of dollars. Oscar lost his job at the newspaper and couldn't get another. We quickly depleted our savings and then Oscar got sick. He died soon after. I hate Howard Wakefield. He's a fucking bastard but I can't beat him. He's seen me a few times at his house and we shared a couple of conversations, but he never knew who I was. At least I didn't think so until the bloody T-shirts turned up and I thought I could finally get some justice. I know for a fact he cut my brake line." Wanda struggled to open the box of chocolates with her broken arm.

"Let me help you with that," Eleanor offered. Wanda popped one pecan cream in her mouth and savored it slowly.

"Did you tell the police all this?" asked Cleo.

"The police asked me lots of questions in the hospital, but not about the bloody shirt. They wanted to know personal stuff about Junie and Rob. Like who came to visit them. When they came and how long they stayed. Did I ever see evidence that Olivia or Eric were in Junie or Rob's bedrooms? Did I ever notice anything unusual about Rob's friends or find things that might indicate he belonged to a gang or something like that. I don't remember what I told them. Probably that he was a slob who didn't have any friends, not any real friends anyway. I tried to tell them my story. They said they'd look into the accusations about the brakes, but I'm not counting on it." Wanda's voice faded and her eyes twitched.

Gretchen returned with the lemonade and she sat on the couch. "How sweet that you brought candy," Gretchen said. "Mom loves chocolate. Can I get you anything else? Are you comfortable?"

"No dear, I'm fine. I just need to rest my eyes. Is there any vodka in that bag? This lemonade needs a little kick."

"Sorry," Eleanor said, "We didn't think of that."

"I thought of it but decided you shouldn't have any until you get off your pain meds," Cleo said. "But I did bring you this magazine about meditative healing." Cleo got back into the bag and pulled out a slick magazine.

"That's not for me," Wanda said. "You can take that back. I don't believe in that crap." Cleo was unfazed by the ungrateful remark. There was an article about yoga she thought Pearl would find interesting, so she held onto the issue.

"Did anyone ever check my brakes to see if they were tampered with? I can't shake the feeling that someone was trying to kill me." Wanda shifted in her chair.

"Do you really think they would want you dead?" asked Eleanor.

Wanda furrowed her brows but then winced in pain. "I've made enemies at the Wakefield house. Turning in the T-shirt was stupid. I should have figured out a way to get back at him without being so blatant. I should have waited until I found something better. Howard Wakefield had one of his secretaries call me to terminate my employment. She said she was sorry about my accident, but they needed a replacement and couldn't wait for me to recover. What a jerk! He couldn't even be bothered to call or send a get-well card. Maybe it wasn't about the T-shirts. I keep wondering if I know something and I don't know I know it. Maybe I saw something I wasn't supposed to see."

"What did you do at the Wakefield's?" asked Eleanor.

"I do what housekeepers do, clean up other people's messes," Wanda said.

"Yes," said Eleanor, "but what did you do?"

"Every day I went there and tidied up, mopped and dusted, changed the bedding, hung up clothes—that kind of stuff."

"Did you work in the kitchen?" asked Cleo.

"I'm not a fucking cook."

"Did they have parties?" asked Eleanor. "I bet if there were parties, you got paid extra to work them."

"There weren't any fun parties, at least not while I was there, but there were gatherings that were more like meetings in the downstairs great room. I only know because I had to clean up after them the following morning. There were just a lot of cigar butts and whiskey bottles. It didn't look like any women were invited either. The room was set up like a classroom with a podium so there was a speaker of some sort. I never could figure out what was going on there. There were always ashes in the garbage can as if they had to burn the evidence of their meeting, so I figured it out. It was some sort of men's club. I was the only one who cleaned down there. There were stories about the basement being haunted, so no one wanted to go there, but I don't believe in that shit so it didn't' bother me. I never saw any ghosts." Wanda began to cough.

"We should let you rest," said Eleanor.

"Thanks for stopping by and bringing the candy." Wanda smiled. Gretchen walked them to the door and thanked them again as they walked down the hill to Cleo's.

"Funny, Bootsy and I just had a discussion about scary stories made up to keep people from going where they shouldn't. Do you think Howard Wakefield made up a ghost story to keep the help away from of his downstairs meeting room?" Eleanor mused.

"Interesting theory, Eleanor, if that's true and Wanda cleaned down there maybe she did see something she wasn't supposed to see."

"She doesn't seem to know what it was though," Eleanor said.

"Oh look, it's my Portland friends. They're early or I'm late. Please stay and meet them, Eleanor. I'm sure you'll like them as much as I do." Cleo hurried to the silver Subaru where two women sat. When they saw Cleo, they got out of the car and hugs were generously exchanged.

"This is my friend, Eleanor Penrose and these are my valley friends, Sue Raw and Arianne Moore."

"I'm happy to finally meet you. Cleo thinks the world of you," Eleanor said. She too felt an instant connection to the two women and understood Cleo's fondness for them. Even after only a few minutes with them she felt an unexpected closeness.

"We thought you'd forgotten about us," said Sue.

"Never. I'm sorry I wasn't here when you came. Have you been here long?"

"No, in truth we just got here," said Arianne, "but we're starving."

"Let's get this feast inside," said Sue as she handed containers to everyone.

That was when Cleo put the magazine down in the backseat of Arianne's car to free her hands so she could help carry in the containers of food. It was just this kind of mindless living that caused people to lose track of their keys and reading glasses. Of course, the love letter that Eleanor copied for Wanda was inside the magazine when Cleo unconsciously put it there before she left Wanda's house. Later, Sue would take the magazine into her house where it would be found by her husband and another man would worry about who loved his wife and wanted her to leave him.

"I should be going," said Eleanor who didn't want to intrude. "I'll see you at the fair later this week, Cleo. Maybe I'll see you too, Sue and Arianne. It was a pleasure meeting you."

As Eleanor drove home she thought about her own friendships and wondered what life would be like without them. Many of those she loved the most were old. Some were already dead. The Do Nothings, her coffee group, book club, Nancy, Gladys—all of them were getting up in years. She had been lucky to have them for so long, but now she couldn't shake an overwhelming fear that something bad was about to happen.

Eleanor's nightmare involved Artemas Chase and Peter Fowler. She didn't really know Peter Fowler and probably wouldn't recognize him if she saw him on the street but in the dream, she knew it was him. He wore a field-grey army uniform covered with Nazi pins and medals and carried a scary looking rifle with a sharp bayonet that caught a flash in the sun's light.

She and Gladys Reyburg watched as Peter goose-stepped down the halls of Riverside Retirement Home and poked those too flawed to live, rousting them from their beds and wheelchairs and forcing them into a large U-Haul truck that waited outside. When the rooms had been cleared of the frail and demented, he turned to Gladys and asked for her papers, which she reluctantly turned over to him. Eleanor looked at the papers and saw the name of the genetic testing company that provided a list of relatives. It was the same company that Angus used to find his lost son. A chill went through her body. She too had willingly sent off her DNA to this very company and now military men were using this information to round up people with infirmities and imperfections in an attempt to cleanse and strengthen the American race.

Never in her wildest dreams did she think this could happen in America. She had to get to her children and somehow protect her grandchildren. Walter's history of dementia and her flawed genes were a danger to them. Eleanor didn't know what markers she had but, in her dream, she knew there were diabetes, cancer, and heart disease. She had to warn Angus. They would be coming for him, too. She looked at Gladys who was the only remaining resident. "My genes are perfect," she said. "I'm sorry, Eleanor."

Eleanor watched as Peter Fowler checked the names on his tablet. "You are on the list of imperfect specimens," he said. "Get in the truck." Suddenly Artemas was there with Ninja turtles who descended from the ceiling like black spiders and somersaulted down the hall. They threw Ninja stars at Peter and the other soldiers. Peter's bayonet turned into a Jedi light saber and he fought a battle with Artemas who suddenly looked a great deal like Yoda. Eleanor was paralyzed with fear and had a difficult time tearing herself away from the fight but realized she needed to run while the evildoers were distracted. She raced outside, opened the door to the U-Haul, and made a mad dash to her car. There was no way she could help all the people in the truck. They were too helpless. She drove away feeling desperate, afraid, and guilty as sirens blared in the distance.

When she opened her eyes, understanding dawned and relief flooded over her. It was a dream—a bad dream and she could wake from it. She lay in bed for a while imagining those who did not wake from that nightmare and would never wake again. How did Artemas Chase sleep with everything he had witnessed? How did any soldier recover from war? Maybe that was why Artemas continued to hunt his enemies. Finding some kind of justice for the victims of war kept him sane. Eleanor wondered if there was anything she could do to recover her DNA, but she knew once it was in the system there was no getting it back.

She looked at the clock. It was the middle of the night and she could still hear the sirens. They were real and nearby. Eleanor rolled out of bed, put on her robe, and went to her window. A fire truck was driving down Main Street, sirens blaring and lights flashing in the night. Eleanor could see the lights come on in the houses below. She moved to the other side of the house and saw a glow from the flames. Someone's house in the village was on fire. Eleanor quickly slipped on a pair of shoes, grabbed a flashlight, and stepped outside to see better. She followed the trail to the east and noticed two more fire trucks and several other residents gathering near Henry Ott's old house. As she drew near, she recognized Angus who was keeping people a safe distance from the burning building.

It was Will and Cynthia's house now and it was fully involved. Eleanor felt a sadness descend as she watched Henry Ott's years of tireless renovation perfected out of love for his wife go up in flames. The vaulted ceilings with the heavy beams, the beautiful custom kitchen, and the secret room. All ruined.

Cynthia and Will stood among the small crowd of villagers holding each other, their faces grim and unreadable, lit by the all-consuming fire. Eleanor wondered where Artemas was. She found her way over to the stunned couple who greeted her with tears and hugs.

"Where's Artemas?" she asked over the roar of the blaze.

"We looked in his room before we left the house, but his bed was still made. He must be at Mattie's," Will said. He didn't seem to be worried.

"Do you want me to go over there and check?" Eleanor asked, surprised at their lack of concern.

"Thank you, Eleanor, but I'll go." Will uprooted himself reluctantly and walked off as if in a daze.

"He's in shock," offered Cynthia. "Everything we had is in that house. I doubt if anything can be salvaged." The firemen continued to pour on water, but they had shifted their focus from saving the house to halting its spread to nearby homes.

"Why don't you come over to my house, Cynthia? There's nothing you can do here and it's sad to watch this destruction. I'll tell Angus to let Will know he's welcome too." Eleanor's offer was heartfelt. Cynthia nodded. In her hands she held the only thing she took from the burning house, a deck of cards.

Eleanor put on a fresh pot of coffee. She was sure no one would be able to sleep after the excitement of the fire. Will and Angus came together bringing the smoky scent of disaster with them. "Dad chose to stay with Mattie. At least he has a bed to go back to there," Will reported. "Neither one of them heard a thing. I almost had to knock the door down to get their attention."

"I have an extra room here," Eleanor said. You're welcome to stay until you decide what you want to do next."

"Thank you, Eleanor," said Will.

"What happened?" asked Angus.

"I'm not sure. I was asleep and then Cynthia was screaming that the house was on fire. There was smoke everywhere. I ran downstairs to Dad's room, saw that his bed hadn't been slept in and tried to find the fire extinguisher but couldn't see anything. The fire was in the living room and was spreading so fast I had to get out. Cynthia ran to the house down the lane and they called 911. I felt lucky that we got out at all."

"I don't know what made me wake up," Cynthia said calmly. There was smoke and I went downstairs and saw flames, so I woke Will and ran out of the house. I suppose we'll have to go back to Idaho now." The four of them sat in silence drinking coffee until Eleanor decided to make a hearty breakfast. Then they sat and silently ate or picked at the bacon and eggs, toast, and fruit.

No one had an appetite except Angus. "I want to go back to see what's happening at the scene of the fire." Angus figured there might be new information about the cause.

"I need some clothes," Will said, "I don't want to go in my pajamas." Eleanor went into action finding a few pieces that once belonged to Walter and something of hers that Cynthia could wear, including some different shoes since she claimed to have stepped in something sticky, ruining her slippers, and they all traipsed back to see what was left of the Chase house.

The villagers had returned to their homes. Smoke rose and embers still glowed, but the house was a shell of blackened debris. The rock fireplace remained standing in stark contrast to the morning sunrise like a monument to Henry Ott's hard work but that was the only recognizable structure. The rest was a mass of blackened shapes. The smell of wet burned things filled the morning air. Artemas limped slowly around the perimeter of the gutted structure talking to firemen who continued to do their job mopping up the hot spots. Will and Angus joined him and huddled together talking while Eleanor and Cynthia stood helplessly and watched.

"There's nothing in there worth saving," Cynthia whispered. Eleanor heard one of the firemen say something about arson and noticed Cynthia's look of alarm.

"Who would want to burn down our house?" she asked. Eleanor caught Artemas' eye and wondered too. Will and Cynthia stayed with Eleanor for two days and then moved into a hotel in Waterton with plans to take care of the details of their misfortune before they moved on to visit their son on the east coast. The fire officials continued their investigation and determined the cause was indeed arson finding evidence of gasoline inside the house and an empty gas can outside.

Eleanor baked her traditional apple pie and drove into town to enter it in the Waterton County Fair. She saw Cleo who was entering a painting of rabbits flying through space and Pearl with a mosaic of her granddaughter's beautiful face. Dede was organizing the church booth along with Helen Pence who was talking in her normal voice. Everyone was busy putting up decorations that declared the theme of this year's fair to be "A Fair to Remember".

Carnival rides grew out of the ground like mushrooms in a forest of cheap games and food carts that offered elephant ears, corndogs, caramel apples and, of course, Waterton ice cream. The barns were filling with Holsteins and Jersey cows, pigs, goats, rabbits, you name it, it was at the fair.

Eleanor met at least a dozen people who wanted to stop to chat delaying her arrival home until late afternoon. She blew her nose and was reminded that the fair was a dust bowl and most of it collected in her sinuses. She could live without the fair, unlike most people who were born and raised in Waterton. For them it was part of their collective childhood memories; the place where they earned their first blue ribbon, won a giant stuffed toy, and threw up on the Zipper. Her grandchildren loved the food and the rides, but if there was one thing Eleanor enjoyed, it was the horse races. If there were no races, Eleanor would gladly stay home where the air was free of dust and the overwhelming scent of cow dung.

This year Elise and Addie were dancing on the main stage on Friday and Saturday afternoon. Eleanor was committed to go those two days. She and Angus planned to go together on Saturday, which was the last day and allowed them to bet on the horses and watch the final heats of the famous pig and Ford races.

The pig and Ford races were a unique feature of Waterton's County Fair. Each evening after the horse races were finished and before the evening concert, several model T Fords lined up on the racetrack. A large wooden box filled with small pigs stood to the side. The drivers would grab a pig, crank up their engines, hop in their jalopies, and race around the track.

When they returned to the box of pigs, they would stop their engines, exchange their old pig for a new one, and repeat the process again to the delight of spectators in the grandstand whose cheers could be heard above the vigorous squealing of outraged pigs.

Every now and then an especially robust pig would wriggle loose and dart across the open field causing the distraught driver to give chase often making him last at the finish line. Needless to say, there was a great deal of friendly pushing and shoving among the contestants. Most of them grew up together and their families raced at the fair year after year, one generation giving way to the next. The winners of the weeknight heats competed on Saturday for the championship which was rewarded with a massive trophy and a kiss from the Dairy Queen. The pigs did not receive a prize and were happy to be back at their farms after the contest was over. Pig kissing was strictly taboo.

Saturday morning brought the sun that glistened on the ocean waves promising a perfect day for the Waterton County Fair. Eleanor finished her daily tasks and was ready when Angus came to collect her.

"Did you bring a bucket load of money?" he asked as she climbed into his pickup.

"Oh yeah," she replied, patting the small cross body bag hanging at her side. "I plan to win big this year." They rode into town to experience what would definitely be a fair no one in Waterton would ever forget.

"Have you heard any more about the fire that burned down Cynthia and Will's house?" asked Eleanor.

Angus gave her a sidelong glance. "Nothing good."

"Do you think Rob and Eric did it?" she asked.

"What makes you suspect them? They can't be responsible for every bad thing that happens in this county." Angus knew more than he was saying.

"Are you defending them?" Eleanor was surprised. "Don't forget they came to my house trying to trace Artemas."

"Is that what they were doing? I thought they were checking up on a snoopy lady who caught an elbow and fell off her barstool." Angus smiled.

"That's what they said, but I think they were trying to find Artemas and get even with him for making Eric's grandfather disappear," Eleanor continued.

"Do I know about this? Do you know for sure that's what happened?" Angus liked to play devil's advocate. He knew Eleanor didn't have the facts to back up her claim.

"Don't tell me it hasn't crossed your mind," Eleanor scolded.

"What exactly?" he asked innocently.

"Eric saw me at Riverside. He suspected Artemas of doing something with his grandfather and came to Sand Beach looking for his house. He and Rob stopped at my house hoping to get information from me about where Artemas lived or maybe even about his work as a Nazi hunter. Then, coincidentally, Artemas' house is burned down in the middle of the night. Tell me honestly you don't think they did it," Eleanor said.

"I can't say for sure, so it would only be speculation. The fire chief thinks it was an inside job."

"What do you mean by that?"

"Whoever set the fire did it from inside the house and they did a sloppy job of it too. The point of origin was most likely in the living room but there were multiple sites where gasoline was used to ignite the blaze."

"So that doesn't mean Eric and Rob didn't break in and set the fire."

"No, but there isn't a lick of evidence linking them to the fire. No one saw them in the vicinity. As a matter of fact, several witnesses claim they were both at the Red Shed well into the night," Angus reported.

"So who do you think did it?" asked Eleanor.

"Think about it, Ellie. Who was inside the house? Who had motive to set the fire?"

"Oh, I hate to think Cynthia would do that, but I guess it isn't that far-fetched," Eleanor said. "She didn't want to be here and now she has the perfect reason to leave, but it's hard to imagine that she would destroy everything they had just to get out of Sand Beach. What will happen now?"

"If they try to collect the insurance money, she could be charged with fraud, but first they have to prove she did it and I don't know if they can. There's always the possibility that some crazy person broke into their house and lit it, but we'll have to wait and see what develops. She might get a good lawyer, or someone may have seen something that could clear her."

"You mean like a drifter who happened to be in the area at the time? I still think it was those two hoodlums," Eleanor persisted, "Cynthia couldn't do that." Angus shrugged. He didn't investigate crimes of arson that didn't involve homicide and wasn't having much luck with the Vargas case. While one was hot the other had turned cold.

The Waterton County Fair was like most other fairs, crowded, noisy, and filled with the aroma of fried onions, cotton candy, and grilled meat. Music from the outdoor stage drifted through the voices of neighbors and friends who stopped to catch up as they strolled down the midway to get to wherever it was they were headed. Little girls in their rainbow-colored tutus hurried to find their place in the lineup of dancers while their families sat on the benches in anticipation. Eleanor and Angus spotted her granddaughters and waved as they took their seats and waited for the show to begin.

As Eleanor looked at the stage, she couldn't help but remember the last time she sat here and watched as Johnny Vargas and Junie Wakefield stood face to face and vowed to love each other until death parted them. Fate had been unkind to the lovers. Tears pricked Eleanor's eyes and she felt Angus squeeze her hand as he too recalled that day in May. Suddenly a pair of pigeons flew overhead evoking another memory of a hawk and a bloody dove. Eleanor remembered Madam Patrusha's words about blood beginning and ending Junie's suffering and sighed as the emcee introduced the first dance number.

"I'm starving," Angus announced when the last dance was finished. "Let's go over to the church booth and get something to eat."

Saint John's Catholic Church had a large booth with picnic tables covered in red and white checkered tablecloths, offering hot dogs, hamburgers, roast beef sandwiches, and a bevy of salads and beverages.

As Eleanor and Angus sat down with their meals, Dede came out of the kitchen and sat next to them. "You won't believe the morning I've had," she began.

"What happened?" asked Eleanor.

"I was doing a load of laundry early this morning and when I reached into the washing machine, I somehow got my necklace wrapped around the agitator. For the life of me I couldn't get loose and I was trapped with my head in the washing machine."

"Where was Mark?" asked Angus.

"He was upstairs somewhere. I called and called and just as I was ready to give up and die, he heard me and came down to the basement. After looking at my predicament he got his saw and cut the top of the agitator off and I finally was free."

"Why didn't he just unclasp your necklace?" asked Angus.

"Well, he could have, but that's not what he did," Dede explained. "Anyway, it made me late and now I can't catch up."

"Is this the necklace?" asked Eleanor as she lifted the sparkling diamond from Dede's neck.

"Yes, it was the first expensive piece of jewelry he ever bought," Dede said. "Now I'll need a new agitator but that's a problem for another day. Are you two going to the races?"

"As soon as we finish this delicious lunch," Angus said, wiping catsup from his mustache with a napkin.

"Bet on the number two horse in the fourth race for me," said Dede. "I'll be here all afternoon. There's no rest for the wicked." Angus gave her the thumbs up because his mouth was full of hamburger and Dede disappeared back into the kitchen.

Finding a spot in the grandstand was easy this time of day with most people coming for the pig and Ford races that took place after the horseraces were finished. Pearl and Cary already secured their spots and Angus and Eleanor sat down next to them, followed by Cleo and Mark who sat behind them.

Josephine and Richard joined the crowd next to the others and the betting and banter began in earnest.

"I'm betting on a Chardonneigh and Ginandtonic quinella," said Cleo as she stood to go, "And then I'm going to the beer garden to get a drink."

"I'll come with you," said Pearl, "but I like Bucktooth to win."

Angus sat studying the racing form. Eleanor knew he would wait until the last minute to decide his bet based on the statistics. None of her friends knew much about horses and most of them bet on the names they found appealing, but she knew what she liked when the horses paraded by on their way to the gate. She looked at the color, size, muscles, and liveliness of the animal. She never bet on a gray horse. "I'm going down to the stalls to look over the horses," she said, leaving Angus and the men behind to talk numbers.

As Eleanor reached the bottom of the steps she noticed the Wakefield box was full of people. Junie sat next to her father and his girlfriend sat on his other side. Rob and Olivia basked in the sunshine with their sunglasses and hats sipping beer from plastic cups. Eleanor nodded and gave Junie a smile as she continued through the crowd greeting many of her neighbors and acquaintances. The Fowlers also had a box and it was filled with youngsters taking advantage of its emptiness. As Eleanor walked by it Edward Fowler approached and began to yell, causing a scene. "You kids get out of there. I paid good money for those seats and I don't need your cooties on them." The kids scattered like field mice and Edward Fowler sat in his box alone squinting into the sun. Eleanor continued on her way to the stables.

The horses for the first race were saddled and waiting for their jockeys to mount them. Eleanor eyed them carefully and chose a bay wearing red colors. It was the number one horse. "See something food and gast?" asked a voice. "I mean good and fast?"

Eleanor turned to see Madame Patruska standing behind her. She looked like an ordinary person without her psychic garb. It took Eleanor a moment to identify this woman whose wild hair was tamed and had traded her scarves and gaudy jewelry for blue jeans and cowboy boots.

"Are you enjoying our fair?" she asked.

"Absolutely," Madam Patruska said. "The elephant ears are my favorite treat."

"Do you have a tip for me for the horseraces?" Eleanor kidded.

"Sure, don't bet on the slow one," she laughed.

"Are you betting?" Eleanor asked as they stood admiring the horses.

"Absolutely, I've got my eye on Inspector Donut," she said. "Oh no, I've pepped in stew."

"Are you staying for the pig and Ford races?" Eleanor asked as she watched the psychic try to clean her boot off on some straw.

"Oh no, the forecast looks grim. I doubt if they'll be able to finish the race. I'll be home before that storm comes. Good luck, Eleanor." Madame Patruska disappeared into the crowd and Eleanor looked up at the clear blue sky wondering what the seer meant then went to the betting window and put her money on the number one horse to win.

By the time she returned with her wager the others sat in anticipation as the horses were loaded into the starting gate. "Which one did you bet on?" Angus asked.

"Bad luck to tell," Eleanor whispered.

"And they're off," the announcer cried. As the horses neared the grandstand people stood stretching to better see the colors of their favorite jockeys. A tight group of racers whizzed past—hooves pounding and dirt flying. Cleo yelled for her Chardonneigh and Ginandtonic as they rounded the bend and the number two horse pulled ahead. Soon they were across the track and Eleanor could see her number one trailing the others.

"Inspector Donut is making his move," the announcer said, and Eleanor watched anxiously as the red horse moved from behind and began to pass each horse one by one. By the time they rounded the final turn and headed for the finish the number one horse was ahead by two lengths.

"Here they come and it's Inspector Donut in the lead. Inspector Donut, Ginandtonic, and Chardonneigh," the announcer called the first three to cross the finish line.

"Aww poop!" moaned Cleo as she realized her two picks were the first two losers.

"Who would have thought to bet on that one?" asked Mark. "He was a long shot."

"I bet the payoff for that one will be good," said Pearl who had bet on the gray Bucktooth.

"Any horse named Inspector Donut shouldn't be allowed to win," complained Angus who had bet on the favorite, Pie-O-My.

Eleanor whispered, "I didn't know the number one horse was named Inspector Donut." "

You bet on him?" Angus was surprised.

"It was just a 20 dollar wager," she said, but when the winning amount appeared on the board even Eleanor was impressed.

"I guess you're buying dinner," Angus said.

That was the last of Eleanor's good fortune. Angus bet on Dede's pick in the fourth race and Mayor, a gray mare didn't disappoint, but on the whole the group didn't win big at the horseraces.

When the last of the horses left the track, the grandstand began to fill with people eager to watch Model T Fords race around the track with pigs squealing under the arms of strong young men. People squeezed together to make room for the fans and clouds began to gather on the horizon.

"It looks like Eric Fowler and Rob Wakefield will race against each other," Pearl said.

"Want to put a little wager on who will win this race?" asked Richard, but no one took him up on it.

Finally, the Fords lined up on the starting line, a gun went off, racers grabbed their pigs, cranked their engines to life, and sped off around the track. One racer's pig escaped and after capturing it he continued around the track without stopping for a new pig, much to the amusement of the crowd. The other contestants horsed around, tripping each other on their way to their cars, and one even pushed another into the pig box. It was all done in the spirit of good fun.

Eric Fowler and Rob Wakefield were in the lead on the far side of the track when it happened. Suddenly there was a crash and both cars burst into flames. The crowd watched in disbelief as Eric Fowler ran from his burning Model T—a man on fire. Two pigs ran squealing away from the inferno miraculously unharmed. Rob Wakefield never left his seat. He died instantly in the explosion. People in the grandstand gasped and cried out in alarm while several ran toward the flames. Angus was on his feet and gone before Eleanor realized what had happened. She looked down to see Howard Wakefield lying on the floor of his private box—his fiancée screaming while Junie tried to administer CPR. Olivia Martin fainted. Cleo's friends from the valley stood nearby in shock. Edward Fowler stood frozen in his lonely box with a beer can crushed in his hand. It was chaos and pandemonium—a fair no one would ever forget. The darkening sky grew darker, lightning flashed, and the air smelled like bacon.

Later that evening after the horrifying events of the day came to their sad conclusion, the coffee group met at Dede's house to debrief and make some sense of the tragedy. They sat around Dede's dining table looking at pieces of pie none of them could eat.

"What happened?" Eleanor finally asked. A long silence ensued while the others wondered how to answer such a question.

Josephine finally spoke. "As far as we know, it was a terrible accident."

"It could have been caused by a faulty gas line in one of the cars. A spark could have ignited it," Mark speculated.

"You know, I saw Rob's car at the Service Center when I had my brakes checked there," Cleo said. "At the time I thought how handy it was his father owned a mechanic shop where his Model T could be serviced. Now I wonder if they did a lousy job on it like they did on my transmission."

"Maybe they did more than that," Dede speculated. "What if they pimped it up to go faster than it could handle and it blew up?"

"I heard someone say Rob's car had been filled with a high-octane fuel that caused it to go faster but was extremely flammable," said Pearl.

"From the video, it appears that Rob stopped suddenly because he lost his grip on the pig and Eric ran into him," Angus shared. "But Mark's right. There must have been a leak in the gas line to cause an explosion like that. I'm sure there will be an investigation."

"A leak in the gas line could have caused that high-octane fuel to drip on the track and ignite when they crashed, torching both cars," Richard said.

"Olivia Martin said Rob and Eric were fighting right before the race," Cleo said. "Do you think Eric nicked the gas line?"

"Anything is possible. Nothing like this has ever happened before at the fair," said Cary.

"Howard Wakefield made enemies too numerous to count," Angus said. "We may never know what really happened here."

"What about Eric? Do we know how he is?" asked Pearl.

"He was still alive when they took him away in the ambulance, but he won't be the same after those burns," Angus said. Eleanor could only imagine the horror Angus must have witnessed when he ran onto the track.

"Howard Wakefield didn't fare that well. He died on the floor of the grandstand," Dede said. Now he could no longer torture her with his desire for the infamous massage parlor. At least she hoped that dream died along with him.

"Wow, that means Junie is the sole heiress to the Wakefield fortune," said Cleo.

"Too bad she doesn't have Johnny to share it with her," said Eleanor.

"Maybe he's responsible for all this. His ghost has come back for revenge," Cleo said, humming a spooky tune.

It was suddenly quiet. "Well, they never found his body. Maybe she's got him hidden in that monstrosity they call their house," Pearl suggested.

"What you're suggesting is disturbing," Angus said solemnly. "It wouldn't be in Johnny's nature to play a part in something like that." The coffee ladies looked at each other under their lowered brows. There was a reason man were not invited to their coffee group. They took all the flippancy out of a mystery.

Eleanor needed to move, so she put on her walking shoes and took the path to the east. Up ahead she saw a crow throwing something into the air. It pecked at some small animal that jumped and fell to the ground so that the crow could peck and toss it again. Eleanor hurried to close the gap making lots of noise as she went hoping to save whatever it was from the crow's sharp beak. The crow flew off as she neared, and Eleanor saw a brown gopher laying on its back panting in exhaustion.

"I see you're alive," she said as she nudged it gently with her toe. The critter quickly turned on its stomach and lunged out at her in defense. Its front leg was injured. Eleanor looked around for the crow. It would come back as soon as she left the animal without protection. Not wanting to touch it for fear of being bitten, Eleanor picked some ferns and covered the poor victim hoping it could recover and move to a better hiding place.

She walked on and came to the burned-out shell that was once Will and Cynthia Chase's house. Someone had cleaned up most of the debris leaving only the chimney standing. So much fire and destruction lately made her wonder what the universe was trying to say. Burning was a way of purifying things. Perhaps this house needed a cleansing that only fire could provide. Rob and Eric were burned as well but she wouldn't let her mind go there. What she had witnessed was too terrible to revisit now and she was in no mood to blame the victims for crimes she wasn't sure they had committed. She hurried on her way wondering what secrets were lost in the house that Henry Ott built.

The sun was setting, and Eleanor saw a glimpse of its light between the storm clouds that were breaking on the horizon. She would have to hurry back or be caught in the growing dusk. As she returned to the spot where the gopher lay hidden, she stopped to see if he was still alive. There was no sign of him under the fern and Eleanor chose to believe that he had scurried somewhere safe until he could heal from his wounds. After all there was no body.

That night Eleanor dreamed about Rob Wakefield and Eric Fowler driving to her house in their Model T Fords. They were boys wearing scout uniforms with sashes covered with Nazi pins and badges. She invited them inside for milk and cookies and watched as someone outside tampered with their cars like the gnome on the wing of the airplane in that horrifying episode of *The Twilight Zone*. Eleanor sat looking out the window as Johnny Vargas wiped his sweaty face on two different T-shirts, leaving blood stains on both. Whenever Rob or Eric turned in his direction he magically disappeared. Then she watched as the two innocent youngsters climbed into their cars and burst into flames while Johnny peered out from the bushes giving her the thumbs up. Eleanor stood rooted inside her house and did nothing to help the burning children. She woke in a sweat. When the awful reality of the day's events sunk into her waking brain and she could no longer rest, she got up, made coffee, and went outside to see just how early the Sunday paper was delivered.

What did her dream mean? Was it just a reenactment of things that had already happened? Did she think Johnny had something to do with the gruesome accident? He was a mechanic after all and knew his way around an automobile. Surely, he could make one catch on fire, but not from the grave. There must be another explanation.

The coffee group met for breakfast on their usual day full of the latest gossip. "Eric Fowler was put in an induced coma to recover from his burns. They cover half of his body and the most dangerous thing for him is infection," said Pearl, who had a friend who worked at the hospital. "I heard they transferred him to a special burn unit in Portland."

"I heard his face will be disfigured and he'll need several surgeries—that is if he even survives," said Josephine who also knew someone who knew someone.

"Well, Howard Wakefield's men at the homeless shelter have all been packed off to wherever they came from. Several buses came for them and now they're gone." Dede sighed with satisfaction.

"Do you think Junie was responsible for that?" asked Eleanor.

"Oh, it was Junie all right. She's taken charge of everything Wakefield. Both funerals are scheduled for next week and she personally met with me to reassure me there will be no more talk of a massage parlor in Waterton. Edward Fowler, who was running against me for mayor, may or may not continue his campaign, but Wakefield money won't factor into it," Dede informed them. "I also heard the Waterton Service Center is up for sale."

"Do you think she was involved in Johnny's disappearance in any way?" asked Eleanor as she recalled her dream.

"Any investigation involving her brother and Eric Fowler is over. They don't investigate dead people, do they?" asked Pearl.

"Eric Fowler isn't dead, but Angus says the case has grown cold and without new evidence they've put the investigation on hold," said Eleanor.

"I'm glad," said Pearl who didn't approve of the busybody ways of her friends.

"I bet we could learn a lot if we staked out Junie Wakefield's house. If she is involved, she might get careless thinking the investigation is over," said Cleo.

"Just what do you think she's done?" asked Dede who was suddenly quite fond of Junie.

"If she's been hiding Johnny in that house, he might slip out where we could see him," Cleo said.

"He's not in that house," said Josephine. "Remember her father and brother lived there as well, not to mention a slew of housekeepers and other employees."

"Plus, the police searched the house looking for evidence after Wanda turned in the bloody T-shirt," Eleanor said.

"So, how long did Anne Frank hide in the attic before the Germans found her?" asked Cleo. "Maybe there are underground tunnels or secret rooms."

"Remember that book we read for book club where that woman hid her lover in her father's house for months?" asked Pearl. The others thought about that for a while.

"If we went on a stakeout it might be weeks before we saw anything if we ever did," said Dede. "Johnny Vargas is probably dead."

"There must be a better way," said Cleo. "Let me think on it." Pearl just put her head down and sighed.

"Eleanor, you're friends with Junie, why not just ask her if we can tour her house?" asked Cleo.

"That's a wonderful idea," said Dede. "I've always wanted to get a look at Howard Wakefield's inner sanctum. It might give me some idea of the workings of his mind."

"Dede, he's no longer a threat to you. Remember he's dead," Pearl reminded. She didn't know that Dede feared Howard Wakefield had a dossier on her and she wanted to see what was in it.

"I don't know," Eleanor hesitated, "It seems coldhearted to ask for such a thing so soon after Junie has lost the three most important men in her life."

"I bet he has a fabulous library," Josephine said. "Maybe we could use that as a pretext for getting into the house. We could say we're looking for donations from his library so we can name a wing after him at our county branch."

"Excellent." Cleo approved.

"Junie loves to read and was hoping to volunteer at the library. I don't know if she even had time to do that before Johnny went missing," Eleanor said.

"Pearl, aren't you on the board of directors of the library?" asked Dede. "Maybe you could get something that looks official for our investigation."

Pearl rolled her eyes. She did not like stakeouts, breakins, or deceit of any kind but was continuously drawn in to all three by these amateur detectives. "I'll do it, but I want to know exactly what we're looking for once we get inside."

"You will be looking for books. Books that might be of value to our Waterton County Library," Dede said.

"We, on the other hand, will be looking for clues that Johnny Vargas is hiding somewhere inside that house," said Cleo.

"I'll make a call," said Eleanor.

"Ladies, please come in." Junie Vargas looked very much like the lady of the manor as she welcomed the coffee group inside the foyer of her grand home.

"You've had so many misfortunes, Junie, thank you for allowing us to intrude," Eleanor said. "I'm so very sorry for your losses."

"It's quite all right," Junie said. "I'm thrilled to think that some of my family's books will be included in the library's special collections. Would you ladies like to get started? I have a few things I need to attend to so if you don't need me, I'll leave you to make your selections. When you're finished, we'll have tea in the dining room." As Junie led them to the library the ladies' heads swiveled as they took in every detail of the Wakefield house.

The foyer was lined with rich dark wood and travertine tiles and featured several stained glass windows above the doors that lit the room revealing a grand stairway that circled gracefully to the second floor. A massive crystal chandelier hung from the vaulted ceiling. The library was off to the right behind French doors that opened into a circular room with a spiral staircase in the center that rose to another floor. A desk with two heavy brown leather chairs sat on one side.

"I'll see you ladies in the dining room in about an hour?" As soon as Junie closed the doors behind her they began their search: Pearl looking for books that would make an appropriate donation and the others tapping the walls for a secret door.

"Every mansion worth its salt has a secret room in the library," said Cleo as she knocked on walls and listened for the telltale hollow sound.

Eleanor hunted for levers like the one in Henry Ott's shelf that unlocked his secret room while Josephine and Dede climbed the stairs seeking other clues. Pearl meticulously scanned the shelves for worthy books and placed her selections carefully on the desk.

It didn't take long for Eleanor to finger a button that caused a shelf to slide open revealing a stairway down. Cleo and Eleanor signaled the others and disappeared down the stairs. "I wish we had thought to bring a flashlight," whispered Eleanor as she felt her way down the steps. Cleo took her cell phone out of her pocket, turned on its flashlight, and followed close behind. When they reached the bottom there was a small room that seemed to have no exit until Eleanor found a similar button that opened a panel into a large basement room that looked like a men's club.

Thick dark burgundy carpets covered the floor and leather chairs were arranged in a semicircle around a podium. Animal heads were mounted on the walls like trophies and lush plants added a tropical flair along with ceiling fans made of solid walnut carved in the shape of leaves. In one corner was a bar, complete with every top-shelf intoxicant available. On the counter was a box filled with Cuban cigars and a case of Black Jack chewing gum. A large pool table filled the other end of the room.

"I don't see any signs that someone is living down here," said Cleo.

"No," said Eleanor. "There must be another stairway down here. I wonder if Wanda ever discovered the secret passage." As if to answer her question voices came from a stairway hidden around the corner from the pool table.

"I hate coming down here," came a voice. "There's something creepy about this place and it smells."

"You've been listening to too many stories. There's nothing down here but spiders and dust bunnies."

Eleanor and Cleo hurried back to the panel and barely closed the door in time before two maids appeared with cleaning supplies. The two snoops froze behind the panel until they heard the sound of the vacuum and felt it was safe to move. Cleo tripped in the dark on the first step and they froze again hoping the maids hadn't heard. Sensing something amiss on the stair, Cleo turned on her cell light and saw that the step was raised slightly. On closer inspection she noticed hinges that allowed the step to open much like a lid revealing a thin brown leather book, a banner claiming *White Makes Right*, and a gavel inside. Eleanor took the book and the two tiptoed up the stairs and reappeared in the library where Pearl, Josephine, and Dede waited nervously.

"It was just a meeting room slash "wreck" room, man cave," said Cleo.

"But we did find this book in a hiding spot under one of the steps," said Eleanor as she undid the strap and lifted the flap. "It's a Bible." Then as she thumbed through it she saw a list of names, much like a teacher's attendance roster, glued onto one of the pages. "They must have held secret meetings down there and kept a list of members in this book. It includes names as well as dollar amounts that could be either donations or debts. I can't tell what it all means."

"I've never seen a Bible that thin," said Dede. "I wonder why they choose that book."

"Dede and I found this hollow book upstairs," said Josephine. "There are several medals and pins with Nazi insignia on them."

"That's like the one they found in Eric Fowler's library. They must not have done as thorough a search here," Eleanor said.

"What do we do with this?" asked Dede.

"Put those two books in my bag," ordered Pearl. "I've put together a classic collection in those boxes that will make the Wakefield family extremely proud as well as enhance our county library. The Wakefields won't get a wing but they can have a collection on a special shelf of honor." They closed all the secret doors that opened up a great many questions, and met Junie in the dining room for tea.

The Wakefield dining room was surprisingly cozy. The long polished mahogany table hugging a fireplace was set for tea for six. Junie sat at its head dressed in a simple sleeveless sheath and presided over the event with poise and grace. Eleanor detected no trace of that young uncertain girl she remembered when Johnny and Junie were first wed.

"How are you holding up, Junie?" asked Josephine.

"I'm fine, really. There's been so much to do planning the funerals and taking care of Father's business dealings that I haven't had time to feel sorry for myself." Junie sighed. "Honestly, we weren't a close-knit family. My father and brother were difficult men to understand, and harder to love."

"Have you had any help from your father's fiancée?" asked Pearl.

"Heavens no, she left as soon as Father was pronounced dead. She claimed it would be too painful for her to attend the funeral so she and her brother, if he was her brother, are gone for good. I really have to admit I'm relieved. It was obvious to everyone that she was only after his money. He probably suspected that and never really planned to marry her at all since he wasn't having a prenup written. He was good at using people. When she realized she wasn't getting what she wanted, she was out of here, but I'm afraid the police may be on her heels. My father's autopsy report showed an elevated amount of digitalis in his system. They found some of the drug in her hotel room. It didn't cause his heart attack, but the medical examiner said it would have killed him over time since he suffered from a heart condition. I'm sure his fiancée was hoping it wouldn't take effect until *after* she married him."

"That's terrible," said Josephine.

"But not unexpected. My father wasn't the loveable sort." Junie shrugged.

"What are your plans for the future?" asked Dede.

"I'll put Father's affairs in order here and travel. I have friends that I'd like to visit. There really isn't anything for me in

Waterton anymore," she sighed. Eleanor thought it was a sigh of relief and not sadness.

"I guess Eric Fowler is out of the picture," said Eleanor.

"He was never in the picture. Let's just say he got me through a painful period." Junie's expression was unreadable.

"We've boxed our selections and left them in your library," Pearl said. "You might want to look through them before someone from the County Library comes to pick them up. I'll be sure to have them call first."

"I'm sure your selections will be fine. It's better for those books to go where people will use and enjoy them. We were never encouraged to use the library. It was Father's special place." Junie said. "I'll have someone here take them to your car."

"The house is beautiful," Cleo said. "It's so huge, I can imagine playing hide and seek here must have been a challenge when you were little."

"Several rooms were off limits. Rob and I were afraid of the basement when we were little because we heard strange things. Even after we grew up, I never wanted to go down there, although Rob often joined Father and his friends for drinks and cards. At least that's what they told me they did down there, although I've had my suspicions."

"What did you think they were doing?" asked Josephine.

"You know my Father was not a nice man and the people he associated with were like him, bigoted and mean." Junie paused, "I just had the feeling that they hurt people."

"But not anymore," said Dede.

"There will always be haters," said Junie. They spent the rest of their time sipping tea and nibbling lemon scones. There was no sign that Johnny Vargas had ever entered these rooms.

"Who are these people and what do these figures mean?" asked Pearl sitting at Cleo's patio table as she tried to make sense of the information in the Bible.

"None of these names are people I know, and they all sound German," said Dede, who knew almost everyone in the county.

"Maybe these are fake names for real people who want to remain anonymous," said Cleo.

"If you combine the information the police found in the Fowler residence, Wanda's description of the meetings, and the medals and pins discovered today, I'd guess we have our very own Nazi organization here in Waterton," Josephine said.

"I agree," said Eleanor. "It's a socially unacceptable group to belong to so it makes sense that they would want to keep their organization a secret and their membership anonymous. I wonder just what these members do. Adolph Eichmann and Josef Mengele were famous Nazis."

"Let me Google some of the other names on this list and see what comes up." Cleo went inside to get her tablet and came back with a large pitcher of sangria.

"Walter Rauff was a Nazi who worked on the mobile gas chambers that were responsible for killing more than 100,000 people during the war," Cleo said as she poured a glass of sangria for everyone. Each of the names on the list turned out to be a notorious Nazi war criminal who made their way to South America.

"I know these aren't the real Nazis. Some of these men are dead or were captured and punished," said Josephine. "This must be a way of acting out their fantasies of racism and bigotry by assuming the names of their heroes."

"What do you think the money amounts are?" asked Pearl.

"What if these are donations used to undercut the progress of people they don't approve of," said Dede thinking of the campaign to defeat her run for mayor. "It wouldn't surprise me to learn that Howard Wakefield donated large sums of money to back white supremacists."

"Now I'm sure Cynthia Chase didn't burn down her house," Eleanor said.

"Oh, maybe these lunatics are responsible for that church fire too," said Pearl.

"Right, the cause was suspicious, but no one was ever charged, even though it opened the door for Howard Wakefield to buy up that property," added Dede.

"I bet if we could discover the real names of these Nazi wannabes, they'd match those running for city council and mayor," Cleo said.

"And they might also include some high-ranking officials who could stifle an investigation into arson," Josephine added. "It seems as if corruption is everywhere."

"How strange that Rob Wakefield died by fire," mused Eleanor. "Do you think that's a coincidence?"

"They say Karma never forgets an address," said Cleo.

Angus sat at Eleanor's dining table studying the book that the coffee ladies found in the step at Howard Wakefield's house. "There aren't any clues to who these people might be in this book," he said. "There may be more documents hidden away that weren't found during the search."

"Are you surprised that Howard Wakefield didn't keep his secrets in his safe?" asked Eleanor.

"We found his safe and searched it, but no one discovered the secret staircase. I'm sure he was counting on that." Angus said. "The police could do another search to see if they can recover more from the secret room."

"What would be the point of that now that both Rob and his father are dead?" asked Eleanor.

"That depends on what they find," Angus said. "The names of those who are engaged in hate crimes might be valuable tools to solving those crimes. There may be evidence of arson, jury tampering, and bribery. We won't know until we look."

"It's not a crime to belong to an organization that believes white men are superior, is it?" asked Eleanor.

"Not in this country," Angus said, "But this could be what the authorities need to link some big-shot names to some small-time crimes."

The funeral service for Rob and Howard Wakefield was an unusual one. It didn't take place in a church but at the Waterton County Fairgrounds. There were no priests or ministers to officiate only a lavish dinner catered by Salvador Dolly who received double payment in advance. In this case, Junie was acting out the role of karma. The entire county was invited through an ad published in the *Fish Wrapper*. In many ways, the funeral mirrored Junie's wedding to Johnny without the dancing.

Junie greeted the guests, many who came out of curiosity or simply to get a free meal and didn't know either of the deceased. The number of people who came to the funeral gave testimony to the county's real feelings for the Wakefield men. Only a fraction of the county residents showed their faces at this somber Wakefield event in contrast with the vast numbers that attended Junie and Johnny's wedding. Each was given a package of Black Jack gum, Rob's favorite, and a deck of cards with Howard's pet quote: *"One should always play fairly when one has the winning cards."* ~ Oscar Wilde.

There were no eulogies given. Junie feared what people might say. In reality, there was little to indicate that the event was held in the honor of father and son. Two oversized photos sat on a table at one end of the large hall, but that was all.

Eleanor and Angus went for Junie's sake and sat at a table with Johnny's sister, Sofia and her husband, Al. "Catch any fish lately?" Angus asked Al as they ate roasted salmon. The conversation evolved into a series of fishing stories the way it so often did when Angus socialized with other fishermen.

"How are you doing, Sofia?" Eleanor asked. "I haven't seen you in months."

Sofia looked up under her dark lashes and smiled shyly, "I'm good. Thank you for asking. I often feel like the invisible grieving woman. Losing your brother doesn't count in the same way as losing your spouse but it hurts just the same."

"I'm sorry, it must be very painful."

"Painful to watch his widow suffer," Sofia said bitterly. "I feel sorry that she has no family now. We all love Junie and have tried to include her in our family. Family was everything to Johnny. It hurt him to leave our parents in El Morro. He would have expected us to treat Junie as family." Eleanor nodded. She felt that listening was better than offering empty words.

"I don't see Olivia here today. She seemed so in love with Rob Wakefield, yet she doesn't even attend his funeral?" Sofia noted. "Eric is alive, and she acted as though she loved him too, but now that his pretty face is ruined, she has abandoned him as well. His recovery will be long and painful."

Eleanor was surprised at Sofia's tone that oozed a bitter satisfaction. It must have shown on her face because Sofia continued to justify her feelings. "It is no more than he deserves. He was a bigot and a coward who tormented Johnny for no other reason than the color of his skin. That's why it was so difficult to watch Junie with him," Sofia said.

"She wasn't with him for long. I'm sure she realized he would never be the man Johnny was." Eleanor tried to apply some balm to Sofia's hurt. "Do you think Johnny was murdered?"

Sofia's head rose with a jerk as she looked around the room. The word 'murdered' seemed to agitate her. "I know he is gone. I know Rob Wakefield and Eric Fowler did things to hurt him and yet he protected them for Junie's sake. I only ever wanted him to be happy. He is my brother and I miss him. I know for sure he is in a better place." Her eyes filled and a tear rolled down her cheek.

Junie chose this time to visit their table and hug Sofia and smile brightly at Eleanor and Angus before she wandered off again. Eleanor couldn't help but notice she was wearing her wedding ring. The large diamond flashed and for the first time Eleanor wondered how Johnny afforded it. Was this her way of telling the community that she had recovered from a brief but miserable period in her life where she had lost her equilibrium? Eleanor reminded herself that she could not judge the way someone grieved. Hadn't she done something similar when

Walter was lost to her by turning to Angus? Surely others had judged her for that. There were some private and personal things in life that you shouldn't have to explain: grief and love were two.

The dog days of summer were upon them. Even the coast was warm and sunny and Sand Beach was crowded with tourists. It didn't matter anymore if it was the weekend or not, they came from the valley in droves to escape the summer heat. Eleanor had risen early and walked the shore before most were awake. It seemed the older she got the less time she had for lying in bed. The sky was a brilliant blue and filled with the cry of gulls and the bark of sea lions that bathed on the rocks beyond the surf.

Eleanor sat at her table studying the Bible they found at the Wakefield house. It wasn't the first time she had looked at it trying to discover some clue that would give her the real names of the members of the mysterious group. The names had been pasted over a page from the book of Romans. Eleanor read the verses on the opposite page:

Let every person be subject to the governing authorities. For there is no authority except from God, and those that exist have been instituted by God. Therefore, he who resists the authorities resists what God has appointed, and those who resist will incur judgment. For rulers are not a terror to good conduct, but to bad. Would you have no fear of him who is in authority? Then do what is good, and you will receive his approval, for he is God's servant for your good. But if you do wrong, be afraid, for he does not bear the sword in vain; he is the servant of God to execute his wrath on the wrongdoer.

Images of Hitler came instantly into Eleanor's mind. If the readers of this passage believed what it said, they might accept that Hitler's authority came from God. Whoa! There lay the danger of blind acceptance without critical thinking. Not all leaders are servants of God. Some serve themselves. Some are tyrants and despots who practice pettiness and revenge. Eleanor couldn't believe this was something written in a book many believed to be the undisputed word of God. She went to her computer and typed in Romans 13 and Nazis. Maybe her interpretation was wrong, but she found that it was not. Nazis and slave owners quoted Romans 13 to justify immorality, bigotry, and evil. The British loyalists used it against the rebellious colonies in their fight for independence, and Southern preachers cited it before the Civil War when Northern abolitionists defied the Fugitive Slave Act.

It was interesting that this passage was next to their list of members. Maybe it was not coincidence, but a plan. Eleanor picked up her phone and called Angus. "Hey, Darling," Angus said. "I was just thinking of you. I've put together a lunch. Let's go to the Picnic Grounds and enjoy a relaxing afternoon by the river."

"I think I've figured something out that might help us identify our Nazis," Eleanor said.

"What is it?" Angus was instantly interested.

"Pick me up in 20 minutes. I'll make a call and then I can show you." Eleanor knew when something felt right the way the last piece of a puzzle just had to fit. After Angus hung up, Eleanor called Junie Vargas.

Angus' punctuality was a trait Eleanor loved about him. He never kept her waiting, and today was no different. On their way to the Wakefield house, Eleanor explained what she had found out about Romans 13 and how she thought it might help them identify the members of the group who met at the Wakefield house.

Junie opened the door and greeted them warmly. Several suitcases sat in the foyer. "Are you planning a trip?" asked Angus.

"Yes," was her only response as she led them to the library. "Is there something in particular you are looking for, Eleanor?"

"A Bible, I'm looking for a Bible. Do you know if there is one in this library?" Eleanor asked.

"There's a family Bible over here." she walked over to a large red leather-bound Bible that sat by itself on an easel.

"May I look at it?" Eleanor asked.

"Yes, it's very old. My great grandfather brought it with him from England. I believe it has a record of our family history in it. I don't think anyone has read it or even opened it in ages." Eleanor opened it to Romans 13 and there stuck tightly between the pages was a sheet of paper with a list of German Nazis and their American counterparts.

Angus looked at it closely and asked Junie, "Do you mind if we take your Bible? It might help us solve a case we're working on. I don't think it has anything to do with your family history."

Junie frowned in bewilderment. "Will you bring it back?"

"Absolutely," Angus reassured her.

"Then yes, of course, take it." It was obvious Junie wanted to be on her way.

"We don't want to keep you, Junie," Eleanor said. "Thank you for your help."

"Where are you going?" Angus asked bluntly.

"I'm going to Rio. I have some friends there I haven't seen in a long time," Junie smiled.

"Well, be safe, Junie." Eleanor felt a hug was in order. Angus merely nodded and wished her well and then they were off down the road to the Picnic Grounds. They had no idea it would be the last time they would see Junie Vargas in Waterton.

The Picnic Grounds was a grassy area by the river that was shaded by a grove of alder trees. It was once owned by the Knights of Columbus, a men's group affiliated with St. John's Catholic Church and used for church picnics until it was purchased by a private owner who was an avid fisherman and friend of Angus.

Eleanor spread their blanket on the grass and Angus unpacked the picnic basket. "I hope you're hungry,"

Angus said. "I packed enough food for four people and two alcoholics."

Eleanor was still savoring the joy of solving the mystery of the Nazi roster. "I can't believe some of those names on the list."

"That was good detective work, Ellie," he said as he put his arm around her. "I'm sure the DA's office can use that list to investigate various hate crimes in this county."

"Do you think it will put a stop to them?" she asked.

"I hope so. Let's celebrate." Angus poured a glass of wine for Eleanor and opened a bottle of beer for himself. They clinked their drinks together, "To justice."

"I visited Gladys the other day," Angus admitted. "No one has died since Peter Fowler went missing. Of course, Artemas has not visited either and she still thought he was linked, so I did a little investigating on my own."

"What did you discover, Detective McBride?" Eleanor asked.

"One very observant resident saw Peter Fowler leaving the room of a woman with dementia during the night. The next morning, they found her dead. No one suspected foul play, and no one asked any questions. Gladys thinks Peter may have become agitated after Artemas visited and it stirred up some residual feelings that led him to commit murder," Angus said.

"But how?" asked Eleanor.

"He probably just put a pillow over her head and suffocated her," Angus speculated. "None of the dead were autopsied, so there's no proof but there will be an investigation and the residents will be questioned. Who knows what will turn up? Gladys' suspicions were grounded on the fact that the nighttime deaths followed Artemas' visits to Peter. The old girl still has her wits about her and she feels much safer now that both of those men are out of the picture."

"Another mystery solved!"

The clinked their drinks together again and toasted, "To curious old women!"

It was a perfect day. A light breeze blew over the water cooling the August air. They feasted on ham and cheese sandwiches, potato chips, and fresh peaches and dozed in each other's arms as the river sang its summer song and caught the sun's glimmer. Eleanor awoke to Angus' gaze.

"Let's take a walk by the river," he suggested as he took her hand and pulled her to her feet.

"I think I'm too old to sleep on the ground," Eleanor complained as she stretched the stiffness from her body.

He smiled at her. "You are anything but old." They walked along the bank, every now and then hopping from one rock to the next.

"This is where I caught the biggest trout I've ever seen," Angus said, pointing to a deep pool.

"I think I see a trout in there now," Eleanor teased. "Did you bring your pole?" She picked up a stone and skipped it over the pool.

"Remind me not to bring you fishing. You'd scare them away. That was a pretty good skip though . . . for a girl." Angus picked up a rock and threw it, besting her by making his stone skip four times and almost landing on the other side of the river. Looking for the perfect skipping stone and trying to outdo each other made the afternoon fly.

"We'd better get back." Angus said, "I'm almost hungry again." He didn't want to bring up the fact that Johnny Vargas most likely would have anchored his boat and fished here or that he was with Johnny when he caught the biggest trout he'd ever caught in that deep pool. His mind was filled with memories of Johnny, but he didn't want to fill Eleanor's head with them and spoil a delightful summer day. He wanted her memories of this day to be filled with him.

When they were almost back to their picnic spot Eleanor spied something blue caught between two rocks. She stooped to pick it up. It was the wrapper from a stick of Black Jack chewing gum. "Was Rob Wakefield a fisherman?" Eleanor asked.

"He was definitely a litterbug," Angus said.

But as for the cowardly, the faithless, the detestable, as for murderers, the sexually immoral, sorcerers, idolaters, and all liars, their portion will be in the lake that burns with fire and sulfur, which is the second death.

~ Revelation 21:8

"This is where we found the list of victims and future victims in the Wakefield's Bible," Angus said as he sat at Eleanor's table. "The family Bible acted as a filing cabinet and documented various crimes committed by the members of this organization. It included several Hispanic families, as well as Artemas Chase, Wanda, and the mayor of Waterton, to name but a few. I don't believe for a minute there is any religious validation here. They simply used these words to justify actions that would get them the results they wanted to suit their own ends. Howard Wakefield wanted the massage parlor so he had his thugs burn down the church so he could purchase the property. It would be an ideal location and when Dede got in his way, she became a target too.

Wanda's brakes were tampered with when they learned of her relationship to the man who exposed Howard's corrupt business practices. They took a closer look at her when she turned in the bloody T-shirt. Being a racist made it necessary to burn down the homes of brown people and when his buddy, Peter Fowler disappeared, they got revenge on the Chase family by burning down their house." He felt no need to worry her with the fact that his name was also on that list along with Gladys Reyburg.

"What happens now?" asked Eleanor who worried for her friend, Dede.

"We turn in this evidence to the police who will use it to make a case against them. Now that the head of the snake is cut off, the rest of it will surely die," Angus said.

"Peter Fowler was the mentor for all these would-be Nazis. Who knows how many innocent lives were touched by his hatred and bigotry? He lived here a long time," Eleanor said.

"We'll never know the answer to that, but we have Artemas Chase to thank for ridding this community of him."

"Do you know what happened to him?" Eleanor asked.

"Who, Artemas or Peter?"

"Do you know about either?"

"No, that's above my security clearance," Angus smiled. He was sure the threat was over, but he was wrong.

Eleanor woke to a day clear of obligations. Summer was turning into fall and the newspaper was filled with ads for back-to-school bargains. She completed her morning routine and set out on a well-deserved walk on the beach. It was early and the sandy expanse was all hers. The cool air felt invigorating after the heat of the last few weeks and Eleanor walked quickly hoping to plan one last dinner with her family before the obligations of their lives began in earnest once again. She would call them as soon as she returned home and invite them, plan a menu, drive to town for essentials, and prepare for a lovely family get together. Her once free day had become one filled with tasks to complete.

As she finished her route, she decided to stop at Suzanna's to see how Mattie was doing now that Artemas was gone. The Do Nothings sat at their table and, surprisingly, Mattie greeted Eleanor with a big smile.

"I'm so happy to see you, Mattie," Eleanor said.

"Sit down, Eleanor, and tell us what's going on in the world," Mattie said, her smile growing larger.

"Yes, sit down and have coffee with us," said Mavis.

"I'm sure you're dying to know what Mattie's so happy about," said Sybil glumly.

"Do tell," Eleanor said.

"Well, I was just sharing this letter I got from Artemas. I think it's the most romantic thing I've ever heard," Mattie said. "Just listen:

My Darling Mattie,

You've pierced my soul. You don't realize how fascinating you are and how dangerously attractive you've become to me. You influence me for the better. You are the one object of my desire. When I am with you, I feel that I am home. I love you without question, without reason, without reckoning. My love has made me selfish I know. I am forgetful of everything but seeing you again yet I am half agony half hope. Am I too late? I love no one but you but if you do not believe it, if you do not trust it, I must convince you of it. Leave your home by the sea and spend the rest of your days with me. Forever and always,

Artemas

Eleanor was speechless. "Close your mouth dear," Mattie ordered. "It's amazing, I know."

After she regained her composure Eleanor asked, "So are you going to take him up on his offer?"

"Absolutely, I feel the same way about him. This kind of love doesn't happen to people every day. I'd be a fool not to go to him. Mattie was all smiles. Mavis sighed loudly.

"I guess we'll just have to make do without you, Mattie," Sybil said. "Believe me, I'm happy for you." "Will you sell your house?" asked Eleanor.

"No, I think I'll rent it. That way if things don't go to plan, I'll have a place to come back to." Mattie was the practical sort.

"Where is Artemas?" Eleanor pried.

"I can't tell you now because I don't know exactly," Mattie confided. "He called and someone is coming for me in two days. They will take me to him. I'll know more then."

"Will you be staying with Will and Cynthia?" Mavis asked.

"No, I'm sure of that. Artemas and I can take care of each other. All this must be kept secret because Artemas says his name is on a list that puts his life in danger. Evidently there are people who don't value his line of work," Mattie whispered. "They may even blame him for the deaths of the Wakefields."

"Is that even possible?" Eleanor was surprised. She was sure Artemas and his family left town before that gruesome affair took place. "You won't be in danger will you Mattie?"

Mattie shrugged. "Life is dangerous, but I plan to live it anyway. I was hoping you would look after my little house, Eleanor. I don't want to leave any clues to my whereabouts."

"Certainly, I'll come over later and get your instructions," Eleanor promised.

On her way home, Eleanor stopped at the hidey-hole and pulled out a note that read:

Dear Ellie,

I am not a poet, but I am a man in love. The words needed to express that don't come easily to me. For a long time, I thought my actions were enough to convince you of my feelings for you, but now I know that words are important to you and since you are important to me, I will try. I love you. I love you. I love you.

Without you my world is a dark and lonely place filled with fish and reruns of NCIS. You haven't pierced my soul; you are my soul.
Angus

Eleanor was moved. This was not some note Angus had copied. These were his true feelings in his own words. She wondered how long it had taken Angus to write this love letter. The image of him sitting at his table, pen in hand, struggling to find the right words made her smile all the way home.

That afternoon Eleanor welcomed her family to the last barbeque of the season. Amy and Taylor arrived first with Elise, Addie, and Wesley who gravitated to the Bosendorfer to play duets and sing songs. Feathers followed repeating words here and there and bobbing to the music causing the children to laugh at his antics. Amy tossed a green salad while Eleanor put the finishing touches on the chicken burgers with barbeque onion sauce and Taylor fired up the grill. Angus came shortly before Erin and Ben and began mixing everyone a drink. Ruby and Mitch found their cousins and set up a karaoke machine they brought in the hopes of entertaining everyone after dinner. It was a lovely afternoon with a cloudless sky that promised a magnificent sunset.

"Sometimes I wish we lived at the beach too," Erin said as she sipped her gin and tonic on the deck overlooking the vast Pacific Ocean. "I just love coming here and having Mom cook for us."

"FYI it isn't always this pleasant at the beach," Taylor said.

"You have to endure many rainy days to enjoy the few we get that are this sweet," Angus concurred.

"What! Are you trying to dissuade us from moving here? I think you just want it all to yourselves," Erin accused.

"Mom doesn't always cook for us either," Amy said. "I think this is only the second time we've been here all summer."

"That's because you're so busy," Eleanor countered.

"Well, we won't be after school starts. I've cut back on my hours at work and the kids are only doing two activities this year. Both Taylor and I are limiting ourselves to one community service so we can spend time at home together. There was just too much busy and not enough joy in our lives, and it was killing us," Amy said. "We will be free every Wednesday for your dining pleasure, Mom."

"I can swing that," Eleanor said. "Perhaps we should keep Sundays open for you, Erin."

"That would be sweet, but I won't be able to swing it. You know I work most weekends," Erin replied, "And I like to stay home when I'm not working."

"I'll take what I can get." Eleanor flipped the burgers onto a plate and announced dinner was ready.

"Knock, knock, Gramma," said Wesley as he filled his plate.

"Who's there?"

"Gorilla."

"Gorilla who?"

"Gorilla burger! I've got the buns!"

"Knock, knock," said Addie.

"Who's there?" asked Ruby.

"Beef," said Addie.

"Beef who?"

"Before I freeze out here, open the door," laughed Addie.

"Why do hamburgers make poor pigeons?" asked Elise.

"Why *do* hamburgers make poor pigeons?" asked Angus.

"They won't talk no matter how you grill them!" Elise answered.

The jokes continued with a mix of laughter and groans while dinner was eaten on the deck. As the evening cooled, they moved into the house and enjoyed the kids singing karaoke accompanied by Feathers who did his best to steal the show with his fancy footwork and bobble head. The grownups were not allowed to participate so they countered by eating Eleanor's delicious blackberry pie and vanilla bean ice cream.

As the sky turned a fiery orange and the sun began to set, goodbyes were said, hugs and kisses were given, and Eleanor was left with Angus and a messy kitchen.

"Knock, knock," he said as he took Eleanor in his arms.

"Who's there?"

"Olive"

"Olive who?"

"Olive you, do you love me too?"

"You know I do," she answered and sealed it with a kiss.

Early the next morning Eleanor woke from a strange dream. She sat next to Angus at the fairgrounds as a couple in white stood on a stage under an arbor decorated with a rainbow of summer flowers. With their backs to their guests, they made their vows then turned to face the crowd. Eleanor thought she was watching a repeat of Junie and Johnny's wedding but when the bride and groom turned it was Mattie and Artemas who stood beaming with happiness while smoke and flames appeared in the background.

Eleanor lay in bed wondering if it meant anything other than that Mattie planned to move in with Artemas. She knew from reading about dreams in the past that weddings foretold of a funeral or some bitter news for the dreamer, but Eleanor was not a believer in psychic nonsense. She shook off the uneasy feeling and convinced herself it was only the residue of past experiences filtering into her unconscious mind. She rolled out of bed and went to free Feathers.

"Good morning you silly bird," she said. "Have you recovered from your night of wild dancing?"

"Good morning, good morning," Feathers greeted her as he stretched and then flew into the kitchen to help make coffee. It was a gray day and there was a chill in the air as Eleanor went out to fetch the morning paper. She thought she could smell rain and hurried to complete her puzzles so she could get in a morning walk before the weather changed.

Walking to Mattie's house seemed a natural thing to do since she had promised Mattie to stop by and get her instructions for taking care of the house while she was away. As she approached the cozy gray shingled cottage, Eleanor felt a sense of dread descend on her. An ambulance sat in the driveway, but no lights flashed. She ran to the open front door almost colliding with an EMT who was about to exit. He gave her a look of sad concern.

"Are you a friend?" he asked kindly.

"Yes, what happened?" Eleanor was breathless.

"We got a call this morning saying she was having a heart attack. When we got here, she was still alive but we weren't able to save her. I'm sorry, but your friend didn't make it."

"Can I see her?"

"No, she's already in the ambulance. Are you Eleanor Penrose by any chance?"

"Yes, I am,"

"She left a letter for you inside. She was adamant that you receive it so it must be important."

Eleanor watched as the man drove the ambulance away with Mattie inside. He hadn't even closed the door to the house or checked to be sure she was Eleanor Penrose. None of this made any sense. Yesterday Mattie was so happy to embark on an adventure and now she was dead. Shock made her numb. She stumbled into Mattie's house and saw the letter on her kitchen table. Eleanor's name was written on the outside of the envelope. She wandered around the kitchen and noticed a teacup broken on the floor. Mattie must have dropped it when she realized she was having a heart attack. Eleanor went into her bedroom and saw the neatly made bed covered with a pink floral comforter and mauve dust ruffle, Mattie's little fuzzy slippers tucked neatly by one side. Eleanor sighed deeply, picked up the phone and called Angus. While she waited for him, she opened the envelope and read Mattie May's last will and testament.

Along with Mattie's shocking death came a moratorium of all things related to Johnny Vargas's investigation and the evidence found about the Nazi organization. Eleanor was consumed by the details involved in managing her estate.

"Mattie May is gone. It's hard to believe," said Dede.

"First it was Eva and now Mattie. The Do Nothings are soon going to be the Nothings," said Cleo.

"I'm not so sure I believe she *is* gone," said Eleanor. "The last time I saw her she said someone was coming to take her to Artemas but she didn't know where he was. We were supposed to keep it hush-hush because he was on a list that put his life in danger. The next thing I know, Mattie is dead and being driven away in an ambulance and there's an envelope on the table with my name on it."

"Do you think she was murdered?" asked Pearl.

"I never saw a body," Eleanor said. "I think they came and took her and want everyone to think she is dead so she can't lead them to Artemas."

"Wow, that's high drama, Eleanor. What was in the envelope?" asked Josephine.

"It was her last will and testament," Eleanor said.

"Did she leave instructions for a funeral?" asked Dede.

"Yes, no funeral. Her body was taken to a medical facility in Portland for research. She left everything she owned to me."

"What are you going to do with all her things?" asked Pearl.

"I'm thinking I'll invite her close friends to her house for a gathering and let them select a memento to keep. I'll serve a lunch or maybe a tea and we can remember her and cry together." Eleanor rested her head on her hand.

"I like that idea. Are you inviting us?" asked Cleo.

"Absolutely, I'll need someone to help me with the food and cleanup." It didn't take long for Eleanor to organize a small tea party in honor of Mattie. The surprising thing was how many people turned up.

Every time she talked to one of Mattie's friends, they suggested two more.

Eleanor selected several knick-knacks from Mattie's house and arranged them on a table with a sign that said 'Take something of Mattie's." She enlisted Sybil and Mavis to help her with this and was gratified when they took first dibs on the things that gave them happy memories of their dear friend. Dede baked a beautiful cake and Pearl and Cleo served it along with tea and mints. When everyone had passed through and shared their Mattie stories, the coffee group ladies sat down with the remaining Do Nothings.

"I'm still amazed I knew so little about Mattie," confessed Eleanor as she picked up an old photo album and leafed through the pages stopping at a picture of a young man holding a toddler. "Was this her husband?"

"Yes, that's Lyle and their son Miles. He was hit by a car and died when he was still a little boy. It broke Mattie's heart. He was their only child. I'm not sure she wanted any more children after that, so she threw herself into her work as a pharmacist," Sybil said.

"Miles died years ago. It was Mattie's idea for Sybil and me to move here after my husband died. She thought it would be fun to be together again, and it was," Mavis sighed.

"What will you do with the house?" asked Sybil.

"Mattie wanted me to rent it so she would have a home to come back to if things didn't go to plan," Eleanor said.

Sybil's eyes grew wide. "You don't believe she's dead, do you?"

Mavis blinked back tears. "If only that were true . . . wait a minute. Have you checked her jewelry?"

"I haven't gone through all of her things. Is there something in particular that you want, Mavis?" Eleanor asked.

"She had a gold locket with a picture of her mother. It was very precious to her. She didn't wear it often but I'm sure she'd take it with her if she could," Mavis said.

They all crowded into Mattie's small bedroom and Mavis went immediately to a full-length mirror that hung on the wall. The mirror swung open like a door revealing a storage place for all of Mattie's jewels. They looked through her treasures: broaches, pendants, rings, earrings, and bracelets—some beautiful gemstones set in gold mixed with cheap costume pieces. Nowhere did they find the gold locket.

"There's the proof!" said Mavis. "She never would have left without it and if she's taken it with her, she must still be alive."

"Unless she was wearing it when she died," said Sybil. "Did anyone pick up her things at the morgue?" "No, I never thought to question it," explained Eleanor.

"So there is no body, no family to check with, and absolutely no knowing if she is really dead," Josephine summed it all up. "Perhaps we should ask some questions."

"If this is true, let's just leave it alone. Mattie wouldn't want us messing up her plan to be with Artemas," said Pearl.

"I agree. If we go snooping around someone is bound to notice and we don't know who it is that's a threat," added Cleo.

"I can guess," Dede said. "Peter Fowler disappeared, Howard and Ron Wakefield are dead, and Eric Fowler is in a coma. That leaves Edward Fowler and the other haters who might want to sniff Artemas and Mattie out."

"I heard Edward doesn't leave Eric's side. He's devastated by what happened," Pearl remarked. "This could be a transforming event for him." No one thought they could be in danger. Their only concern was keeping Mattie safe, if indeed she was still alive.

Eleanor remembered the crow pecking at the gopher who fought to stay alive and how happy it made her to think her intervention gave the small furry creature a chance to escape. There was no body there either and no proof that the gopher succeeded in finding a safe haven. For all she knew it might have died from its injuries, but she continued to think it got away. Thinking Mattie was with Artemas made her happy too.

"As much as it disturbs me to let a mystery go unsolved, I think we need to agree to go on as if Mattie is dead." Eleanor looked at each of the ladies as they nodded in agreement and raised their teacups in a toast that sealed their secret.

The next day Cleo called bright and early. "Eleanor, you'll never guess what happened last night. The Wakefield House burned down. It was a horrendous blaze that lit up the whole neighborhood. There must have been five fire trucks here. You could see it clear out to the highway. It was a total loss."

"Was there anyone in the house?" Eleanor asked.

"I think it was closed up. Junie left for parts unknown. I can't help thinking about all the beautiful things we saw there all gone up in smoke."

"It was just stuff, Cleo, although there were so many books. I wish now we had taken more for the library," Eleanor said.

"I thought the fires would stop now that the Wakefields are dead, but now the Wakefield's house has been burned. What does it mean?"

Eleanor thought for a while. "I don't know Cleo. Do you know what caused the fire?"

"I haven't heard," Cleo said, "but the whole thing is very disturbing." When Cleo hung up, Eleanor called Angus to find out what he knew. The last time they spoke he seemed sure the threat was over.

"The Wakefield house has burned to the ground," Eleanor said as soon as Angus answered the phone.

"I'll make some calls," he said. Thirty minutes later he was at her door.

"Got coffee?" he asked as he made his way in with Feathers flapping around his head hurling insults.

"Better than that, I made eggs." Eleanor set the table and they sat down to ham and cheese omelets with toast and fresh blackberries.

"It was arson. The entire house up in a ball of gasoline-inspired arson." Angus frowned. "I don't understand it. If the Wakefields were responsible for creating the other fires, why this? I was sure with the death of their leader the Nazi organization would lay low hoping the investigation wouldn't touch them. There must be something we aren't seeing." Angus' bushy brows descended in puzzlement.

"Could it be revenge of some sort? Do you think Sofia could do something like this?" Eleanor said the first thing that came to her mind. "She seemed really bitter at the funeral."

"She found a wad of black gum in the wreckage of Johnny's boat. The police missed it. It convinced her Rob was in the boat. I had to tell her there's no convicting a dead man. She's bitter, but she didn't do this. This was more than one person. That house was huge." He paused, "It could be revenge, or we missed something inside that house."

"You mean something someone didn't want found?" Eleanor too was puzzled. "Blackmail?"

"Possibly, that might explain the money amounts recorded in the Bible. The reasons for blackmailing those people on the list may have been in the house. We won't find it now. The house was a total loss." Angus popped the last bit of toast in his mouth.

"That reminds me." Eleanor left and came back with a slipper. "I found this under the bed in the guest room. Cynthia must have left it when they stayed here after the fire." She turned it over and showed Angus the black tar like substance stuck to the sole. "It's Black Jack chewing gum." In both of their minds Cynthia was exonerated.

Eleanor sat at her desk. The rain pounded against the windows washing what was left of summer away along with the dust that covered the greenery outside. Eleanor didn't mind the rain. It smelled fresh and clean and gave her a rest from watering the few plants that grew on her deck. She was warm and dry in her office with the glow of a fire to cheer her as she paid her bills and organized her paperwork. Feathers supervised from his perch by the window and eyed her carefully as she filed away Mattie's business. Eleanor had visited Mattie's house several times over the week boxing and storing her treasures, deciding what to keep in the house for renters and what needed to be thrown out. It was tedious work.

She picked up the phone and called Pearl. "Pearl, it's Eleanor. I was cleaning out Mattie's garage yesterday and found some glass and other things you might use in your studio for mosaics. I don't know if you want any of it, so why not come over later and take a look?"

"Great, I remember when Mattie developed an interest in making mosaics. She bought some beautiful glass and tools too. For several weeks she came to open studio, but she didn't pursue it for long. Some of her work was pretty terrible. Actually, all of it was awful. I've never seen anyone make such ugly art."

"Yes, I noticed a couple of pieces she has stored out there." Eleanor hated to critique anyone's art, but Mattie's mosaics were sparse, colorless, and heavily grouted.

"I have open studio all afternoon, but I'll come over this evening," Pearl promised.

"Great, I'll see you then." It felt good to have one more thing out of the way. By the time Pearl arrived, the sun was setting over the ocean between the darkening clouds, casting a silver lining and a sparkle on the water too bright to view. Pearl backed her car into Mattie's garage and began her inspection.

"This is beautiful glass," Pearl remarked as she lifted a large sheet of dark blues and greens. "Here's a box of glass snippers and some small tiles."

Under the box of glass, Eleanor spied something that caught her eye. It was a thin tattered book, *The Winterstein Family Tree*. Tied to it was a journal belonging to David Winterstein and included his memoirs.

"How did that get in Mattie's garage?" asked Pearl. "Who are the Wintersteins?"

"It looks as though someone was hiding it here," Eleanor remarked as she leafed casually through some of the pages. "Oh my, there's a picture of Artemas in here. His real name is David Winterstein and this is his family tree."

"Why would Mattie keep it out here?" Pearl asked. "Books get moldy in a garage."

"I don't know," Eleanor said, "In this diagram of his family tree, he's changed the name of Peter Winterstein, his cousin, to Peter Winter and then Peter Fowler. According to this Artemas and Peter Fowler were related."

"I don't understand," said Pearl.

"I'm not sure I do either, but maybe after studying this it will make more sense." Eleanor put the book aside. "I can only guess that Artemas asked Mattie to keep it for him. I bet he told Peter Fowler about it when he visited Riverside since it's his family tree too and took measures to protect it," Eleanor said.

"Peter Fowler didn't want anyone to know he was Peter Winterstein. I wonder why."

Pearl picked up the book and looked at the family tree. "Someone wrote the Fowler name right next to Winterstein. There's a whole list of them going back to the early 1700s."

"I find it odd that Artemas was hunting a Nazi war criminal who was related to him. It's like two brothers fighting against each other in the Civil War," Eleanor said. "I'll definitely have to take those books with me."

"We better get back to work," said Pearl. "I have to be home to watch *This is Us*.

"Look at this," said Eleanor holding a framed piece that showed what could have been a sunset in oranges and reds. "I can barely lift it."

"She overdid the grout," Pearl sighed. "I'll take this bag of gout by the way, but it's open. Is there some tape around here?"

"I saw some in the house. I'll get it," and Eleanor disappeared inside.

The sun had set and darkness surrounded the little cottage. Eleanor's eyes caught movement outside the kitchen window, and she remembered the night of the bear's visit at Cleo's but this was no bear. It was a man carrying a gas can. It was a man Eleanor recognized. She stepped quickly away from the window but too late. He was already at the door.

"Open the door, or I'll have to burn the house down with you in it," he growled, but he didn't wait and kicked the door in.

"Edward Fowler, what are you doing?" Eleanor took a step back.

"I've come to cleanse this house," he said.

"This is Mattie May's house, it has nothing to do with you." Eleanor took another step back.

"I don't believe you haven't found something here. I know Mattie shared secrets with that man called Artemas and if he left a clue here, I have to destroy it."

"There's nothing here but the remnants of an old woman's life," Eleanor said.

"I don't believe you. Artemas Chase came here looking for my father because he knew about us. He was a Jew. Did you know that? Did he tell you that? He was a Jew and he hunted us down so he could tell everyone we were Jews too."

"That doesn't make any sense, Edward. Artemas worked for the Counterintelligence Corps. He hunted Nazi's, not Jews."

Edward snorted, "You think you know everything, but you don't. His real name is David Winterstein and he and my father were cousins. They were Jews. We developed superior genes, but they remained flawed. My father stayed in Germany but David Winterstein's family fled to America. During the war my father collaborated with the Nazi's because they were right."

Despite her panic, Eleanor tried to appear calm and decided to draw Edward out some more. Maybe she could give Pearl time to escape and get help. "But Edward, you said your branch of the family developed superior genes, couldn't the same happen for others?"

"No!" he shouted without explanation before diving back into his story. "My Dad changed his name from Peter Winterstein to Peter Winter. Some say he was a traitor to his own people, but he was enlightened. That proves his superior genes. He did what he had to do to make Germany great and purify the race, and when he was accused of war crimes he escaped to America and became Peter Fowler. He was a hero who had medals to prove his loyalty to the cause."

"But that was so long ago, and the war was lost." Eleanor said.

"He was a man who wanted to remove the weakest of the human race to make us all stronger, smarter, and better. He worked to make that happen in America. It doesn't help any country to pamper the weak and inferior. Those with genetic deficiencies need to die. They need to be disposed of to make room for the strong and the fit. Even nature does this. It's only humans who insist on rescuing the afflicted who then pass on their flaws to the next generation. Our kind has become weak and stupid because of people who do this in the name of kindness."

David Winterstein hunted father down and took him away. I'm sure there is a clue here that will tell me where he is. Do you know? Have you found it?"

"No, Edward, I don't know. I'm sure Mattie didn't know either. Why would you want to burn down her house if you're looking for clues to his whereabouts?"

Edward ran his hands through his hair, "Don't you see? No one can know that we are Jews. Most of the Jews are inferior. We aren't. The Fowlers are superior to the Jews. We don't exhibit the characteristics of them. My wife was blonde and blue-eyed and so was my mother. Over time we've obliterated the hook nose and the stupidity and other flaws, but not everyone can see that. If they knew we were Jews, they would think we were weak and destroy us."

Eleanor shook her head. None of this made sense. Eleanor didn't understand hate and intolerance. However, she fully understood that Edward Fowler had just told her that there was no way he planned on her living to tell the story to anyone else.

"I'll help you look, Edward. Honestly I haven't seen anything that reveals your ancestry here in this house. If he told Mattie, your secret died with her."

"No. It'll never die. Secrets like that never die. I've lived all my life with this secret. Howard Wakefield found out and he held our shame over us. He made us his dog army. You won't believe what we've done for him to keep this secret and now that he and his son are dead, I can't let anyone find out . . . now you know, and I can't let you tell either. Not after all we've done . . ."

He never got to finish his sentence because Pearl took that moment to step through the open door and bash him on the head with Mattie's framed mosaic. It was quite heavy but Pearl was tall and she did yoga. It broke and left a dreadful mess of glass and grout, not to mention blood. Eleanor quickly took the duct tape and bound his hands with it while Pearl stood over him and looked on in shock.

"I can't believe I did that. I'm not a violent person, but I heard most of that conversation from the porch when I stepped out for a cigarette," Pearl said. "I figured he'd have to kill you, Eleanor, since he told you his secret, so I grabbed Mattie's art. As ugly as it was, at least it was good for something."

"I'm glad you did, Pearl. I'll call Angus." Eleanor went for her phone.

"He'll probably claim he was framed." Pearl smiled at her own joke.

By the time Angus arrived, Pearl and Eleanor had made tea and were sitting at the kitchen table. Edward Fowler was still unconscious. "Good grief," Angus said when he saw the carnage, "What happened here?"

"Edward Fowler tried to kill us," Pearl began. "He came to burn down Mattie's house to destroy any evidence of his connection to Artemas Chase, who is really David Winterstein."

"Evidently Artemas and Peter Fowler are cousins and the Fowlers have been hiding the fact that they're Jewish— probably paying blackmail and committing crimes for Howard Wakefield so he would keep their secret," Eleanor added. "I bet he's responsible for burning down the Wakefield house as well."

Angus checked Edward's pulse, "He's alive." Pearl continued to ramble repeating everything she had heard as she listened outside the door. When the police came along with the ambulance, Angus drove Pearl home. It would take two days for her to recover from the trauma of almost killing someone. She swore she was finding a new group of friends.

The news of Edward Fowler's arrest spread quickly through Waterton County. Pearl and Eleanor were heralded as heroines for at least a week. The ladies of the coffee group met at Suzanna's for coffee and planned to help Eleanor go through Mattie's things after breakfast.

Pearl put her head on the table and pleaded, "All I want is a quiet, uncomplicated life without drama."

"You would be bored in no time," said Dede. "Then you'd be complaining about how dull and simple your life is."

"Life is light bouncing off of dark," said Cleo. "You can't appreciate quiet and simple without loud and complicated."

"This Nazi business has certainly stirred up a hornet's nest of questions for 'Just Josie,'" said Josephine.

"I'm literally buried under queries about Jewishness. People want to know if it is a religion, a race, or an ethnicity. They are concerned about their ancestry and many wonder why someone would care so much about being Jewish that they would kill to keep it a secret."

"Maybe you should just write a column explaining it all. I'm not sure I understand it either," said Cleo.

"Judaism is a religion, but its beliefs are very flexible," Eleanor said. "There are many people who consider themselves secular Jews and don't believe in God."

"Jews are not a race," said Dede, "and they're more than a culture or ethnicity. They're like a tribe or family."

"The shame for Edward Fowler came from his father who denied his family to avoid persecution from the Nazis. Peter Fowler must have bought into Hitler's belief that Jews were an inferior race and needed to be eradicated. He became a tool of the Nazis and then was hunted by his own cousin for war crimes," said Eleanor. "It must have been personal for Artemas."

"Keeping that shame a secret gives it a great deal of power and over time it becomes more powerful and difficult to dislodge," Josephine said.

"Imagine starting a whole organization of haters and being one of the people your group hates," said Cleo.

"Each of those members may have had their own secret and were probably paying Wakefield to keep it not knowing that everyone else was keeping something hidden too," said Pearl.

"There aren't many Jews living here—at least that I know," said Dede. "Their organization seems to have discriminated against anyone who was different. Here it focused on the Hispanic population. They were more about purging their community of those that didn't fit their ideal than anything else."

"Their feelings of inferiority must have driven them to belittle others to make themselves feel superior. Their actions make more sense in that context," said Pearl.

"Just like any bully, they're insecure and afraid on the inside. I wonder how Howard Wakefield found out about their secret and was able to use it to manipulate them," mused Eleanor.

"They did a lot of drinking and partying. Someone was bound to spill the beans eventually. The Fowlers and the Wakefields have socialized with each other for generations," said Dede, "And Howard Wakefield's nature was always to use and manipulate. He probably learned it from his grandfather."

"I bet he hired people to find out about everyone in this town. If you had a secret you could be blackmailed," said Cleo. "Maybe the members of his group weren't haters, but just had secrets they didn't want exposed. They might have been victims of Howard Wakefield's intolerance."

"It's a good thing Edward burned down the Wakefield house. Now everyone's secrets can remain secret," said Dede. "Those whose names are on that list must feel free."

"I don't think so," said Eleanor, "we still have the list and Angus said an investigation will be done and some of those names may be implicated in hate crimes or corruption. The Bible held a great deal of information about a number of people and what they did to protect their secrets."

"You know I still have those books from the Wakefield library," said Pearl. "Maybe there are more secrets in them." The ladies all looked at Pearl. They knew she didn't really want a simple life.

When they got to Mattie's house, Eleanor unlocked the door that had been replaced since Edward Fowler had kicked it in and they got busy boxing up the rest of Mattie's personal items. Pearl scoped out the books while Cleo and Dede went through her closet bagging clothes for Goodwill. Josephine and Eleanor scoured the kitchen clearing out cupboards and leaving only those things that might be useful for renters.

"Are you planning to rent the house long-term or by the week?" asked Josephine.

"I hadn't really thought about it. I assumed it would be a long-term rental. Renting it by the week might be more lucrative but too time consuming. I'd have to hire someone to clean it," Eleanor said.

"It really is a sweet little cottage," Josephine said. "Maybe your friend Wanda could clean it. How is she doing?"

"She's still healing," said Cleo, "Her daughter plans to sell the house and move. After the police told her that her brakes were definitely tampered with, she's become very paranoid. She lost the love letter her husband wrote her for the second time and thinks someone stole it. Now she won't leave the house, but she did go to the beauty salon to get new eyelash extensions."

"It's easy to bag up all the clothes when you don't have to decide what to keep," Pearl said. "None of that touching everything to see if it evokes a special feeling. I can honestly say nothing in her closet gave me any joy."

"I've decided I'm keeping this fur thing," said Dede as she appeared modeling a genuine fox stole.

"Don't let Doogie get wind of it. He'll tear it to bits," said Pearl.

"I'm hungry," said Cleo. "What's left to be done here?"

"There's just one more cupboard to go through and then we can go to my house for soup," Eleanor offered.

"Why does this look familiar?" Josephine asked holding up a postcard she pulled out of a drawer. There was a fish swimming in clear water among green mossy rocks.

"I used that picture to inspire the mosaic Angus bought at my exhibit," Pearl said. "I bought it at the flower shop."

"Oh, double oh," said Dede. "That's the postcard Sofia was writing on when I mistook her car for mine. I remember she was so startled she threw it up in the air. I knew I'd seen it somewhere before when I saw your mosaic."

"That's like the postcard Angus got saying Johnny Vargas was murdered," Eleanor said. "Do you think Sofia sent it? She was angry and totally convinced that Rob Wakefield deserved punishment for his intolerance. I bet she helped plant the bloody T-shirts. Wanda told me she visited Junie at the Wakefield house. They could have planned it together with Junie planting the shirt found in Eric's room."

"Maybe, there must be dozens of those postcards around town and what difference does it make now that Rob is dead and Eric is suffering in the hospital?" asked Josephine. "There's nothing written on this one. Mattie never got a chance to use it."

They finished by separating boxes to store from boxes to give to charity. All the while Eleanor kept the hope that Mattie was alive and would return in the forefront of her mind and saving those treasures that might bring her comfort.

Eleanor had made a fall soup of borsch the day before and had it chilling in the refrigerator. She warmed it, topped it with a spoonful of sour cream, and served it with crispy toast. "That was delicious. Can I get the recipe?" Cleo knew Eleanor didn't share her cooking secrets but asked anyway. One never knew when you might catch someone off guard.

"Sure," Eleanor replied, "I think the recipe is in that red cookbook called *Basic Cooking* on the shelf in the kitchen."

Cleo couldn't believe her good fortune. She found the book but was disappointed when she saw the ingredients. One can of beef broth, one can of shoestring beets, there was no way Eleanor would make a soup out of canned foods. She sighed and noticed a photograph stuck in the cookbook.

"Did you find it?" asked Eleanor who was coming in for a plate of deluxe chocolate chip cookies.

"I found this photo stuck in the cookbook. Isn't that Johnny Vargas?"

Eleanor glanced over her shoulder. "Yes, that's the cookbook Junie borrowed when she and Johnny were first married. She wanted to learn to cook. It makes me sad to think that she marked the page with his photo. I wonder what she was cooking." Cleo put the cookbook on the shelf but left the photo on the counter and hurried back to the table for a cookie. She knew she would never get the recipe for Eleanor's deluxe chocolate chip cookies so she had to enjoy them while she could.

After the ladies left Eleanor cleaned up the kitchen then sat on the couch and turned on the television. An Arnold Schwarzenegger marathon was airing. Feathers perched on the back of the couch and murmured parrot words of love. She only meant to rest her eyes for a minute and woke when she heard the doorbell ring. As usual, Feathers alerted her to the ever-intruding pirates and scallywags. Angus stood at her door with bags from Hung Far Low's Chinese Restaurant. Eleanor had totally forgotten their Friday night dinner date.

"Angus, come in. I'm sorry I must have fallen asleep." Eleanor looked at the clock and couldn't believe how late it was.

"Don't worry Ellie, I saw Dede in town and she told me how busy you were today so I guessed you might not want to cook tonight. Besides, I was in the mood for Chinese." Angus took the takeout into the kitchen and got out two plates. "What's this?" he asked picking up the photograph of Johnny Vargas that was left on the counter.

Eleanor was still groggy from napping too long. She had forgotten about the photo and hadn't really looked at it only noticing that it showed Johnny with a big fish. "Junie must have left it in the cookbook I loaned her. Cleo found it this afternoon." She peered at it while Angus studied it closely, his lowered brows attesting to his intensity.

"That's a yellowfin tuna that Johnny's holding," Angus said calmly. "Look what's in the background." Eleanor took the photo which showed Johnny standing in a boat smiling into the camera holding a big fish. Behind him was a hill with a statue and some buildings. It wasn't clear. Eleanor knew she was supposed to be seeing something important, but she wasn't sure what.

"Is that Mexico behind him?" she asked. "I don't know very many places in the US that have statues of Jesus looking over the city."

"Right, it's a small town called El Morro, just south of Rosarito, Mexico," Angus said. "That's Christ of the Sacred Heart in the background."

"Okay, isn't that where Johnny's family is from?" Eleanor seemed to remember Sofia saying something about being from there. "It must have been taken when he was visiting his parents."

"No," Angus was excited now. "look at his left hand."

Eleanor looked closely and noticed the gold band on his ring finger. "It's his wedding ring. He didn't visit his parents after his wedding. There wasn't enough time." She was beginning to understand.

"Right, Johnny Vargas is alive and he's living in El Morro with his parents." Angus began to laugh. "I bet Junie is with him right now and I hope they're spending all her daddy's ill-gotten money on margaritas and fancy dinners."

"You mean Johnny faked his death?" Eleanor said. "That doesn't seem right."

"There's nothing illegal about leaving the country without telling anyone. Johnny wasn't responsible for people jumping to the conclusion that he was dead." Angus was pouring them each a celebratory drink. "Who knows how it happened? If someone tried to kill him and he survived, playing dead could have been his best chance to stay alive. Maybe his boat capsized, and he took the opportunity it offered to escape the Wakefield's torture."

"He wouldn't do that to Junie. She must have been in on it too. You don't think they had anything to do with Rob and Howard's death, do you?"

"No, they couldn't know Rob would die in a crash or predict that Howard would have a heart attack. They probably hoped Junie would get back in Howard's good graces and get some money so she could go to Johnny. With Johnny dead to Howard, she'd be free to travel on daddy's dime. It was a clever plan that unfortunately ended badly for Howard and Rob."

"Do you think Junie planted the bloody T-shirts?" Eleanor wondered. "That would explain why she hung out with Eric Fowler. She told me not to judge her."

"Hmmm, she must have known the T-shirts wouldn't be enough to convict either of them. She might have done it out of revenge. I bet it scared those two hoodlums though. Johnny didn't want her to know how they bullied him but the night he disappeared I bet Rob tried to hurt him. His gum *was* in the boat. Something happened that night and Junie must have found out about the earlier attacks. They knew Rob and Eric wouldn't quit until Johnny was dead, so they came up with a plan to beat them."

"Sofia was in on it. She must have sent the postcard saying Johnny was murdered to make people realize how badly he was treated and force Eric and Rob to suffer. I think she's still angry about the racism," Eleanor added. "Even at the Wakefield's funeral, she was still acting the part of angry sister saying Rob had done him wrong in an attempt to keep Johnny and Junie's plan a secret." Eleanor smiled. "She told me Johnny was in a better place."

"Johnny would have needed help getting out of town. Sofia and Al probably hid him at their place while everyone searched for him. I'm just happy things turned out in their favor." Angus smiled and raised his glass of Crown Royal and they toasted, "To Junie and Johnny."

It wasn't long before Angus received a check in the mail for the exact amount he had loaned Johnny Vargas to buy a diamond engagement ring. The check was signed by Junie Vargas and the envelope was postmarked Rosarito, Mexico. The note inside simply said, "Thank you."

Two days later, Angus picked up Eleanor and Feathers and drove to a rental facility to get a travel trailer. While he hooked the trailer to his truck Eleanor read an article in a well-known newspaper describing the capture of a Nazi war criminal who had been living under an assumed name in a small town on the West Coast. Evidently, he was returned to Germany where he awaited trial and punishment for his crimes.

Angus climbed in the truck and the three adventurers headed for Mexico.

"Habla usted espanol?" he asked.

"Si, lo hablo un poquito," Eleanor answered.

"Maybe we should practice on our way there," Angus suggested.

"What if we get there and they aren't there?" asked Eleanor. "Can you drive this thing clear to Rio?"

"You are traveling with a trained professional whose detective skills are unparalleled," Angus replied.

"Yes, but it's a long drive. I hope you don't get tired of me," Eleanor said.

"Imposible novia." Angus reached over and squeezed her hand. "Te quiero." A rustling of feathers and a voice came from the back seat, "Hasta la vista, Baby," but this time it didn't sound like Walter—more like Arnold Schwarzenegger.

Acknowledgments

Of course, my thanks go out to every literary teacher I ever had, my friends and family who endured my endless chatter about the book and provided fodder for my pen, especially Suzanne Weber, Kathryn Christensen and April Petersen, my first readers who inspired and encouraged me.

A special thank you to my publishers, J.V. Bolkan and Sharleen Nelson at Gladeye Press, who took a chance on me. And my husband, David, whose clever quotes appear without end as the voice of lovers and parrot.

About the Author

Patricia Brown was born in Oregon City, Oregon, and was educated at Oregon State University, graduating with a degree in elementary education, a career she pursued for 28 years.

She lives in a small town on the Oregon coast with her husband, where she dabbles in the arts and enjoys the company of family and friends. *Dying to Win* is her fourth novel.

Get all the books in the Coastal Coffee Club Mysteries series!

A Recipe for Dying

The old people are dying, but no one seems to notice—after all, that's what old people do, isn't it? Eleanor and her friends set out to discover what the heck is going on!

Dying for Diamonds

When a mean-spirited mystery writer visiting the sleepy coastal town gets murdered, family secrets and the bonds we share are tested.

Under A Dying Moon

A girl washes up on the beach and two women are found murdered. It's up to Eleanor and the gang to solve the mystery.

ALSO FROM GLADEYE PRESS

Available for purchase at: www.gladeyepress.com and wherever fine books are sold.

The Time Tourists, A Novel
Sharleen Nelson

Step into time with Imogen Oliver in this first book in the Dead Relatives, Inc. series as she investigates a young girl who disapeared from home with her boyfriend in 1967 and never returned, and then travels back to the turn of the 20th century to locate a set of missing stereoscopic glass plates with a mysterious connection to her own life.

Teaching in Alaska
What I Learned in the Bush
Julie Bolkan

Among the first outsiders to live and work with the Yup'ik in their small villages, this book tells Julie's story about how she survived the culture clashes, isolation, weather, and her struggles with honey buckets—a candid and often funny account of one gussock woman's 12 years in the Alaskan bush.

10 Takes: Pacific Northwest Writers
Perspectives on Writing
Jennifer Roland

From novelists to poets to playwrights, Jennifer Roland interviews a variety of authors who have one thing in common—they have all chosen to make the Pacific Northwest their home.

Tripping the Field: An Existential Crisis of Ungodly Proportions
Ian Jaydid

An irreverent action adventure with quantum physics, philosophy, religious shenanigans, monsters, unabashed drug use, and a love story all rolled into one action-packed novel.

COMING SOON

FROM GLADEYE PRESS

Look for Book #5 in the Coastal Coffee Club Mysteries series, late 2021

Time Tapestry, the second book in the Dead Relatives, Inc. series featuring
The Time Tourists, coming 2021.

- Visit www.gladeyepress.com for fantastic deals on these and other GladEye Press titles.

- Follow us on Facebook: https://www.facebook.com/GladEyePress/

- All GladEye titles can also be ordered online or from your local bookstore.

CPSIA information can be obtained
at www.ICGtesting.com
Printed in the USA
LVHW050103080421
683806LV00003B/6